T0367133

MARYAM

MARYAM
KEEPER OF STORIES

Alawiya Sobh

TRANSLATED BY NIRVANA TANOUKHI

LONDON NEW YORK CALCUTTA

SERIES EDITOR

Hosam Aboul-Ela

Seagull Books, 2016

Originally published in Arabic as *Maryam al Hayaka*, 2002
© Alawiya Sobh, 2002

First published in English translation by Seagull Books, 2016
English translation © Nirvana Tanoukhi, 2016

ISBN 978 0 8574 2 325 2

British Library Cataloguing-in-Publication Data
A catalogue record for this book is available from the British Library.

Typeset by Seagull Books, Calcutta, India
Printed and bound by Maple Press, York, Pennsylvania, USA

CONTENTS

1

The issue is over, as far as I'm concerned.

I have despaired of the answer, given up on the question and lost any hope of finding her again.

The visa is finally in my hands and a few days remain before my departure. There is hardly enough time to make the preparations, to complete the necessary farewell visits with family, cousins, neighbours, to say goodbye to Ibtisam and Yasmine and to Alawiyya and the rest of the characters in her novel.

But where is Alawiyya Subuh that I may say goodbye to her?

If I see her again, I will not ask: 'How's your book coming, Alawiyya?'

I will certainly not ask her.

Whenever we met in the last few years and I asked her what became of our story, I felt as though my tongue were a hot blade that opened a soft wound inside her. As she looked away from me, I glimpsed a gust of hidden pain fly across her eyes, and I watched her gaze falter and melt into the earth's rotation. But her eyelids would stop fluttering and her eyes settle again on mine. Then she'd fumble for a question, ask thirstily about my latest with Abbas, news of Ibtisam, or recent developments in the lives of her characters—those characters about whom I had once told her everything I knew, many years ago. But, since then, they've all passed on to new fates, fates unknown to her. And all that I told her passed into nothing.

I wonder now why I told her all those stories and why she listened if she never wrote any of it down.

Has Alawiyya really disappeared, like Ibtisam, or has she just transformed herself for the new life she chose? Or has she, like

Yasmine, abandoned her youthful dreams of outgrowing the place of her birth?

I want to know if she has changed like all the others, or if she has withstood it all, as if outside the time and space of the war. Did she forget everything, like our village neighbour Abu Yusuf who forgot his name after his wife Khadija died? He started calling all the other men 'Abu Yusuf' and whenever anyone said to him, 'But you are Abu Yusuf!' he would weep and say, 'No. You're all liars. All of you are Abu Yusuf.'

She disappeared just like Zuhair, her hero and counterpart in the novel, leaving all our fates to be lost in her unfinished book. I could no longer find her name on the pages of newspapers and magazines, or even on the door to her old flat at the top of Hamra Street. Later, I discovered that the whole building where she and her grandmother had lived had been razed to the ground.

When new novels came out, I rushed to the bookstore, pored over the titles and the authors' names, but I never found her name or our stories. A few times, I bought all of them, persuading myself that she could have written our story under another name. But as I leafed through the first pages, my fears would be confirmed—that she had disappeared and our story with her.

I no longer need to read my life in her book, because my story ends here. I just want to find her to say goodbye, to tell her that I have chosen a path for myself outside her novel. I only want to know about her fate and the reason she disappeared.

She vanished, and no more news of her reached me.

She no longer visited me at home, like Ibtisam or Yasmine. Each one of them used to come separately, stand at the flat door and ring the bell, or tap with her fingers when the electricity was off. I could tell which one of them it was from the way they rang or knocked and because I knew their routines by heart. My room is now empty of their chatter. The visits have dwindled and the talks dried up, as the river dwindles to a trickle after crossing a long distance. I don't believe this has happened because they are busy with their new lives. It seems that sometimes people become mementos to one another. Like a familiar piece of clothing, a shoe, or a scent, they evoke an occasion or an emotion in all its minute details. In avoiding the others, each of them flees from the war and its memories.

Before the war ended, Alawiyya did come by sporadically. Sometimes, she would be gone for days, weeks or months, but in the end she would return to knock on my door. I rarely left the flat. Often, I would only go to the firm to collect my salary at the end of each month, since regular attendance was not enforced. Particularly during the early years of the war when the fighting was at its worst, I spent most of my time at home in my room, unless I had arranged to meet Abbas. Ibtisam and Alawiyya, for their part, went to the fronts and disappeared for days. They wandered off like sheep and grazed in the war's meadow only to be brought back to my little stable where they regurgitated their tales.

Back in those days, I could not have foreseen in Alawiyya the inscrutable darkness that later pervaded her features. Whenever I opened the door, her smiling eyes met me behind the thick glasses that I loved on her and which, for me, were just another part of her face. That was before she had the corrective operation to get rid of them. I don't know whether she took that risk out of boredom, to play with her eyes and gamble with them as she did with her life. Or perhaps it was the obsession with beauty that infected her while working at the women's magazine.

In the old days, she would come to my place with her dirty military cap and the same old pair of jeans that she had owned for years. She would sit cross-legged on my living room sofa, the flesh bulging inside her jeans around her bent knees, and tell stories of battles and war fronts. Lifting her cap with one hand, she would run the other rhythmically through her limp hair, separating locks that stuck together with oil and sweat, airing out the scalp and roots and urging them back to life. She would stop abruptly in the middle of her story and say, 'God, Maryam. It's been so long since I've taken a shower.'

Later, when she began disappearing for months at a time, I knew that she was busy with her writing or some new friendship or affair. Only Ibtisam would tell me everything down to the last detail, maybe because she and I went back the furthest, to the days when we were children. She had always been an open book to me until she closed the book one day and the river of stories dried up in her mouth. Even when Ibtisam was rapt in one of her private struggles, I could read the gestures hidden behind the glimmer of her eyes. As for Alawiyya, her mystery increased with time. Her absences grew longer and she would return only when her mouth had filled up with the water of a story that she could not swallow. But even then she would come to listen more than to talk. My room, this room of stories, was in my father's house. The brown wooden cupboard with a mirror glued onto the centre leaf was paired with a wood-veneer bed. I had bought it as a temporary solution when the old bed was destroyed in an explosion; and the temporary had become permanent with time. The pillows that I had sewn with my own hands lay scattered around the old sofa with its slipcover stained with red and green flowers, and on this sofa and these pillows their stories gathered like water in a well.

In the old days, my room was a shelter for their stories and secrets. I took them in and they spread themselves out carelessly on my floor and on the sofa that remains in the room until this day, scarred by little black cigarette burns. I simmered coffee on the stove-top and the stories rose from their mouths with more fervour than the steam rising from the large pot. We needed to tell each other everything, even the most intimate of details. Each of us needed to tell our story in the presence of the rest, so we could be mirrors in which to discover *their* many faces and ours.

How we conspired and schemed with one another! I remember the day I told them all about what Mustafa had done to me, how he left me after I had adored him and done everything he asked. The curses hurled down on him so violently—'*The son of a . . .*' '*That piti-less bastard*'—that they piled up quickly on the sofa and all over the room. Only Alawiyya Subuh remarked, 'God! Men are impossible,' but then she fell back, laughing so loud beside me that it seemed like machine gun fire.

Where did all those stories go?

I'm not sure why, but while it strung us together like the beads of a necklace, the war drove others apart. Then the necklace broke, and I came to wonder if we had come together to create our own world when the one around us had collapsed. Was it the war that destroyed our dreams, or was it peace that came and pushed each of us into her private world? Or was it age and the way of things?

I'm not sure I understand it completely. All I know is that our conversations are different now. Words are thrown like stones at each other's head, or they curl out preening like a cat's tongue, or coil like a snake anticipating a strike. Our speech is no longer speech but something different. The concerns expressed by this new language are superfluous beyond belief, like the echo you hear, after shouting into a well, rising from its depth.

Where has everything I told Alawiyya gone? She moved among us like a thief, picked up our stories as they slipped from our mouths into the room, pocketed them and stole away. She even took her own stories with her before she vanished.

I'm the one who wouldn't stop babbling, telling her everything I knew about myself, about her and all the characters of the novel. It started when she came to me towards the end of the war and said: 'The war is over. I want to write the experience of our generation. No. Not the experience of our generation. That's too ambitious. I want to write your story, because you are the shadow, the shadow of all the protagonists in the novel, and the shadow of all our memories. I find your character enticing.'

'We've been friends a long time, Alawiyya. You know everything about me.'

'No. I want to see things through your eyes.'

'But I'll just say things that you already know.'

'I know, I know. But I want to see things the way you see them—now that the war is ending.'

'Why don't you write about yourself? Isn't your story worth writing?'

'Not now. Maybe I will—in the sequel. I need more time to understand what has happened. I can't write about something that I don't understand yet.'

That's how we were before the war ended. We wanted to buy the fish while it was still in the water. Now I want to see the fish in front of me before I pay.

* * *

And so she disappeared after I told her everything. Just as surely as the novel remained unwritten, my story remained unread. Neither I nor any of the rest of us ever read what we had told Alawiyya. My words were wasted. I had been speaking into empty ears. She reduced me to a mouth that spoke on her behalf and ears that listened for what would profit her. I would steal others' tales and offer them to her as gifts. I became so accustomed to hearing with her ears that every time a scene, a conversation, or any piece of news caught my attention, I would think to myself: 'Where is Alawiyya to hear about this and write it down?' Even when I watched my shadow alone in the dark—and it was only in the dark that I ever saw it—even then, I would say to myself: 'Where is Alawiyya now, to watch my shadow with me?' As the years went by, I became an expert in spotting the kinds of stories that intrigued her. Alawiyya discovered in me the refuge for these women's secrets. She envied me for this gift and sometimes admitted so.

'How come they tell you everything, and not me?' she asked.

'I don't know,' I would answer, laughing.

I truly did not know. At the time I suspected that they told me things because they didn't fear my shadow. I listened to and nursed them until they felt they could trust me. But, with time, I became like the priest to whom everybody confessed everything. Not only did I become a refuge for women but men too began confessing to me, revealing intimate details that they would never discuss with another woman. Even our neighbour, Abu Talal, who boasted of the sexual virility of his youth when he prowled the neighbourhood, confessed to me that he had become impotent. Of course he never used the word 'impotence'. Instead, he just said: 'Maryam, I can't seem to get it up . . . '

'Get what up?' I asked.

He pointed to his member and said: 'Him. Who else would get up?'

He started telling me about his wife, how when he took off his clothes and was naked as God had made him, he would stand in front of her rubbing it between his hands, saying, 'Please help me. If you won't have mercy on me, have mercy on him.' But she never granted mercy. She certainly did not show any when she overheard him telling me all this. She told him in front of me, 'What good is it going to do you, complaining to Maryam? Are you hoping she'll beat me up for you? You and your little guy can both rot for all I care.'

I didn't spare any details either when I told Alawiyya about my life or the lives of the other characters in her book. I even introduced her to my parents and my aunts. She kept nosing around in my neighbours' affairs until she had befriended all of them and learnt all the scandals of the building and the neighbourhood. I was happy to help at the time, because I believed that by doing so I would secure my place in her novel.

Could she have forgotten about us?

Whether she has or hasn't, the fact remains that she never wrote anything. Now, I must tell the story before I leave. You see, she has lost touch with the particulars of our fates. A few years ago, all she could remember about her characters were generalities; her indifference was clear to me. After all, Alawiyya is one of the novel's characters and I know her well. I can tell when she's actually listening; her mind opens up like the leaves of a tree. Just as I can tell when she recoils; her cheeks slam shut like the covers of a book. In the old days, she listened with her eyes too, not only with her ears. Her pupils soaked my stories like two round sponges—one my words and the other the gestures that I made while I spoke. In them, I saw reflections of my anger, calmness or silence.

I want to know—did she die like so many of the characters in her novel, or is she still among the living? Did she die in '75 after the war broke out and she discovered in herself a talent for politics and combat? Or did she die in '78 when Israel first invaded Lebanon and occupied what it initially called 'Free Lebanon' and later became 'The Security Belt'? Or did she die before that, when the Syrian army entered Lebanon in '76? Was it then, when she fought in the mountains and stood at a checkpoint on Behamdoun Road armed with a Siminov machine gun that came from the land where all proper names ended with that same 'ov'? Or did she fight and die in '82 when the Israeli army entered Lebanon again, driving all the way to Beirut?

No, she could not have died before '87, because I read her book *The Slumber of Days* when it came out that year. Perhaps she went missing afterwards. But can't the dead also write?

I do not know what died inside her, what altered her so permanently, whether she decided to take a stand against our memories or her own. Did she despair and come to loathe writing, or her characters? It is not clear whether she fled from our stories or from us. I asked her these questions many times, long before she disappeared, but she would not answer.

Could she have lost her mind, like her friend Zuhair? I almost believed Zuhair when he confided to me a long time ago saying, 'Alawiyya is a cheat. She wants to drive me crazy. I know it. I've heard of a hero scheming against the novelist to set himself free, but a novelist conspiring against her own heroes? Why? She should know that if I go mad she will be next, and that if I disappear she will be gone too. She should know better than to play these petty tricks.'

But I did not tell her any of that.

I don't know why Alawiyya changed towards him. She introduced us all to him when he returned to the country at the beginning of the war. He had just graduated from medical school but was obsessed with movies and theatre. In Beirut, Alawiyya met him at the party's newspaper headquarters, where he told her that he was dreaming of writing a new kind of theatre, and the two became inseparable. Alawiyya and Zuhair, a writer and a playwright, in the making.

She called me one day and asked me to meet her in a public cafe on the Rouché seashore. As we sat in the fading light of dusk, Alawiyya shooed a fly away from the bottom of the windowsill and lifted the curtain to peek at the sunset. I ordered my usual cappuccino and she, a cup of Arabic coffee without sugar. A little later, Zuhair appeared, and Alawiyya's face lit up as she introduced us. I shook his hand and studied his dark face and black eyes, brimming with energy and intelligence.

She said, 'Maryam, this man is talented and *au courant*, unlike most. Our idea is to collaborate on a piece. I'll write a novel, he'll write a play, and the two works will be about the same characters and the same story.'

'Really? Tell me more.'

'And so, we will meet jointly with you or any of the other characters in my novel. We will listen together to the same stories, but each in our own way. Neither of us will meet alone with any of the characters. The only difference is that I will start my novel with a comma at the beginning of the first line and Zuhair will start his play with an "and".'

At the end of her explanation, she asked, 'Isn't that a superb idea, Maryam?'

And what happened afterwards drove me mad. Each of them did their best to betray the other.

Zuhair started calling me in secret, asking me to meet him alone. And when I asked: 'Why alone?' he answered, 'You know. Maybe you could tell me something about yourself that would be different—something that would give me an edge over her. Also, maybe you want to tell me something that you didn't feel like telling her?'

Alawiyya, unfortunately, did the same.

At the beginning, I told myself that they were either the same person or adversaries. It was also possible that they were playing each other against me, to see if I would tell my story twice in the same way. But I obliged and entered the game. Maybe I did so because I hoped to discover my shadow in a novel or my character in a play. As I talked to the two of them, I found that what I told Zuhair was in fact different from what I told Alawiyya. I discovered new faces for my mother, my neighbours, Abbas and the rest of the characters in Alawiyya's book. Maybe it's true that a woman will tell a man what she won't tell a woman, and tell a woman what she won't tell a man. They certainly managed to draw my story in two opposite directions. Sometimes, I realized that I was lying. I do not mean lying in the usual sense but lying as Alawiyya did whenever her imagination interfered in any story.

What was stranger and what puzzled me was Zuhair's question.

'What do you think of Alawiyya?'

'Why do you ask?' I answered.

'Because I am about to surprise her by making her a character in my play. But keep this between the two of us. Don't tell her,' he said and winked at me.

And later, when I met Alawiyya, she winked the same way and said precisely the same thing.

I could not figure out their motives. I would have lost my mind if the novel hadn't been lost first, along with Zuhair's story and mine.

The novel was lost when it was stolen. That's what Alawiyya claimed, at least. Each morning, Alawiyya would go to the same bustling cafe on the Rouché seashore to write all day and return home exhausted in the night.

One evening, she returned home after midnight when a storm was raging, and the electricity was out in the neighbourhood. Rain was pouring in stark darkness when she turned off her headlights and got out of the car. She decided to leave the manuscript in the brown leather suitcase on the front seat. She was already nervous about climbing the stairs to the fourth floor and making her way into the flat in the dark, guided only by the dim flame of her cigarette lighter. She did not need the added worry of carrying the suitcase up the old building's dizzying circular staircase.

She did not discover what had happened until the next morning when she ran down the stairs to her car. No sooner had she reached the entrance of the building than her eyes fell on the tiny pieces of broken windshield scattered all over the ground and the leather suitcase flung open alongside them. As she picked up the suitcase, her eyes followed the trail of papers sprinkled and scattered from one end of the alley to the other. Then she rushed up the alley to gather the papers. She searched the smudges where ink marks had been erased but found nothing in them except shadows of ink, lost letters and missing words fallen into the dirt. The rain and the wind had written the end of the novel.

She stood watching our memories float on water and mud, as words dissolved in the rain and erased our shadows, hers and mine. Our endings swam in the dirt, and the madness of the playwright swam along with them. Alawiyya lost her mind and went almost as crazy as Zuhair.

She said, 'The manuscript is gone, Maryam. Our stories have been washed away by water and mud.' As she told me what had happened, water and mud flowed from her eyes and erased her features right before my eyes, just as they had erased the words on her papers.

For weeks, Alawiyya would wake in the night, finding her pillow wet with mud and water. The tears would flow down her cheeks against her will and onto her papers every time she approached them and sat behind her desk to start the novel again.

When I asked her to rewrite the novel, she said, 'I tried but I can't. A person can't be reborn, and neither can a story. A story retold is not the same story.'

Alawiyya and Zuhair became strangers once she stopped calling and asking about him. Every time she ran into him on Hamra Street, she would cross to the other side and look away. The poor guy was probably relieved by her manoeuvres. He wished never to set eyes on her face again, in those last years before his own face disappeared for good. He did not want to press her with the same questions, which she had never answered, even before their relationship had ended. 'I beg you, Alawiyya,' he used to plead with her, 'tell me who made you do this to me. You tell me and I promise not to be angry. Just tell me.'

'What do you want me to say?'

'Tell me. Is it the Russians, the Americans or French Intelligence that put you up to this?'

She slowed down as the sadness weighed on her footsteps. 'Take care of yourself, Zuhair,' she said, laying her hand on his shoulder before walking away.

*

No, I no longer believe her about anything. Once she disappeared from the world of writing, I started having my doubts about the story. Had she lied when she said that the manuscript had been stolen, or had she dreamt it up to be finished with the novel? Were our memories truly erased by rain, or had she intentionally left the car door unlocked so the thief could come and set our memories free?

In my mind, her face is an inverted triangle with the tip pointing downwards. I can still remember the way she acted when she stumbled on an exciting story or a secret worth keeping to herself. Her pupils would expand and she would get that mouse-look on her triangular face. She would move her eyes about, cautiously, attentively, and devilishly, then lose herself in the crowd. I would watch the triangle dipping into the mouths that whispered in her ears.

Some time ago, when I went to the Canadian Embassy to pick up my visa, I found myself, out of sheer habit, scrutinizing the faces lined up at the little application window. The faces were devoid of all questions save one—How close am I to the window, to my dream of leaving? I let my eyes wander from face to face, listening to the stories they told as they stood waiting. I asked myself, 'Where is Alawiyya Subuh to listen to these stories and see the rivers of human hopelessness flowing at the Embassy gates?' For a moment, I could see her standing in the crowd, waiting to submit her own application.

I was drawn to the back of a woman with round shoulders, a somewhat plump backside and scruffy hair like fuzzy wool. I studied her profile and her face, inspected her features. Then I backed away when I had made sure it wasn't Alawiyya.

A few days ago, when I was crossing Tayyuni Circle on my way to visit Ibtisam, I remembered Alawiyya. I don't know why but, at that moment, it seemed possible that an explosion lay behind the secret of her disappearance. Perhaps she was blown up during the war as she was crossing the roundabout in the night. I looked around, right and left, just as she would do whenever we would leave the little nest of her neighbourhood. Every time we would cross a circle that, during the war, had been notorious for the constant shelling overhead, she would turn to me and ask: 'What was the name again of this circle? Was it Tayyuni or Qasqas or Sodeco, or what?'

And when I'd tell her the name, she would say, 'That's impossible! Where's the bombing? No, this can't be the same one. If what you say is true, there'd be a bomb falling over our heads at this moment.'

She would say that and look nervously around, with a hand sheltering her head.

'But the war is over, Alawiyya. What are you still afraid of?'

'Well, even if it's over and that's the case, they should change all the names of the roundabouts and neighbourhoods that are associated in our minds with violence and death. Otherwise, we're still going to be scared. They'll have to change the names so that we can discover these places all over again and not be afraid.'

Alawiyya is gone, and our names and faces are gone with her. Even her face has disappeared with our stories.

How can I find her features again?

What has been her fate and how does it compare to ours, the heroes of her novel?

I am the one who asks questions that have no answers. I am the one who speaks to imprint her memory on her white papers, before flying away with a blank memory . . . maybe it can still be done, if I can find just the scent of those memories.

But will I find it?

2

The whole city gave up on sleep that night. Explosions sealed ears and filled the city sky, turning the anticipated *weekend* into a nightmare. Then Monday came and the shelling calmed, so I goaded my body out of the apartment and down to the empty street. I headed in the direction of the office, not because I was expected there but to pretend that there was still life not far beyond my reach. As I drove through deserted streets, I felt as though I was descending into a vast cavern beneath the earth, like the hollow of the old well in our village home. It had once swallowed me and thrown me into hidden depths until I swallowed the water of my death and the emptiness inside my skull. Now the bones of my skull had grown loose by the deep booms of the shelling and felt disjointed like the skeleton of the old house.

The whole city seemed to me like a bottomless well that day and what seized me was my childhood fear that Mother would fulfil her threat and 'take care of me' in the water of the well if I wasn't a good girl.

The scene replayed itself before me. She had dragged me by my hair to the edge of the well, lifting the lid and pointing inside. 'I'll throw you in there,' she had said, her finger pointing into the darkness and flinging my heart right into the well, making it sink deeper and deeper inside. After that, each time the lid was taken off for a cleaning, my heart would slip away from me once again. It would scramble into the house and I would hurry inside, following the path of my heartbeats.

The streets titillated me and summoned me outside to peer into the secrets of their hollows. It was the same as when Mother would be away and my fear of the well at my childhood home would move me to seek what was hidden under its lid. Gazing into the darkness with my face fixed at the water's surface, I would lose myself in the dread and pleasure of finding secrets. I would stare at the water's unbroken darkness interrupted only by the reflection of one narrow beam of light. Then I would lift my head a little, move it right, then left, to watch it sway before me inside the water.

Father had dug the well more than sixty years ago, before water ran to the village homes. The cover of the well kept changing with time. It took on numerous shapes before finally assuming the form of a tile that lay at the level of the courtyard floor. In the beginning, the mouth of the well had been covered with the lid of a barrel that was set aside each time water was being raised. Then Father replaced the lid with a piece of tin that he cut to be larger than the opening, after my cousin Halima fell inside.

The well had been left open that morning. Mother was crossing the courtyard when she glanced towards the well and saw a small pair of legs disappear inside, then heard a splash below. She thought it was my sister Zainab.

She screamed at the top of her lungs, 'Oh my God. She's gone. The girl is gone.' She tore the scarf off her head and started pulling her hair out with her hands. The women and men of the neighbourhood raced into the courtyard after hearing her screams to stop her from throwing herself after her daughter. My uncle and his wife ran upstairs. They lived in a little room on the lower level, with a window overlooking the valley. My uncle's wife started wailing passionately in a shrill voice. She snatched Mother's veil and began to wrench and wave it through the air, telling her in a dirgeful rhythm: 'Ya Fatima, you wretched thing. Ya Fatima, you miserable thing. Ya Fatima, you unfortunate thing. Ya Fatima, you have already enough misery and misfortune. Ya Fatima, may God give you patience.' Her husband, my uncle Daoud, who was a strong swimmer and had served in the French army during the World War, jumped into the water with shirt and trousers on. He pulled the struggling girl out of the water and folded her body around his neck like a scarf. The men gathered around and pulled him out with a thick rope, circled several times around his wrist.

The surprise came once the rescue was complete and the girl slid down from his shoulders. Mother was mute with shock and my uncle, trembling from the cold water soaking his clothes, looked down incredulously at his own daughter. As for his wife, her wailing suddenly halted and transformed into something like the howl of a siren, 'That's you, ya Halima, when all this time I thought it was Zainab, you miserable little thing? How did you get yourself in that water, you wretched dog?'

She lunged at her daughter to beat her but they held her back. Lying on the ground, the little girl shivered from cold and fear, and the big black eyes in her round brown face froze at the sight of her mother's rage. Halima had to be turned over and her belly emptied of the water and secrets she had swallowed.

Then the cover of the well changed again into a concrete slab, but the new shape did not change my fears.

Ever since that day, the threshold of the well sends a certain trepidation creeping through me, a different kind of fear than death by water. According to Mother, the lady jinns were not comfortable except sitting at the very mouth of the well, the place where the secrets of the unknown world lay. I inherited this fear of the unknown, of wells and thresholds, from Mother ever since we gathered around her as children to listen to the stories of the lady jinns. She would caution us, my sisters and me, to take refuge in God in every step we took and to always say: 'In the name of God, the Kind and Merciful.' She warned us that it was not enough to whisper the words in our hearts, because only loud voices were heard by the jinns and kept them away. She said to call on God every time we approached the threshold of the well or crossed into the house, or the bathroom, or any other kind of threshold, especially if it led to water, or any kind of hole that could fill up with water or in which water was used.

And when I used to ask her, 'But why is that, Mother?' she would say, 'Because they like to sit with their children on thresholds and in places where there is water.'

'They who?'

'*They*. I mean, In the name of God, the Kind and Merciful. You should never utter their names or you'll be possessed by one of them. Say "they" or "her" or "In the name of God, the Kind and Merciful" and they'll hear you and know that you're talking about them.'

I have heeded her advice to this day and take refuge in God, as she always did, whenever I cross any kind of threshold. She would call on God whenever she turned on the hot water tap at the sink, just in case 'In the name of God, the Kind and Merciful' was sitting there. Mother would make sure to give 'her' fair warning so 'she' would not get burnt, and God help Mother should 'her' child be hurt, because the retaliation would surely be much graver than the offence. And so Mother would always call on God, even as she poured the dirty water down the toilet after washing the floor.

All thresholds led to secrets that frightened Mother. Any crossing or change signalled to her the possibility of arriving at the unknown. Mother often swore to us that she had seen 'her' more than once; 'With my own eyes, I saw her,' she used to say, 'believe these eyes of mine, which will be eaten one day by the worms of misfortune.' She would see 'her' standing at the threshold of the well whenever she woke up in the middle of the night and crossed the courtyard to relieve herself in a remote place.

And there 'she' would be standing, flesh and blood and wild hair, at the mouth of the village well. Mother would see 'her' brown eyes shimmering under the moonless sky. But it was after what happened to my sister Zainab that she became truly convinced that 'In the name of God, the Kind and Merciful' sat at the edge of our well.

*

That morning, Mother had finished baking and her round face was as red and warm as the loaves she had just made. Before she went down to the field to help Father harvest the wheat, she appointed Zainab watchguard of the fresh bread. Zainab was to make sure that none of the other children could steal the bread before she got back.

'Ya Zainab, be careful,' she instructed her sternly, 'God help you if I get back and find even one loaf missing. I nearly killed myself kneading and baking. You wait till I get back and I'll feed you. I know what big stomachs you all have. Each one of you needs ten loaves to fill up.'

We knew why she was so protective of the bread. She would have to wake up before daylight to finish the kneading, then wait for the dough to rise, then start baking at dawn. She would sit on the floor with her legs spread open, flatten the dough with her hands on the wooden board in front of her, then toss and turn each loaf between her hands until it became a wide slim circle before throwing it lightly on the flat oven.

My sister prepared to carry out Mother's orders and stood guard over the bread for fear of punishment. But my older brother Ahmad slipped by her, stole some loaves and escaped down the valley to eat them there. My sister ran after him, but he was faster and soon disappeared from her sight. He devoured the loaves in the orchard while, back at the house, fear devoured my sister. When Mother returned and heard about my brother's 'big belly', she broke into a rage and ran after my sister to thrash her. But before Mother's hand could reach her hair to tear it out, Zainab fell at the threshold of the well and blood oozed from the back of her head. The ground coffee pressed to the opening could not stop the blood's flow and neither could Sayyed Ali's readings, which were said to heal the ill, bring her back to consciousness. Zainab kept pushing towards the outer gate of the house, lunging her little body in that direction, while everybody held her still. She cried out, saying she wanted to go to her Mother, her brothers and sisters, her home.

Mother became hysterical and almost fainted out of fear for Zainab. She held her and sobbed, 'This is your house, my child, and I am your mother, may you live to bury me, you balm of my soul.' But my sister answered with fire flashing in her eyes, 'No, you're not my mother. My mother is there, far away. My brothers and sisters are there. I want to go to them, they're waiting.'

'I am your mother, and you, you are the first candle that lit this home. I am Fatima, your mother.'

'No, you are not my mother. You, your name is Khadija,' she said, 'my mother is Fatima. She's waiting for me over there!' And listening to her, Mother wept until she finally fainted.

She stood vigil at my sister's side day and night, hugging her close so Zainab knew that it was she, her mother, holding her and not the other one waiting over there. Mother hugged my sister, her arm covering the short distance between her young breast and neck while her stomach pressed firmly against Zainab's waist to keep her from running to the other mother.

She cried and cursed herself and damned the hour she had chased after her, until Zainab regained her senses. Mother told everybody the story, swearing that it wasn't she who hurt Zainab, that it was 'In the name of God, the Kind and Merciful' who had been sitting at the edge of the well. She convinced everybody including herself, by telling the same story each time without adding or changing anything. To wrap up the story, she would press the tips of her fingers together and make a dot in the air, as if putting a full stop at the end of a sentence.

'And this is the truth, as truly as you see me and I see you this minute,' she would say. 'Because "she" had slipped and fallen at the edge of the well, "she" got up and pushed my daughter until "she" opened her head. God help us.'

Years later, whenever we would visit the village in the summer, we saw everything the way Mother told us. With time, we learnt to see with her eyes because we were certain that her eyes never lied.

Like Mother, we would catch a glimpse of the lady jinn. Mother's stories had to be believed,. Otherwise, her faith would be shaken and her fears would grow. 'God watches and sees everything,' Mother used to say, 'and He will make sure "she" gets her due.'

Mother believed that she was the wronged one in all things, because the ways of right and wrong were clear to her. If she had the slightest doubt, she would go to the sheikh and he would advise her on what she needed to do. With Father, she would ask his permission first for everything, since that is how he had 'disciplined' her from the very beginning. When they first got married, she would ask him how much she should bake, and if she wanted to have a new dress made, he would have to give his consent before she could go to the village seamstress. Otherwise, he would give her a beating to set her straight, as he often did when she was still a young bride. One time, she wore a new slip for him that hung loose and fell to the knees. When she lifted her dress and he saw the slip, he asked her:

'Where did you get that from?'

'I had it made by the seamstress, Manahel.'

'And why didn't you ask me first?'

'Because the old one was worn out.'

And he wore her out with a beating so she would never get another slip made without his permission. Later on, he explained, as he made up with her, 'You see, Um Ahmad, it's for taking off, anyway, not for wearing. If no one other than me is going to see it, what's it for? Worn out or new, what do I care?'

*

Later, Mother told Alawiyya the story of Zainab's accident. She leant closer to her and, putting a hand in Alawiyya's lap, she whispered, 'Each of us has a double, my child. It was probably my daughter's double who made Zainab fall and hit her head on the edge of the well. Why else would Zainab's head have opened just like "hers"?'

Mother heaved her heavy frame from the sofa and moved with weighty steps into the kitchen. A sadness dimmed Alawiyya's face, and when she spoke, she stared like Mother—into nothing: 'Do you think Zuhair is my double? When I made him lose his mind at the end of the story, the novel too was lost. How else can you explain that it got lost when he lost his mind?'

Did Mother invent stories to believe in them? And did Alawiyya also invent the end of her story in order to believe in it? I am not certain about Mother's motive, but I know that she spoke to me plenty about her fear of wells, and that I too am afraid of the edges of water, and of empty spaces.

I can still remember my fear when I saw Mother's eyes disappear into the hollows of two wells in her aged face. I stood in front of her. I looked at the colour of her face and saw that it had come to resemble the soil in which she was about to be buried. Her closed eyes, surrendered to the final absence, were different from when they would be closed to open again. They were no longer Mother's eyes. Had they become Grandmother's? Mother's eyes used to be surrounded by fleshy, generous lids. Then suddenly there appeared two deep hollows that swallowed her eyes as soon as the curtains of the eyelids were drawn over life. As I sat next to her body saying my final farewell, her eyes sank deeper and deeper with the night. She had faded into the hollows of her eyes and could no longer see me. Her eyes were lost to me.

*

For two days the constant shelling had held my breath captive in my chest. When I left the apartment that morning, I felt that I was descending into a dark space filled with water. The chill in my body seemed natural but my lungs felt forlorn in the seclusion of my chest. My eyes that had been lost on the roads, and I thought had drowned just as Mother's, returned to me when I saw Abbas, and a fire rekindled in my veins, softening the chill of my dim shadow.

Abbas was alone at the office. The firm, which was owned by a well-known lawyer, was supposed to give us some experience before practising law on our own. But jobs are merely titles during times of war. So, Abbas arranged a second job, monitoring prices for one of the ministries. There too, supervision was slack and he would get paid at the end of the month whether he went or not.

As soon as I walked in, he remarked casually that his head was killing him and complained that even a cup of coffee might not be enough to take care of the headache. With profuse courtesy, he asked me to make him a big pot of coffee, since the woman who came every morning to clean and to wait on the employees had not yet arrived.

I walked into the small kitchen to find the sink full of dirty cups and glasses. While the coffee brewed on the stove, I washed two coffee cups and a little plate to cover the pot. I wiped the tray with a napkin and carried it to the office where Abbas sat waiting at his desk for the coffee that would thaw his frozen mind.

I sat on the chair in front of him and poured the coffee into the cups. I asked him how he had spent the night during the shelling. I don't remember what he answered, or if I even heard what he said. I remember that it was the first time we had talked about ourselves. He did not talk about his wife or his children, and I did not tell him about my past relationships. He just said he was tired, and I said I was too.

We talked without thinking about what we were saying, something that resembled children's talk. He said he missed falling asleep on a wooden bench in a beautiful park full of flowers, trees and the songs of birds. He said he wished he could still lie on his back and look up to the sky and sleep—sleep and dream—then wake up and find out that this park was Lebanon, and I said, 'Yes, me too.'

He didn't ask if I was involved with anyone, and at that moment I didn't think about the fact that he was a married man. Suddenly, as I got up from the chair, I said, 'You know what? I feel like loving someone.' I paused a moment and asked, 'Is this talking dirty?' I looked at him, smiling.

He laughed with me and said, 'Love has to be dirty.' And when I asked, 'Why?' he didn't answer. So I talked about my loneliness, and how I felt vulnerable and violated. I didn't say any of this with the intention of exciting him. But little did I know that I was turning in my keys, entrusting them to him without stopping for a moment to ask 'Why him?' Was it a coincidence? Or was it that in this city that toyed with everything—including lives—everything could start as a child's game?

As I spoke, the exhaustion was visible on Abbas' face and he looked older. He seemed like my father even though he was my age and I had said things to him that a girl would not say in front of her father. Although I spoke innocently, the room filled with a musky ripeness. For the first time, I noticed the little wrinkles around his small round eyes, his pallid skin and the full black beard covering his thick lips.

So, I transformed his frail arms in my mind into the muscular arms of an athletic man and I imagined that his long ears were invisible behind his earlocks. Beside him, my short and thin frame felt even smaller, the size of a pistachio nut. It was as if I were Maryam, but another Maryam. I could turn over his hand that was stretched on the table and sit in his palm like a little bird.

When I drew close to him to pour his coffee, he raised his eyes from the desk to the ceiling and stretched out his hand to stroke the warmth between my thighs. Without looking at what he was touching, he was reaching the dark recesses of my body and opening up new spaces. He kept his eyes fixed on the ceiling as if he didn't want to see what he was doing—the spaces hidden beyond the barrier of my skin under his hand.

A thick sweat seeped from within me, from the openings and pores of my body and clung to my skin. It was unlike normal sweat. It stuck like oil, and I wiped it from my face, neck and arm all the way down to my wrist.

While Abbas' hand played with me as if with the thighs of a doll, I grew fond of the game and began to go along. All my life, I never let myself play; I no longer asked for much. But at that moment I was not thinking, and I played with my body as we did with the wounded city.

When he reached out to me, the heat of his hands changed oil into water, and it dripped onto the floor. It was not the water of wells but of seas that met a distant sky stretching far above his gaze. Silently, he stroked my thighs, and my legs responded as if they wanted to learn to walk all over again. I imagined him standing close by, poised to catch me if I fell to the floor.

But Abbas did not imagine any of this.

He entered the well between my thighs, floated and swallowed the fear of leaving the water inside me, or the fear that he may never leave again.

* * *

There's nothing like playing to escape death.

What began as a diversion ended in love. Seeing him every Sunday became a thirst and a hunger that fed the hollows in my body, until the world redeemed itself in my eyes as a few warm secrets. I merged into his mass until my isolation vanished with the loneliness of my shadow. Because this shadow had limits in his life, the limits tempted me. What I wanted was 'a real man, not the shadow of a wall' as women say in Egyptian films. I wanted someone from whom to draw the illusion of anticipation and virile secrets, a companion once a week who would always be passing through my life. As for him, my weakness was all he wanted from me. He had found in my loneliness the key to my body.

Even though I met him every Sunday, he would become enraged if I left the house without his permission to see Alawiyya, Ibtisam or any of my friends. Every Sunday, he fled from his wife and the tedium of his home to indulge in my dependence on him. That was Abbas. He needed me to be the eyes in which to draw the picture he imagined of himself.

These Sundays pass slowly without Abbas, and I am condemned to the world of family gatherings and the formal visits that I have always detested. Now, the fava bean breakfast is the highlight of my Sundays, not because it reminds me of the fava beans I ate with Abbas during the Sundays of the war but because it reminds me of Mother. Its smell in the morning reminds me of Mother and the Sundays that we dedicated more to the mashed fava bean dish than the fact of our being together.

Mother and the rest of the family treated Sunday breakfast as an opportunity to satisfy some timeless hunger. Like frenzied little birds we snatched the food from her. There were nine of us children, Mother, Father and all the visitors who appeared unannounced on those mornings. They were lucky, those guests whose mothers-in-law must have finally remembered them in their prayers.

Round, flat thyme pies stood like a tower on a platter beside the large bowl of mashed fava beans that Mother had prepared from scratch. She cooked the beans slowly through several stages, each of which had a special name. When the beans softened, she called it a *hallouta* and when it fell apart, she called it *tiryak*, or even better, she described it as the 'moon of all time'. Her face would brighten at the ripe fullness of 'the moon' as she held up a steaming bean between fingers that had become so hardened and dry with the laundry and hot dishwater that the skin had become numb to fire itself. She would blow a little on the bean, then pop it into her cool mouth, to be sure that it melted on the tongue. The beans would start cooking at dawn when she rose for the early prayer and simmer all morning, 'God's blessing on the Prophet.'

For a few moments the food looked abundant but it soon transformed into a scattering of unwanted scraps. Mother would spread a big plastic sheet in the middle of the living room floor where we would all gather. A satisfied smile would spread across Mother's face as bowls and plates were spread on the sheet. Her eyes watched vigilantly to make sure that the piece of bread reaching for the large platter would be big enough for a heap of fava beans, fried eggs or raw pounded meat to sit comfortably on it. Nothing angered her like when she spied one of us daintily eating undersized mouthfuls. She would not hesitate to nudge whoever was sitting next to her, and say, 'Make your hunks bigger or you'll never fill up your bottomless pit of a belly.' Or she would yell the same to those of us sitting far across from her, and when no one would listen, she would lift her eyes to the heavens and say, 'God, you hear and see everything. You are the witness for those who give and those who refuse what they're given.'

Mother complained that our hands would never reach first for the beans, nor for the thyme pies or the vegetable dish. Even though we lived in a country blessed with greens, the plate of vegetables was always neglected. First to go was the plate of raw spleen that Mother would dice into little cubes to be sure there was enough to go around. As soon as eyes caught sight of the little black diamonds, the most valuable of edible jewels on the sheet, hands reached out swiftly and snatched them. Left with only streaks of red blood on the plate, Mother would retreat into silence until someone noticed and asked what was wrong.

She was always the last to join us, which is why she was always left with the scraps that we did not want. She would tarry on purpose. As soon as we would gather on the floor, she would start shuttling back and forth to the kitchen or the bedroom for no reason. Something in her body compelled her to avoid the food. I noticed that this happened whenever there was any meat being served. If meat were served as a stew, she would sit down and eat with us without any anxiety. But when a proper meat dish was served, she would come and go nervously until we called out to her and invited her to eat. It was as though she was not entitled to eat like the rest of us without an explicit invitation. For some reason, she felt most comfortable eating in secret, but she would always say, 'No, I'm not hungry. I don't know why people are such gluttons. Look how my stomach is stuck to my back. I would sooner die than make myself eat like that.' I would listen to her and look at her paunch that did not seem stuck to her back.

The words 'not hungry' were heard from her only when there was a meat dish served.

'Come on, Mother, we're waiting for you.'

'You go ahead, I'm not hungry.'

'Why don't you come sit? What are you still doing?'

'Coming, coming. Just a minute.'

She cast quick glances in our direction yet avoided our eyes. She hovered busily, waiting for us to urge and plead with her to join us. She would come only after all of us had begged her repeatedly, if the food was 'at the level of meat'. She considered meat a luxury, an indulgence for which she needed to excuse herself.

I used to hate the holidays on which we grilled meat because it was certain that Mother was going to be troubled and ill at ease. Eventually, she would get irritable and pick a fight either with Father or one of us. Sometimes, she would confront us angrily, saying we didn't remember her at lunch by leaving her even a little piece of spleen or a skewer of grilled meat.

'I'm not eating any more. You all go ahead and fill up.'

'Why were you late then?'

'Because I'm not hungry.'

'Not hungry? How can you not be hungry? Why did you get mad then?'

'I got mad because—why could none of you remember me enough to leave me a little piece of meat? Oh God, you hear and see everything. You are the witness for those who give and those who don't.'

She would keep stalling and join us only after she was certain that she had been wronged. Once she was certain, she was satisfied. But her indignation at not being offered even a single piece of meat did not make us feel guilty because she never threatened to die if she didn't have her fair share. But we did feel guilty should one of us reach for the heart of the onion, the heart of which had to be saved for her while we contented ourselves with the outer layers so our Mother would not die.

Since we were children, we learnt to avoid eating the heart. I remember very well how she warned us against it. The layers of the onion and its heart lay next to the pounded meat on the plate. Mother's mouth would water as she stared at the soft heart sitting next to the hard shells. Before anybody's hand could reach for the heart, she would say, 'Children, never eat the heart of the onion.'

'Why not, Mother?'

'If you eat the heart of the onion, your mother dies.'

'Really?'

'Of course, or do you want me to die?'

'No,' we answered.

'Then never eat the heart of the onion or I'll die.'

And after that, the heart of the onion was Mother's. She delighted in the crushing sound it made between her teeth, as we delighted in knowing that our mother would not die.

All my life until Mother died and even after then, I have avoided eating the heart of the onion. I let it glow in my eyes with the memories of Mother. When I reach the heart, I put it aside so Mother will not die all over again.

* * *

When my mother died years ago, I began liking grilled meat, raw spleen and fava beans, even though before I had always refused to taste any of them. I came to desire the foods that she had craved, as though I could conjure her through my cravings and fill the void she left behind. A nagging feeling makes me go early in the morning to a famous fava bean shop, and the smell of their home-made recipe leads me to the lost scent of her hands.

These aromas will perish from memory when I fly away to Canada, just as when I emigrate, I will take with me the sweet fragrance of the last grape in the bunch. My scent will fade from the house and the office where I worked, just as my sister Maha's smell left our room to give way to a new smell and new secrets in her husband's home, and a life whose details I did not know.

Her smell left the room to live on in my head and I could barely recall this old smell when I kissed her on the cheek. She had a new smell after marriage—whenever I entered her bedroom for some reason or opened her closet—but her new smell lacked the old muskiness. I had thought that human smells, like fingerprints, never changed and remained unique for each person.

I cannot tell exactly how the smell changed. Did her smell mix with those of her husband and children? Or was it just a matter of change in hormones with age and marriage? Maybe hormones are secreted differently under pain or happiness, anger or silence. Or maybe her scent has changed in my head. Maybe.

But that Sunday, I noticed something like her old smell when she sat next to me on the living room sofa of Father's home. I had not seen her for weeks and did not know that her husband had left for Kuwait to look for a job, planning that she would follow him if things worked out. Her two boys, Hussein and Mohammad, were sitting on her lap. Her arm was stretched along the back of the sofa behind me, the white sleeveless shirt exposing her underarm hair.

Her old smell crept into my nose. I don't know if I sensed it when she mentioned that her husband had left or when I saw her laughing.

Since her marriage she laughs modestly. Actually, she smiles constantly but never really laughs, as though she has become afflicted with a kind of laughter amnesia. My friend Ibtisam was struck by the same affliction—funny, considering her name. But then I saw my sister laughing like she did in the old days. She was roaring hysterically, so that her head swung from side to side and her mouth stretched so wide that her dimples disappeared into her cheeks.

At first she did not explain why, but my aunt who was visiting that day insisted on knowing the reason. 'Why are you carrying on like a madwoman?'

'Because I've been sleeping without a blanket.'

'What's so funny about that? It's hot as hell outside. Why would you cover up with a blanket anyway?'

After we pressed her, my sister finally confessed the story of the blanket to my aunt Samiyya and me. She told us that during their seven years together, her husband would not sleep with her except under the blanket.

'What do you mean under the blanket?'

'Just like I am telling you, he needs to do it all under the blanket. The blanket has to be covering us both even if it is pitch dark in the room. I tell him, "Just let me take my clothes off before we cover ourselves" but he says, "I just can't do it that way".'

But I could not laugh. I looked at her as she told the story and her old smell wafted from her body. My aunt volunteered her advice, saying, 'It's better under the blanket. Why not? Besides, your body is white and beautiful, my dear, and you never know when one of us is naked and "In the name of God, the Kind and Merciful" could see and desire you. That happened to your great aunt Tuffaha a long time ago, and her marriage was ruined because "he" would never let anybody, including her husband, touch her after that.'

She poked Maha's thigh and said, 'It's all right, child. It's more modest that way, and safer too.' She winked and nudged her, and among the wisdoms she offered was that for the woman to undress during marital obligations is a burden because then she has to strip off all her bodily hair with boiled sugar. She said that her late husband—God rest his soul—did not cause her any trouble because he never took off any of her clothes. She would just take off her slip and he would lift her dress or nightgown and take care of his business. For that reason, she would only use the sugar down below.

'One minute and we're done—end of story. No muss, no fuss.'

I suspected that my aunt was lying. I remember visiting her as a child and watching her boil a big batch of sugar that filled the whole house with its sweet smell. I was certain that such an amount was needed to remove the hair from her whole body. I said, 'Why did you always boil so much sugar then?'

'Oh, you be quiet now. Do you think it's just peach fuzz that a woman's got down there? It's *this* much,' she said cupping her hand, 'like a jungle, I tell you. You would think that I enjoyed the sugar, but it was all for the sake of cleanliness.'

Then she looked at my sister and said, 'Child, don't be upset with your husband about the blanket.'

'But I get so hot that I can't breathe and my heart almost stops beating.'

'I tell you it's better for you that way, and faster. If he sees you naked in the light, he'll want to take his time, and he'll wear you out and leave you exhausted. Yes, of course. What else did you think was going to happen? This is the burden that we all have to carry.'

* * *

I told Alawiyya about that Sunday, what my aunt said about herself and my sister's story about the blanket. I also told her about my sister's old smell which disappeared again with her husband's return from Kuwait.

My own smell too has changed of late. Ever since my hormones decreased, the odour between my thighs has become clean and light, like the smell of clean air. Sometimes, when I smell my hand after masturbating, it is as if I am smelling some odourless, clean skin. My panties no longer have that musky smell, that scent which I think was the reason the plumber did his work with the door closed behind him the time he came to fix the broken bidet.

Was it the smell of the panties or the sight of them flung carelessly on the floor? Or was it the exchange that had taken place between him and Mother?

I was lazing half-awake in my room across from the bathroom when I was roused by a conversation between Mother and the plumber. Mother, the Hajji, stood at the bathroom door with a hand on her waist and the other resting on the frame of the door. The plumber sat his bony young rump against the edge of the tub and leant his hand on the edge of the sink. Cigarette smoke rose from between his fingers as his bulging eyes stared at Mother, the Hajji, whose nervous body shook like frothing milk about to spill over the rim. I still remember how the words poured from her mouth in front of the plumber, repeating the phrase 'no meaning' in every sentence, to demonstrate her modesty and purity to a boy whose beard had hardly blossomed. She was talking like our cousin Nabiha who, whenever she described anything as 'long', would make sure to add 'No meaning'. If Nabiha said 'round' or 'thick' or 'this width', she would always say 'No meaning', and if she said 'this big' or 'went in' or 'came out' or 'stood up' or 'opened', she would quickly follow with 'No meaning'. Descriptions of any sort burnt her cheeks and face, and her tongue sought to quench the burning with the phrase 'No meaning'. I remember the day when I visited her in her family home in the village. She was putting away the thin sleeping mattresses, so I got up to help her, and she said to me, 'Stuff it well in there—No meaning. Because if it doesn't go all the way in—No meaning—it will slide out again—No meaning. Know what I mean?'

Throughout her conversation, Nabiha would always remind the listener of her modesty and that she did not intend a second meaning.

That day, Mother spoke just like her. Explaining the problem, the plumber said, 'This pipe I put in, it works like between a man and a woman. There's a female part and a male part.'

'Yes—No meaning.'

'No meaning, ya Hajji.'

'They say that since it was the carpenter who made a mess on the knot, only the carpenter can clean it up to undo it. You figure out how to make it fit—No meaning.'

'But, ya Hajji, I can't put him inside her because the hole has to be bigger—No meaning.'

'No meaning. You figure out how to take care of him.'

'If the male can't fit in the female, it won't work. Then the water starts dripping out from the hose—No meaning.'

'But how can you fit him inside?—No meaning.'

'If you don't want me to get a new pipe, I'll try to fix the old one. But then I'll have to set it upright, for it to go in—No meaning.'

'Come on now. You figure out how to fix the old one so I don't have to buy a new one and make a second hole because the opening's got too big—No meaning.'

I climbed out of bed and headed down the corridor to the kitchen to make the afternoon pot of coffee. Mother followed me with unusually quick steps, as she did only when she was unsettled by something. She tugged at the edges of her scarf around her flushed face to make sure that all her hair was tucked in and not a single hair could be seen.

The plumber closed the door behind him, locking it from the inside, and did not come out for a long while. Mother knocked more than once asking him:

'What's wrong? Why's the door closed? What's holding you up in there?'

'Just a minute, ya Hajji. I'm almost done.'

'Leave him alone. Let him do his work as he sees fit,' I yelled to her from the kitchen.

When the plumber appeared again, his eyes were misty and his skin had a peaceful and earthy shine. Smoky haloes enveloped his eyes, different from the dark circles of work and exhaustion or the kind that afflict politicians and officials because of the secrets stored in the blood around their eyes.

The haloes around the plumber's eyes faded before I could understand what had happened. Had the exchange with Mother aroused him? Was it the smell of the underwear or was it just the sight of the underwear on the floor, which can sometimes excite more than the presence of the body that wore it?

I was not sure. All I knew was that the underwear that lay on the floor was found in the tub after the plumber was finished fixing the bidet, and I found traces of dried semen on it. Did smelling my underwear excite him as it did Abbas? When I used to meet Abbas on Sundays, he would push me onto the bed as soon as he saw me, part my legs and close them around the sides of his face. He would nuzzle and sniffle at me like a cat at her kitten.

'Why do you do that?' I would ask him.

'Shut up and don't say a word. If you want to talk, you know what to say.'

He would reach up with his hand, cover my mouth and start sniffing again. When I would fall silent, he would lift his face to mine and say, 'Talk.'

'What do you want me to say?'

'You know what to say.'

'What?'

I would stay quiet.

'Say it. Say, "Put it in."'

I would not say anything.

'Talk. What is this called?' pointing at his member.

And he would insist every time until he heard the answer. He would repeat the question like a teacher to his student until he got the correct response. But I would not laugh while repeating the answers or naming our things when he pointed to them with his finger. As I spoke what he wanted to hear, I would sometimes press on his head with my hands and let him sniff me. Then I would smell the semen on his thigh or on my inner thigh, and sometimes, I would rub my face in it.

Finally, Abbas explained to me one day that he disliked the smell of clean underwear. It was the smell of bodily fluids that excited him, and not the smell of Camay or some other soap. He loved it because it reminded him of the aroma that emanated from his aunt Tuffaha in the village, whose lap smelled of fermented apples. In the late 50s, when he was a little boy and still lived in the village before his family migrated to Beirut like my family, Abbas used to curl up and fall asleep in her lap every time he had a headache. Hajji Tuffaha would sit cross-legged on the floor and Abbas would rest his head in her lap. She would read verses of the Koran and stroke his head and shoulders, reaching around his neck with her plump hands and gold bracelets as he pressed his face into the folds of flesh between her thighs and the bottom of her belly. From the openings of her loose underwear would escape a damp smell, hinting of a viscous substance impenetrable by light. Sometimes, he would peek under her skirt and she would say, 'You naughty boy!' and pinch his ear, then continue her stroking. And one day, for the first time in his life, he saw that bushy triangle between the thighs after peeping quickly inside. 'You little mouse,' she said to him, laughing, 'I'm sitting here praying for you and you're sneaking a look, you peeping Tom. By God, no man can ever be trusted. But it's all right,' she said, 'what's important is that you get better. You're still young and must be forgiven.' He was ten years old at the time.

Her smell came back to his nose as he told me the story, the smell that had disappeared from the village after she died and took it with her.

All smells disappear, following those who create them. But the scent of memories remains, and disappears only with the flight of its author. I recount these memories so the scent will stay right here. That is the only kind of smell that never leaves. As for my other smells, those will disappear and leave with me.

3

It is Ibtisam whom I feel compelled to say goodbye to before anyone else. For she continues to be the sea of my memories, even though her marriage has darkened its waters and broken the rhythms of its waves, keeping her away from my shore, my shadow and all my years.

I must call to let her know that I finally have the visa and am making preparations to depart. I will go to the Gevinor building in Hamra Street to the Middle East Airlines office or any other airline where I can find a seat to Canada. I will say to her, 'For the first time, Maryam will see Beirut from above!' But will I find the strength to kiss her and say 'Goodbye'? Or will I say, 'I will see you soon. Take care.'—as on any other day?

Will Ibtisam have time to see me, or will she evade me as she has done in the last few years? 'I'll talk to you tomorrow,' she says, 'and we'll see if we can plan something . . . ', and I say, 'OK, whatever you like.'

I know Ibtisam like I know myself. From the start, I have been nourishment for her heart and she, the window through which I saw my life's beginnings. I remember the day when I drove her to shout in my face. 'You kill me with your weakness!' She had said. 'How can you let your father and brother hit you?'

That morning, Alawiyya and Ibtisam had convinced me to march in a student protest, as a way of overcoming my fear. That was in the days before the war and the idea terrified me. 'What if my father or brother saw me?' I said, 'They would bury me alive.'

'Why should they bury you? Is there anything wrong with expressing your beliefs? Besides, it's none of their business.'

'In our house, there's no such thing as "None of their business." And "express my beliefs"? That's a good one! The last time I forgot to slip the scarf on my head before leaving the bus, he saw me and pulled me all the way up the stairs by the hair. Since then, I make sure it's on as soon as the bus turns towards our street.'

But they would not leave it alone. They kept arguing with me about the march until they convinced me. I would never have dreamt that my brother Ahmad would see me on the street in front of the Parliament, chanting with all the others. For freedom!

I tried to stay close to Ibtisam, locking arms with her on my left and a young man on my right. As the march started, I was mute with fear; but slowly, as the chanting caught fire around me and soared, I was moved by its electricity. My shoulders, once bowed with timidity, straightened gradually until I raised my head high and thrust my fist in the air. My lips, which had begun by murmuring weakly, grew bold and passionate until my voice erupted and my body became weightless like a fresh breeze. I found myself shouting, shouting, shouting:

'Oh Freedom,
We are your men.
Oh Freedom . . . '

I repeated the words exactly as I heard them chanted, and wanted the rhythm to grow faster and faster.

But as soon as my eyes fell on my brother watching me from far away, and I saw the anger burning in his eyes, I melted into the crowd in a flash. Afterwards at home, I had to 'stomach a beating' that I have not forgotten—one slap because I was not wearing a scarf on my head, and another because I was at the march.

*

I know that Ibtisam loves me.

Her mother did not know anything about me and had never seen me when she asked her, 'This Maryam, is she pretty?'

'So pretty. Like the moon.'

'Really? With long legs and big eyes?'

'She is just gorgeous. Like the moon.'

The day I met her mother for the first time, I was wearing my blue school uniform. She stared at me for a long time, at my bowed legs and crooked teeth, scrutinizing me as if she were examining a bride for her son. I hid my hands in my pockets and asked Ibtisam, 'Why is your mother looking at me this way?' 'She is looking at your beauty,' she answered, pinching my cheek, 'I told her so much about you.'

Her mother laughed loudly after leaving the room. 'How can you not see those bent legs?' she asked Ibtisam. 'And that mess of teeth!' Ibtisam told her mother that she did not know anything about beauty because I was lovely like the moon.

Like the moon . . . !

When we were little, we sang of the whiteness of the President Jamal Abdel Nasser whose face, we thought, was drawn on the moon. I was four after the events of '58, when I played a game with the children in the neighbourhood. They stood in a circle, each with their hands around the waist of the next in the chain, singing and swaying from side to side. I would slip my little body into the circle and sing along with the rest of them. We would stretch the word 'Jamaaaal' as we sang:

'Jamal, how beautiful his wife,
Beautiful just like him,
Fair like him, blond like him,
Shamoun, how ugly his wife,
Black like him, black just like him.'

One night, the family gathered around the television to listen to Abdel Nasser's resignation speech after the '67 war. I noticed for the first time that Abdel Nasser was dark, not white at all, and not blond. I was struck by the darkness of his skin; I had never thought to doubt that he was fair. And I noticed that Shamoun was blond, and that his wife was a beauty.

*

I will call Ibtisam before I make any preparations, and whether she says goodbye to me with old eyes or new, I will hold her and press her tightly against my chest. How can I not go to her, when she has been the keeper of my secrets? She knows my whole story with Ali and Mustafa and the others . . .

Yes, she was the first one I told about Ali.

I met him at Yasmine's house in South Beirut. Ali was a relative of her husband Dr Kamel, and rented a room nearby when he moved to the city to finish his degree. As he gazed at me adoringly with his passionate dark eyes, a fire ignited in my body. Every time he kissed me on my forehead or in that little point between the corner of my mouth and my cheek, I discovered a wealth of affection that got lost when he was killed. After that, only Ibtisam was there to listen while I talked to myself. She taught me how to walk all over again, holding me by the hand as I crawled, then stood up, eventually walked the ground by myself again.

The Israeli army began its invasion of Lebanon in 1982 as its tanks started creeping into the south of the country. No one knew that the invasion would continue to Beirut in order to occupy it. Ali called me and said, 'I'm taking the car to the village to bring my family to Beirut.'

'You can't go, Ali. The Israeli army is advancing. I'm sitting next to the radio and listening to the military reports. They're saying that the army is still moving north. Please don't go.'

'How can I not go, ya Maryam? Should I just leave my family there to die? In '78, when they came in, we lost both my brother and sister in the bombing, and the house too. I can't leave them there.'

'I beg you, Ali, forget about going. Driving around on the roads is more dangerous for them than staying at home.'

'I can't, Maryam. I have to go. When I get back, I'll call you.'

'All right. Take care of yourself. I love you.'

'Me too. Bye.'

'Bye.'

When the Israeli tank crushed Ali, his mother and sisters on the way from the south to Beirut, and no one survived except the little girl whose mother threw her out of the window in time, I too had to learn to walk again and rediscover my limbs. First I heard the news on the radio, then I saw the car on the television screen—crushed on the Southern highway. His name and the names of his family members were repeated on television and radio stations. I could not believe it at first, and I could not make myself go to the funeral. They were all buried in one mass grave while Ali's father, who had been waiting for them in his room in Beirut, had nothing left but the baby girl with her broken bones and wings.

The world collapsed for me. Months passed before I could say a single word, since the shock had extinguished all my desires, even the desire to speak. Cigarettes burnt my throat but sustained me. Ali was the only person who had ever adored me and had become my whole life in just a few months. I did not mourn him because he had promised me marriage but because he *was* the promise.

*

Two years had passed since his death when I met Mustafa, the brother of a friend from the office where I worked. When I met him at her house, he explained that he was just back from Switzerland. He was a young man of thirty-five, very dark and tall, with a heavy frame. He had thick black hair, black eyes and a cigar always in hand that added to his pride. He had a noticeable weight at the bottom of his belly, unlike most men whose body fat gathers and swells at the middle of their torso. His legs were full at the top, which made his thighs rub against each other when he walked.

I was at the stage where I had recovered from my shock over Ali, or, more correctly, at the stage when I wanted to overcome my pain and the fear of loneliness.

I knew him for almost a year during which we met several times. He would call me, saying that he had just returned from Switzerland to spend a week or two in Beirut until he could sell some of the merchandise he had brought back with him. Then he would leave again and I would wait for him, wait for his phone calls, and his *hello*, which he said with an affected English accent. When he would finally return, we would meet and he would give me a load of merchandise, towels in various colours and sizes, women's underwear, pyjamas and sometimes, alcoholic drinks. I would sell it to whoever I could and give him the money.

One day, he called at seven thirty in the morning, saying that he had got back from Switzerland a couple of days earlier and that he wanted to see me and had some things to say.

'Now?' I asked.

'Now. This minute.'

'Should I meet you in a cafe?'

'Come here . . . to my house,' he said, 'I'm tired of travelling. What, don't you trust me?'

'No, that's not it.'

I went without fear. His home was a furnished flat at the end of Hamra Street, which he had 'moved into' as happened to so many deserted flats at the time. As I drove through the city after the long night of shelling, the streets were empty except for a few cars and pedestrians. The Valium that I had taken to sleep the night before was still weighing on my head and body. I parked the car in front of the building and went up to his flat on the third floor.

He opened the door and wrapped his arms around me. Then keeping a hand on my shoulder, he closed the door. In the mirror hanging on the hallway wall, I saw myself—a miniature figure on a key chain, attached to his corpulent waist. In a moment, he was throwing me on the bed. He was on top of me, panting on my face as he wrestled with my clothes. I did not resist, not when he kissed me on the sides of my neck or ears, nor when his fingers unbuttoned my trousers. I do not know why I did not resist. I had loved Ali for two years and I often visited him alone in his room. We would make food and eat together, and when he would kiss me, I would feel all my joints melt. But there was never a day when he tried to unbutton my trousers.

Ali used to lie on top of me with his clothes on. He would embrace me and squeeze me with his hands until the sweat dampened our clothes and mixed with the fluid that wet his trousers between his thighs, until we could no longer tell our smells apart. Until this day, when I visit his grave and burn meadow safflowers, all I can smell is our shared scent. Sometimes, he would undo a few buttons of my shirt and kiss the tops of my breasts, or he would touch me between my thighs over my trousers. But that was all. Not because he was shy but because he did not want to hurt me. He said he wanted me to become his on our wedding night. Though his politics were progressive, Ali's peasant roots kept him from wanting more from me, and that made me feel safe with him.

*

It was the first time that I had been naked in front of a man. Clouds seemed to have gathered around my body, then dispersed to reveal it to me only in that first moment of nakedness before a man's eyes, as if it had fallen from the sky and suddenly become a reality. He lay on top of me and I felt his alien eyes swallowing the surfaces of my face and body. As he ran his lips over my skin, I found corners, curves and protrusions that I had never noticed before. But since the discovery came to me through Mustafa's mouth, eyes and hands, it left me feeling violated by him and estranged from my body.

And it was the first time that I had seen a man's member. I glanced at it to make out its shape, to comprehend the secret that attracted me whenever I found myself staring at the front of a man's trousers.

When he finally climbed off me, I stayed lying on the bed. Naked, he walked to the kitchen to get a bottle of cold water. He stood in front of me in the middle of the room and, throwing his head back, emptied the bottle into his mouth, as if it were a thick wide sewer. The sound of water poured into my ears. I gazed at his nakedness and felt ashamed of my body. As I began gathering the bed sheets around me, my body diminished within itself while Mustafa walked comfortably around the room, unconcerned with his sagging belly and his member which had now softened and shrunk.

I was not only ashamed of my body but of all its flaws, not only of my droopy bottom but also of the large mole on my breast. At that moment, I envied men's careless ignorance of their bodies. My body had never repulsed me like it did that day, naked before me, and before a man who only saw in it flesh for his satisfaction.

A feeling of dejection took hold of me, not because I had hoped to lose my virginity with a man whom I loved as I did Ali but because of the callousness with which Mustafa took me. Not that it had happened in spite of me; the truth is I did not resist him. Because with Ali's passing and the death of many others, the very idea of waiting had lost meaning. With this absence of time, all things became confined to the 'now' and the fear of death rendered all other fears senseless. Afterwards, even the shell of my loneliness cracked, and my values collapsed like the city's buildings and streets. But my cravings for romance endured in spite of everything, and I still longed for some affection and a little poetry.

I returned to my room, took another pill of Valium, and slept. I did not awaken until I heard Mother's voice. I opened my eyes to a dim light seeping under the window curtain, and time became muddled to me: Was I at the day's beginning or the night's end? I tried to discern the amount of light in the sky and the amount of darkness in my eyes. The last time I looked at the watch, it was twelve, noon. How long I had slept, I was not sure. But I knew that I was standing on the threshold of the evening when I heard Mother saying: 'Get up, ya Maryam, the sun has caught you off guard. A thousand times I've told you that if the sun catches you off guard, you'll be in a foul way all day and the world will look dark to you.'

And Mother was right.

The sun had ambushed my heart and my mood, and I wanted to cry. My chest clenched and the tears gathered in my throat. I rose from the bed and stood like someone wavering between waking and sleep, between dreaming and reality, and between pleasure and plight. The burning between my legs was kindled not only by shame for myself but also for Mother and Father. As I walked, I imagined them staring between my thighs, smelling nothing on my body except the reek of Mustafa's odours.

A headache wrapped itself around my head in the house, caused by the Valium, or maybe by Mustafa's smell, or the request he made of me after he rose and walked away naked. He returned with a big plastic bag and placed it on the bed beside me. I was still lying down, my body wrapped in the sheet. He sat at the edge of the bed and began emptying it in front of me—women's clothes of all shapes and colours and cheap underwear in bright red, yellow, orange and purple. I will never forget that underwear which reminded one of those poor imitations of outdated Western styles that a tourist to Syria would see hanging in the shopfronts at the Hameediyya market.

I looked at the clothes spread around me on the bed, panties with an opening or a zip fastener at the front, or a small design covering the groin, like a heart, or butterfly, or feathers. Mustafa almost died laughing as he explained to me the purpose of the zip fastener, and demonstrated by zipping it up and down. He said, 'Look here my sweet, with this one she can have sex without even taking off her underwear. We are living in an age of speed where time is valuable. Besides, we men like strange things like that.'

I needed the illusion of love. I took the merchandise and, despite everything, sold it all. And the one who liked it most was Yasmine.

'How can I wear something like that?' she would ask, then add laughingly, 'Is this what you've come to, Maryam? Selling underwear after studying law?'

Yasmine told me that that day her husband, Dr Kamel, went crazy when he unzipped the zip fastener and his desire bordered on insanity before the 'match', as she called it. And another time, when she wore the panties that flicked on and off with any movement or touch, he became a madman.

I sold countless bags of Mustafa's merchandise. Each time I saw him after a long absence abroad, he would be carrying a bag of new merchandise. 'This way,' he would say to me, 'we can save money and get married.' But my own 'match' with Mustafa, our final battle, was of another kind, and it is one that I will never forget.

I had never known that my voice could be that loud and shrill.

That day, I thought Mustafa was in Switzerland. I was passing by the Ghandoul Café on my way home from my new job at the public notary's office when I saw Mustafa sitting close to a young blonde woman with light brown eyes, holding her hand on the table. I could see her eyes shining from far away, and Mustafa's gaze devouring her as they talked in whispers.

At first, I stood there paralysed by the shock. Then I drew closer to their table with slow steps, and after making certain that it was Mustafa, I said, 'Excuse me, Mustafa, I would like a private word with you.' He left the girl sitting at the table and followed me outside, where my questions fell on him like the beads of a broken rosary. 'I thought you were in Switzerland. When did you come back and how come you didn't tell me? And who's that girl you're sitting with, you filthy cheat?' And many other questions that I no longer remember as much as I remember my choking voice as I tried to scream in his face.

He did not answer my questions. He just said: 'Enough. Enough of you. Keep your voice down and get out of here. Whether I travel or not is my business.' Then he said the sentence that I will never forget, 'Did you really think that I would marry an old maid like you?'

His words struck me like a thunderbolt.

'I'm an old maid?' I repeated.

'Yes, an old maid and a half. Or did you think you're still a young girl with a future and marriage waiting for you?'

I fumbled in vain for a deadly retort. 'You bastard!' I heard myself saying, 'You're the old man, you piece of shit!' I walked calmly to my car, but as I drove away the tears erupted, washing over my bitter laughter. I was twenty-eight then and he was thirty-six.

That evening, Ibtisam consoled me, 'It's all right, ya Maryam, we all make mistakes. Leave it all behind you.' Then she laughed and said, 'But you deserve it. If only you could've seen yourself, going around from house to house making us buy those rags from that donkey.'

To cheer me up, she took out the zip fastener panties and raised them to her face, peeking through the zipper and saying, 'Peekaboo! Wake up, ya Maryam, wake up!' Then she put the underwear away and said to me in a sad voice, 'Forget the whole thing. In war, and out of war, we can all get carried away and make mistakes. We can all be stupid sometimes.'

* * *

Whether Ibtisam awakens from her slumber or not, I will still love her.

I try to understand her life from the little she says about it, and the lot that she swallows, hides or chooses to forget. I see the words diminish in her throat and watch her vocabulary get lost in the narrow world she has entered. I discover that her pond of words has dried up, the water evaporated under the sun.

I hear her confuse her children's names as she calls them, the same way our names were mixed on Mother's tongue. I can tell that Ibtisam does not believe she is entitled to express her desires. Like Mother, she has to believe this in her heart, or she will suffer. She does not need more suffering; in fact, she does not need any. I notice that she says—'My children will miss you'—before she says that *she* will miss me. I look at her and wonder how she can only talk about what her children and husband love and hate. I no longer hear her say 'I'. And she never says 'we' as she once did.

In the old days, I would ask her, 'We who?'

'We, the people,' she would sometimes answer.

And at other times, 'We, the revolutionaries.'

'We, those of us who dreamt.'

'We, the ones who refuse . . . '

And the last time she spoke of 'we', she said 'We, who have been defeated.'

Since then, the word 'we' has acquired new usages. She says, 'We Muslims', 'We Arabs', 'We the Lebanese', 'We, those of our sect', 'We women', and finally, 'We the family'. She would say the word and get scared, quickly changing the subject, just as she did when I went to her, raving, the day the Israeli forces committed the Qana massacre. As soon as I stepped into her living room, her eyes wandered from me to some other place that I did not know. Finally, she jumped to her feet and I thought she was going to say something, that she was about to explode in pain, or scream in anger, or open the door and walk out. But she stood in front of me, and started babbling about her problems with her Sri Lankan maid and her children. She jumped from subject to subject, about how the meal had burnt on the stove, how the oil had splattered and burnt her. She opened her hands to show me her burns but her hands were soft, without a mark.

'Look at my hands, how they were burnt by the oil . . . ', 'I topped off the tank yesterday . . . ', then, 'Jalal is the best, isn't he? There's no one like him.'

In her hallucinations, she would flee from her fears, reciting to herself things I could not understand.

4

If I find Alawiyya, I will not ask her about our story. I will tell her
that the comma with which she had intended to begin her novel, to
separate the present from what had preceded it, had drifted away
and split into little pieces. I will tell her that the clauses are no longer
dependent, and that predicates no longer concern me . . .

*

In truth, I am most concerned about visiting Mother's grave, about
saying farewell, and cleaning it well. Then I will sit next to it and tell
her that I am leaving. I will talk to her like the others who visit graves
in my village. They sit beside the graves, and talk more to their dead
than the living. I see them on the holiday mornings, talking to their
dearly departed. I hear a voice asking the grave: 'How are you today?
Are you well, God willing? You slept comfortably, God willing? Are
you comfortable down there, or is it uncomfortable? I saw you yesterday in my dream and you said that you were comfortable and
happy, and when you told me so, it comforted me.'

I overhear many of the stories told to the dead. The visitors deliver
news about who has left, who has emigrated, who has died and joined
them there, asking sometimes whether the newcomer was welcomed.
The women speak to the dead while the men rarely speak. A woman
tells the one lying in the grave about her longings for him and gives
vent to her worldly cares. She apologizes for the delay in visiting, 'Here
I am, washing your grave and scrubbing it because you like cleanliness
. . . Forgive me for staying away for so many weeks. I have missed
you and missed talking to you. But my pains and illnesses have kept
me away from you. From doctor to doctor I've been going, and I still
feel the same. There's no doctor but God.'

The graveyard became a meeting place for the villagers, taking the place of the square which had once been a living room for them. No longer that dreadful and lonely place where old graves were eaten by moss and time, it became a retreat for the visitors of mortality.

Its domain expanded and spilled into neighbouring fields that the county eventually transformed into an extension of the old cemetery. Even so, some were afraid that they would not find a spot in which to be buried next to their father or family, so they dug their graves in advance, to secure the proximity.

My uncle, the mayor of the village, chose his grave at the foot of the mountain, at the head of the graveyard. He dug a two-level grave, but, instead of being flat and even, the hole slanted steeply to one side.

My uncle took his wife to the grave and told her: 'Ya Hajji, this is my grave and this is yours. I don't like my space to be angled downwards. I like the other one better.

'And which one is mine?'

'The one at the bottom, of course.'

'So you want to be above me in life and in death?'

'Of course. Where else would I be, you on top and me below? Listen to that madness. That would be something! What would the people of the village say? How could they respect me after that?'

My uncle, the mayor, was four years past one hundred when he dug the grave for himself and his wife who was two years his elder. Some time before my uncle died, Kameel, the village idiot, discovered that the mayor's grave was a pleasant place to sleep. He would climb in at night and lie peacefully there until dawn. Kameel rarely slept in his mother's home. During the day, he would visit all the village houses whose owners would offer him charity in food and cigarettes; then at night, he would sleep in the valleys, meadows, or my uncle's grave—when sleep overtook him nearby.

When my uncle found out that Kameel had taken a shine to his grave, he went mad. The Hajji Diba told him that she was gathering wild mallow early one morning, and she reached the foot of the mountain when she saw two legs stretching out of the grave. She screamed and fainted, thinking it was 'In the name of God, the Kind and Merciful.'

Kameel sat next to her, as she lay on the ground, saying, 'It-s-s-s It's m-m-me, ya D-D-iba.'

When she regained her senses and saw that it was Kameel, she went straight to the mayor and told him the story. On the same day, the mayor closed the two graves with two molded concrete slabs. He grabbed Kameel and scolded him, 'Who would have thought that a halfwit like you would dare. I myself have not yet slept in it, and you thought you could, you dog?'

Mother too asked that she be buried next to her brother's grave, even though her last request was that we would take her to see her mother. She snapped her head off the pillow, and though she looked towards us, her gaze wandered beyond:

'Take me to my mother . . . I want her. Take me home. Where are you, Mother?'

'This is your home, Mother.'

'No. This is not my home. Take me to my mother. My home is over there.'

Those were her words, even though she had rarely mentioned her mother to us, and whenever she did, it would be to curse her and her uncle Akeel for marrying her off. And when she would visit the graveyard, to complain to my brother and her brother about her sorrows, she would pull out the weeds that cast shadows on their graves and wash their headstones with water, but she would walk past her mother's grave without a glance.

When I go to say goodbye to my mother, I too will pull out the weeds before watering the jasmine that she asked me to plant around her grave.

At her deathbed, my sister Zainab asked her, 'Where do you want to be buried?' but she did not answer. She turned tearful eyes to the wall next to her bed.

'Why aren't you answering, Mother? God desires that we choose the place of our graves.'

'I don't want to die, ya Zainab. Leave me alone.'

'We're all going to die. We're all on the way, and no one will stay behind. You'll be ahead of us, and we will follow.'

'Whoever wants to die can die—I don't want to.'

'You need to make your request. Refusing to choose is a great sin in God's eyes.'

She answered after a long silence, the pain wringing her pallid face, 'Next to my brother, Abu Ali—Daoud.'

My sister was satisfied but I had grown impatient with her questions. 'Leave her alone,' I screamed in her face. 'Leave her alone. What do you want with her? Is it not enough that she's dying, you also want to turn her grave into a burden? Don't you see that she's refusing death, that she doesn't want to talk, but you have to keep torturing her with your questions? It's criminal.'

'You keep quiet. It's blasphemy not to let the dying request where to be buried. She's the one who will have to sleep in her room, not us.'

Then she turned to Mother and said, 'Carry my regards to my brother and uncle, and tell them that their absence is always felt and that we miss them.'

When the crackle of death sounded in Mother's throat and her eyes bulged, my sister Zainab bent over Mother's face, trying to make out what and who was going through her frozen gaze.

Suddenly, she turned to us and said with wide eyes, 'Mother must be seeing whoever has come to take her. What do you think she's seeing, and who? Is it the Angel Azrael himself, or has he brought with him Grandmother and Grandfather, our brother, Uncle Abu Ali and others who knew her? No, he must be alone. But no, that can't be, because when you're dying, you see before your eyes those who died before, coming to get you. When my mother-in-law was dying, she called out to them each by name. Mother sees them but she can't talk. Oh, if I could only know what death is like.'

I told Alawiyya about Mother's passing, and she listened to me attentively like she still did in those days. A bitter feeling, yellow, rose from her depths as she listened to me. The same feeling that rose from within me every day since my childhood mornings. As soon as I would get to school, Ibtisam could always tell what was on my mind. She would nudge me before we got into the classroom.

'What happened? Did your father and mother have a fight again this morning?' she would ask, and I would nod my head 'yes', and sometimes I would not even have to respond because she could guess the answer in my vacant stare.

I would get up in the morning to their screams flying around the house. They began their morning with a quiet chat over a pot of coffee on the veranda adjacent to our room. They would take turns recounting their dreams of the previous night but soon the exchange would slip into old quarrels about events that took place more than a quarter century ago, conjuring up the names of people whom they had not seen since the late 40s.

'You would not believe what I saw in my dreams, woman!' Father would tell her. 'I was travelling to Palestine and the camel stopped in his tracks, the son of a dog, because he was tired of the load that they had thrown on him. He just dug himself right in and nothing could get him moving. That's camels for you. When a camel hides things in his heart and gets angry, he will only do what's in his head, and he'll take revenge on his owner at the first chance he gets.'

'And I saw in my dreams that I had a fight with Um Ismael,' she would say. 'I've been in a rotten mood since I got up, all because of that bitch of a dog.'

The dream banter would only be a warm up for the main event, the way morning exercises start with light callisthenics in preparation for more serious efforts.

Whenever the opportunity presented itself, Mother would remind Father, with all the wrath in hell on her side, of the times in the 40s, when he used to go to Palestine on his camel to sell the carpets he had brought from Syria, or the barley and other grains from his aunt's fields. She never tired of berating him for leaving her behind while he went on those trips.

'What difference would it have made taking me along?' she would demand. 'The camel was going either way. You wouldn't have had to carry me on your back. What's your excuse? Let's hear it.'

'Can't we sit in peace, woman? I couldn't take you, and that's that. If I could have, I would've taken you. I used to roam the country from beginning to end, stopping at every street and corner in all of Palestine. Why make you suffer all of that?'

'Like you hadn't already made me suffer a thousand times! How could you have added to such suffering? What have you given me except suffering? From the very beginning of my life with you, I've been loaded with troubles. I call on God, and He hears and sees everything. Now it's between you and Him!'

'Are you going to shut up or should I smash your head on the wall, you ass? But then your head and the wall are one and the same. You've spent your whole life thinking like an ass and never smartened up. Who's the one who's been burdened with troubles, you or me?'

'You could have taken me with you, but you're a tyrant.'

Father would then leap up and lift his hand to her face to slap her, 'I said shut up. I couldn't take you. Won't you understand that once and for all?'

She would raise her hands to shield her face, with one eye open and the other shut.

'No, I will not understand it! Even if I forgot about the trips to Palestine, you would still have to explain to me why you didn't take me along to the Bayk's funeral. Each time I tried to get behind you on the camel, you threw me on the ground like a dog. God forgive you for your tyranny. The whole world was there at the Tayba. All the women poured onto the roads and made their way on foot for the chance to tear their hair out in mourning for the Bayk. Only I was forbidden from seeing it all, you tyrant. I will carry the sting of it in my heart for all time.'

'How did you expect me to take you there? And your children, you ass, were we supposed to leave them all alone?'

'Nothing would have happened to them. All the women left their children behind. You should know that I stood at the door that day and took off my scarf and said, "Hear me, ya Saint Zainab. Just as he deprived me from seeing the Bayk's funeral with my own eyes, may God never forgive him or accept his repentance." And may your tyranny come back to you, God willing.'

'You've spent your whole life cursing, and what good has it done you?'

'I will keep cursing and lamenting my burdens, because the day is bound to come when He will hear me.'

I would hear them as soon as I got up from my bed. With closed eyes, I would walk to the veranda door and plead, 'Do you have to fight every day about things that happened five thousand years ago? Does it have to be every day beating the same dead horse?'

'Look who's here to tell us what to do,' Mother would say. 'Like it's not already enough that they come out of your ass, they have to cry boohoo on top of it! Be off with you, girl, if you know what's good for you!'

Of course I would be off and go to school and tell Ibtisam about Mother and Father's morning, and how Mother kept needling Father as if she was determined to take her revenge and make him as miserable as he had made her during their life together.

Ibtisam could tell from my eyes whether Father had hit Mother. I would describe to her how he had held her by the hair to strike her head against the wall, and how Mother would scramble like a chicken with her round body as he shuffled after her on his crippled 'leg and a half'. I would tell Ibtisam how long Mother had wept and describe her tears in detail, remembering each and every moist line that had run down her cheeks.

I never told Ibtisam, nor did I ever pretend to Alawiyya, that I came from a happy family. I grew up thinking that, inside the home, one could not know laughter or quiet or calm. For me, home meant clamour and screams and roosters' quarrels. Often these family battles led to the tearing of clothes and even the flashing of kitchen knives, so that Mother would run to hide them as soon as the fighting erupted. But when it peaked, she would shriek at the top of her lungs, 'By my ashes, my children are gone.'

Sometimes, she would let herself fall to the floor and her eyes would start rolling backward and the ceremony of reviving her would begin: 'Run. Run and get a matchbox,' everybody would start shouting. We would either burn the tip of her nose or slap her on her round cheeks to rouse her. There were times when she would open her eyes before we could use the matches, and we would realize that she had been acting all along. But there were other times when her nose would singe and black traces would mark her nose for days.

I thought that laughter only lived outside the home until I entered Ibtisam's house for the first time and saw her mother laughing. I was so stunned that I had to run my eyes about the house to make sure it was happening. Her mother's calm face and demure smile matched the illustration of the mother in my school primer. I had thought that mothers only smiled in front of the cameraman's lens, that perhaps photographs could not come out without their smiles.

Every time I passed by the Armenian photographer Asfadian's shop and looked inside, I would find myself smiling, because Mother had bequeathed many of her smiles upon his lens. I still remember when she pulled back her black georgette scarf and stood in the midst of my older sisters who, instead of scarves, had worn hats that made them look like film stars from the early 60s, and their cherry-painted smiles did not match the sadness in their eyes.

Mother's scarf was not like the scarves worn by girls and women today. It was a sheer scarf that did not hide her hair or cover her quiff. When Father saw that black-and-white photograph, her loosened scarf and my sisters' hats provoked an attack by him on all of them. Each generation of sisters paid a price through these beatings so that one day my sister Maha and I could take off our scarves in the mid 70s.

*

I had thought that all mothers, like mine, never smiled, that they believed laughter was shameful and impudent for girls, and always reminded you that only tears paid off on Judgement Day. It is crying for the Hussein, the Prophet's family and the Imams that profited you in the end; not laughter.

Mother used to tell me that each of us had a bundle that held the tears we had shed for the Hussein and the Prophet's family. And on Judgement Day, we would find our bundle of tears awaiting us. The larger it was, the more tears to wash away our sins with. That is why when I was a child and would go with Mother to Hajji Fatm's house for the observance of *Ashura*, I would always cry my eyes dry to make my bundle grow.

Once as I cried I asked her, 'Should I keep my tissue with the tears in it, and take it with me to Heaven?'

'No, you silly girl,' she said, 'these tears will dry up. But every drop that falls from your eyes goes straight into your bundle up there, and you'll find it waiting for you later.'

Whenever Mother cried, she would say, 'I dedicate my tears to Hussein, peace be upon him. God knows me best and He knows what's in my heart.' Even when my brother died of cancer during the war, the women gathered around her as she cried and urged her, 'Ya Hajji, dedicate your tears to Hussein, peace be upon him. Crying is forbidden except on his soul. Only that will profit you. Crying for your son will not bring him back to you.'

'I know, I know,' Mother answered, 'and I did dedicate them to Hussein, peace be upon him. But parting with the fruit of one's toil is not easy, and God knows that well.'

On the few occasions when she did laugh, it was when we had passed our grade or she had made a dish that she liked. The laugh would glint in her eyes like a flash in the dark, then quickly disappear.

The only thing that made her throw her head back with laughter was hearing someone 'fart' or a 'squeaker' escape. She would roar until tears flooded her eyes but then suddenly become troubled, wipe her cheeks dry and erase the smile from her face. 'I don't know what's wrong with me,' she would say, 'why am I laughing so much? God knows what could be coming tomorrow. May God let our laughs bring only goodness upon us.'

I did not discover why farting was so amusing to her until many years after she died, when our neighbor Um Talal told me a story that Mother had confided in her.

It was back in the days when we still lived in Burj Hammoud, before we sold the building and Mother had to give Father her life's savings so we could afford one flat in Zuqaq Liblat. In those days, Mother would sleep with us in the girls' room, spreading a wool mattress on the floor in the narrow strip between our two beds. Father would sleep on the sofa in the corner of the living room while my brother slept in the family room. When Father wanted her, he would send her signals, and when she did not understand them or ignored them, he would sneak inside and nudge her while she slept until she got up and followed him to the living room.

Father loved sex, like our neighbour Abu Talal, but he was shy to discuss it, unlike Abu Talal who constantly bragged about his virility before it finally failed him. Whenever a woman from the neighbourhood would joke with him, 'How's he doing these days, Abu Talal?' he would lift his head high and hold a finger up straight, 'He is just fine,' he would say, 'at his best, in fact. If he poked a wall, he'd knock it down.'

But Mother did not share Father's fondness for intimacy. 'If your husband likes you, he dirties you,' she used to say, 'and if he doesn't like you, he shames you.' Naturally, she neither wanted to be dirtied nor shamed. In her view, sex was a predicament. If she followed him into the living room, she would be dirtied, and would have to get up in the middle of the night to heat water on the stove and wash herself. She could not go to bed after having sex without doing her ablutions because evil spirits would prey on her soul in the night. Sometimes, she would wash herself quickly in the night, then shower fully before the dawn prayer. She also worried that one of us might wake up to use the bathroom, find her showering and know what had happened between them.

Nothing could save her from him, said Um Talal, until one day Mother discovered that farting was the weapon that could rescue her from opening her legs to him.

One night, as she lifted them, a fart surprised him right in the face. Immediately, his desire withered. He pushed her away, swearing angrily, 'God damn you! Get out of here, you ass. You beast!' He threw her out of the room, cursing her and her parents and the day he had married her.

After that, whenever she noticed Father leering at her in the evening, she would slap her hand on her stomach and say, 'Oof, I'm full of gas all right. That big plate of lentils and all those radishes . . . My intestines are swollen to the limit.' Hearing that, Father would relent and go to bed early.

I never saw Mother indulge Father the way Ibtisam's mother did her husband. Mother dreamt of education, and especially after my sisters had been forbidden from finishing their studies, she dreamt of the day I would become a lawyer as big as the world itself. My sisters had learnt to 'unknot the letter' with Sayyed Ali who taught the village children to read the Holy Koran. The first generation of sisters became mothers, the next completed primary school and the third finished middle school. My sister Maha got her baccalaureate and married while I, the last grape of the bunch, managed to reach the university. Mother had wanted to educate all her daughters but her circumstances did not allow her to see the dream through. She believed that education was a woman's only defence against the 'rule' of the husband.

She would often tell me how she saw me in her dreams, dressed in a lawyer's robe, raising my voice to the judge in defence of the oppressed. Ibtisam's parents also dreamt of educating their children. Her father worked overtime in his job at the port and, from time to time, sold a piece of land to pay their tuition.

Not only did Ibtisam's mother smile but her father did too. He was of the calm and simple type. I would always hear him tell her mother, 'Leave the girl alone, let her have a strong personality. I'm not worried about her, even if she sleeps surrounded by a hundred men.'

The fights began in their home when the war started in Lebanon and her brother stopped being a Nasserite. He became enamoured with the Phalangist Party and began worrying about the future of Lebanon while Ibtisam would go secretly to the Palestinian refugee camps to train with the soldiers. Now, each member of her family had to choose their allegiance.

Even I did not know that she had joined the ranks of fighters, until I saw her on television one day, wearing a red keffiyeh around her neck. With the men, she leapt fiercely to the aid of an injured man who had fallen in front of the statue of Habib Abu Shahla at the UNESCO, pushing him into a military vehicle. That was at the beginning of the war, when people sat glued to the television to follow the news.

That day, her brother went mad. Her father stood with her while her mother sided with her brother. With Alawiyya's parents, the loyalties were reversed, her father siding with the Phalangists and her mother, like her, with the Palestinians and the Left. Her father would clasp his hands behind his back and shake his head from side to side, saying to her mother, 'You fancy yourself a militiawoman now, do you, ya Um Ayyad? You're going to destroy it, this home. Why, we would be worthless without the Christians. What flavour would this country have without the Christians?' And she would reproach him thunderously, 'What do the Christians have to do with anything? You stupid man, don't you realize that I love them more than you do? Nobody is going to ruin the Christians of this country except your stupidity and the stupidity of the Phalangist Party. You and all enemies can die in your heart's misery. You'll remember Um Ayyad's words. You just stay by your bully Pierre Jumayyil, and we'll see what comes of it.'

'None other than your Abu Ammar is a bully. I spit on you and those who begot you.'

But the road ahead of Ibtisam was easier than the one lying ahead of me.

When she would wear a short dress to the university before the war, her father's smile would reach the back of his ears, and he would tease her admiringly, 'What is *this*, ya Baba? What's all this beauty? Even Najla Fathi couldn't compare.' And I would envy her, not for her long legs, but for her father's tenderness. When a groom approached her family in her teens and she snubbed him, her older brother said, 'You will marry him, whether you like it or not.' 'In your dreams,' she said, 'go marry him yourself!' and she hit him with the barbecue skewer she was eating from when he tried to hit her.

Her father stood in his son's face, 'What, you're going to hit your sister in front of my eyes?' he said. 'She is free to marry whomever she likes.'

Inspired by her stance, I rejected Ameen when he approached my family for me. Like Ibtisam, I dreamt of marrying a man whom I loved, one from outside the family whom I chose with my heart and mind. But here I am today, after all these years, marrying Ameen after having rejected him 25 years ago.

Only Mother stood by me, though her motives were obscure. Did she secretly want me to marry for love, or did she want the last grape of the bunch, the last of her daughters, to stay by her? 'All my daughters are gone,' she would say, 'they took them all away from me. Maryam's all I've got left.'

*

Mother was always a mystery to me, a maternal spring of murky depths. She didn't know how to express herself in words because speech was foreign to her. She expressed herself by cleaning, washing dishes and cooking, or, as she did one year when I did not mark at the top of my class, by beating me with a water hose.

I told Ibtisam and Alawiyya about one incident that I will never forget. The Arabic teacher dedicated a lesson to motherhood on Mother's Day which we had never celebrated in our home. The teacher spoke passionately about mothers until her eyes almost welled up, explaining how much they suffered and so had Heaven at their feet.

I was deeply stirred by the teacher's presentation, and felt a swelling of emotion towards Mother that day. On the way home, I cried because Mother did not use the same loving words with me that the mother in the textbook spoke to her child. Neither did she say to me what Ibtisam's mother told her daughter, 'May you live to bury me, my little joy, you grass of my heart.'

But then I remembered her tears and exhaustion. I saw her in my mind as the loveliest of all mothers, her eyes the sweetest eyes and her tears the purest tears.

When I got home, the desire had not left me to embrace her, to pull closer to her breast and kiss her rough hands. I drew near to her while she stood silently at the sink, and I contemplated her face, her hands, her belly and the cracked heels of her feet. But the second my body touched hers, she shoved me with her elbow and pushed me aside. 'What's wrong with you?' she asked, 'why are you pawing at me like a cat? May a sickness tear you to pieces. This is the stupidest daughter I have, right here.'

When she pushed me away, I cried out and starting sobbing, 'I just wanted to kiss you and love you.'

'And you could not find a better time than when I'm up to my ears in dishes? May God take all of you and this world that broke my back. Are you always going to be stupid, girl? I told you a million times that I don't like kissing. I hate nothing more than to be kissed.'

*

Still, her last wish was that I would kiss her. She spoke to me with her eyes and whispered some broken letters before her breath gasped, then faded into its last rattle. I gathered the letters in her eyes and understood that she was calling me to kiss her.

'May you live to bury my heart,' I said to her, and assaulted her with kisses on her face and hands. I felt her desire to kiss me. But she lacked the strength.

In the last days, I discovered that the word 'Mama' did not leave my mouth freely. I was now uttering it with the knowledge of one losing a mother and a word. The taste of it had changed in my mouth. I knelt beside her bed so she could kiss me, and when I called out to her—'Mama'—the word left my mouth filled with fear.

5

I remember telling Alawiyya the story of Ibtisam's marriage, back in the days when she still listened and wanted to see the fish with her own eyes.

The day Ibtisam decided to get married, tears shone like pearls in her eyes. It was a crisp morning in the winter of '86. I met her at that cafe on Hamra Street, at the intersection between the Central Bank and Nahar Daily. The cafe was a landmark visited by businessmen, intellectuals and journalists. On the spacious terrace, tables surrounded a fountain. Traces of water from the workers' early morning labours spotted the terrace and reminded one of October's cool—its calm and transparency.

Ibtisam, though, appeared anything but calm. Her face was dark like muddy water and her words reeked of despair. She said she feared that one day she might find herself *out* and not *in*, as she said in English. She told me how she had been lying in her bed, watching an Arabic movie with a romantic story, of the kind that she had mocked in the days when she was a revolutionary. She had always found those movies unrealistic, without revolutionary potential or purpose. She said she had felt a deep sob as she watched the hero touch the heroine affectionately on her back, gazing at her as if the world's light were in her eyes. She found herself moved by emotions that she had once considered reactionary.

She asked me many questions. 'Is it possible that all along the fighters had seen us as imported whores in ready-made revolutionary packaging? We have been defeated in politics—but have we been defeated in love and hope too? Didn't we reap twice the disappointment from the men who we believed to be progressive, partners wanting freedom for us and themselves? Or were they just the embodiment of emotional

schizophrenia weighed down with past eras and revolutionary carica-
tures of Harun al-Rashid?

'As women, were we true to ourselves in our dreams? Or did we
carry our own contradictions in our bodies? Cloaked under robes of
revolutionary struggle, did we conceal the scents of concubines inside
its folds?

'Was it all a lie? I never lied. And I am sure that a lot of those who
died or were defeated did not lie. But, then, why were we defeated?
Was it because we were liars or because we were too earnest? I don't
know.

'What I know is that I'm lonely,' she said. 'Today, I'm lonelier
than ever. I need to feel love, even if it's just a ruse in a movie.'

She said she felt an emptiness. She bought a lace nightgown and,
at bedtime, put it on and looked at her bare breasts from both sides
in the mirror. A sob lingered in her chest as she pressed her breasts
together with her hands and looked at them. Then she turned off the
lights and slept, her breasts spreading carelessly under the gown,
freed from the clutch of the bra that she hated wearing while she
slept.

Barely two months had passed when Ibtisam decided to marry.
It was five o'clock, early in the evening, and a cold storm threatened
the country. Each drop of rain was 'the size of a marble' as my stepmother used to say, bringing three fingers together to demonstrate.
The phone rang more than twice. I was in my room tracing the pat-
tern of a tailleur that I had picked out from the *Burda* magazine. That
way I saved money, passed the hours of boredom and could show up
in a new outfit every time I saw Abbas.

I ran to pick up the phone and was surprised by Ibtisam's warm
voice. She stammered a bit, then asked whether I had time to get a
drink later that evening. I was happy to see her after such a long time,
even more because she said that she had missed me from her heart,
and it had been a long time since I had heard someone say so. Even

Abbas never said it except when we met at the end of each month, so that it became a sort of salary that I would collect at regular intervals.

The darkness was unyielding when I rushed out of the house to meet Ibtisam. With thunder and rain assailing me, I wondered what water filled Ibtisam's mouth. We sat on the second floor, behind the large glass window facing the intersection. I wrapped my fingers around a cup of warm tea, encircling it with my palms to absorb its heat while Ibtisam swirled a glass of vodka in her hand, a spark of hope dancing in her eyes.

She told me that she had finally agreed to marry Jalal who, many times over the years, had asked for her hand to no avail. She tried to summarize her position to me. She said he was a good man and that he loved her and, more importantly, that they had arrived rationally at their decision to build a life in which they would decide everything 'together'.

Next followed a host of rhetorical questions: 'Isn't family more important than love—after love's faded, and all else has failed? Should I simply keep *out* of everything, ya Maryam? Out of all circles and life itself? And if I don't marry, will I be able to fall in love again, to take the risk of being thrown into another unknown?

'No, no. I can't,' she answered herself. 'I will fall in love with the man I marry. I'm too tired for anything else. I need *one* man who will love and accept me—one who will embrace me. Jalal has been waiting for my answer for years. I will not love someone else. I will only love the one I marry. I will take him to that point in our relationship where the thought of return can no longer be a source of fear. Perhaps marriage is the only way to the point of no return.'

I asked her, 'But aren't you one thing and Jalal another?'

'No, why do you say that? Jalal is educated and loves life, and he also has political commitments.'

'To?'

'He was involved with a number of parties but politics is no longer his line of work. Now his priority is his business, but he is still open-minded and liberated. It's enough for me that he said "I don't care about your past. We will start all over, and we'll do everything and make all our decisions together".'

'What about Kareem? Doesn't he still mean something to you?'

'I would rather not talk about that. It still hurts. He's no longer part of my life, and I prefer not to look back.'

For a moment, Ibtisam's serenity washed the fear from my eyes and heart, and I started breathing more easily. I could see her standing before me on firm ground, not dreams of dust. But I was scared that she saw Jalal as a saviour through the illusions of love and would only be disappointed.

My relationship with Abbas taught me that the point of no return cannot be reached merely through the harmony of naked bodies. One must follow one of two paths, marriage or love. Abbas had travelled one way with his wife through marriage and the other, with me by exposing his deepest desires.

On our way back from the hotel, he would regard me cautiously, even though hours ago he had shed the leaves of his desire before me, and we had shone radiantly in our sin. He would never have spoken to his wife about the things he told me, nor would he ever have shown her the faces he revealed to me. With Ameen, I now fear reaching the point of no return, but this time through the concealment of our true faces.

As Ibtisam spoke about Jalal, his face came back to me. His was a face brimming with ambiguity—cheeks puffy in their egg-like roundness, surrounding his coy greenish eyes. His complexion was reddish; but his neck and hands, a dusty white. Long hours of sitting, at his desk during the day and at restaurants and nightclubs in the evenings, had loosened the flesh on his neck, and the bulge of his paunch did not flatter his average height or advancing age. Jalal, who had studied economics and business, became the head of the bank where Ibtisam's brother worked as manager of one of its branches. The two had been good friends for a long time, and Jalal thrived in his position during those periods when the Lebanese pound deteriorated. He would take out a loan in pounds, exchange it for dollars, then pay the loan when the dollar was high again. He also made use of his connections at the bank to speculate in real estate and made a fortune there.

When I first met him, he seemed devoid of the smallest trace of the sensitivity or romance which I knew Ibtisam wanted in a man. And this passion for life that she spoke about seemed more like a taste for lavish feasts of stuffed courgettes and grape leaves, accompanied by intestines prepared with lard, and a desire to consume all he could. Ibtisam's love of life was something different. Like a bird, she sang to the world so it would sing back to her. In spite of her hard exterior and her stubbornness, there had been a time when her poetic innocence transformed her into a hatchling in the palm of a man she loved and who loved her back transparently, as Kareem once did.

I remember how, when she met Kareem at the beginning of the war, a new Ibtisam, glistening with femininity, had been born. It seemed as if another Ibtisam who had been sleeping inside her suddenly awoke before my eyes. I remember her in those tight jeans, the white blouse unbuttoned at the top and the black sweater she used to tie around her shoulders.

She would study in the cafeteria of the Education School and wait for Kareem and me to meet her there after we finished at the Law School. Whenever we were late, she would be upset. In those days, she lived and breathed through him and, in his presence, her eyes shone and her walk became the dance of a lover for her beloved. Kareem had only to look at her to make her feel every part of her body anew. Her face would flush and glow and her gaze wander restlessly, unable to settle on one place. She would leave us sitting at our table, walk to the jukebox in the corner and pause. Then she'd lift her hair from her face and let it drop again, at a loss for the right choice from Fairuz's old love songs, something that would express her exact feelings at that moment. Sometimes she would pick 'My handsome, how I fear losing you', playing it over and over again, and telling him with her eyes how she feared losing him. At other times, she would choose 'See how vast the ocean? That's how vast my love is for you' and let her eyes say how much she loved him.

I remember her standing in front of Kareem in the college quad, fiddling with his shirt buttons, looking up into his eyes with a new playfulness, and saying to him, 'I love you, I love you.' Kareem would smile broadly and say to me: 'Look at her, this crazy friend of yours.'

'Yes, I'm crazy. Much more than crazy. I'll always be crazy about you,' she would say, lifting a finger to his face, then walking away.

Kareem never belonged to any militia. Even though he came from a Christian family that always supported either the Communist Party or the Nationalist Syrian Party, he constantly found himself wavering between the two, in spite of their differences. His secular beliefs pushed him towards the National Movement whose banner drew together all parties of the Left.

But towards the end of the 70s, after being victim to a sectarian kidnapping in the area of Ras al-Nab'a in West Beirut, Kareem had to leave Beirut for Saudi Arabia. A rotating sectarian checkpoint surprised him one Sunday. As soon as he handed them his identification card, they took him out of the car and led him to an unknown place, but the card that identified him as a supporter of the National Movement did not absolve him. He disappeared for three days during which Ibtisam tasted neither food nor sleep; only bitter coffee and an endless chain of cigarettes sustained her. Her anxiety was unbearable because of an incident she had witnessed just a day before Kareem was kidnapped. She was crossing the Barbeer Bridge when a pair of militiamen forced two civilians out of their car on their way to East Beirut. First one, then the other—they were lifted by the arms and legs, then flung off the bridge to land lifeless beneath it.

The memory of the sight froze the blood in her veins. She kept going back and forth to the bathroom to vomit, as if she wanted to physically expel the image from her memory. But the scene never left her; instead, it endured—the corpses of the two men lay with her on her bed and the eyes of the militiamen glowed before her like burning coal, painted on the wall of her room. She could remember their voices, shouting: 'For disposal. We'll have to throw out today as many as they killed of us yesterday.'

She did not rest until Kareem was freed, as a result of numerous calls at the highest levels.

He went directly to Saudi Arabia where one of his relatives had arranged a job for him. Kareem's absences kept getting longer until finally his visits became just brief summer trips. Ibtisam would await his return and when the time came, she would trade her jeans for a dress and undo her hair. She'd touch up her face with a little make-up and the musky scent of love would envelop her body.

She would talk in whispers whenever she was with him in Beirut; and when he was away and would call from Saudi, she would shout over the bad connection, 'I love you, I love you.'

But that night, her screams were those of a mad lover.

It was 1982, and the Israeli army was holding Beirut under siege in preparation for the invasion. Tanks and armoured cars crowded the streets, planes shadowed the sky and shelling showered from above. The resistance created a belt around Beirut with the bodies and breasts of men, and the city held together feebly under the ideas of resistance and survival. Lips trembled in thirst for water, and ears filled with calls for rescue, as ambulances moved frantically among the injured, and hospitals could no longer accept either burnt bodies or bloody wounds.

Ibtisam worked at a clinic in the Watwat area—quickly turned into an emergency room—while Alawiyya volunteered a few hours there after her long days at the newspaper. That day, the two left the clinic at ten in the night. Ibtisam went home and Alawiyya continued to the house of a poet where friends and writers gathered to spend the late hours of the night laughing, debating and arguing. Everybody was hungry that night and fantasized about a cold glass of Arak. But in the absence of running water and electricity, where would the ice cubes and cold water come from? Where to get enough bread for the crowd? The poet had already knocked on all doors in the building, until one household donated a loaf, perhaps taken away from the mouths of their children.

After drawing straws, it was determined that Alawiyya and the poet would venture out to Marroush Restaurant, the only possible source for a bottle of Arak, cold water and ice. The busy restaurant had a large generator to keep the refrigerators running, the food fresh and ice for its customers.

They stood waiting in the middle of the night, nestled in the crowd in front of Marroush, many waiting to buy a hard block of ice, or a fraction of it, for the precious pleasure of drinking cold water during times of siege. It seemed to them that preserving this pleasure under these circumstances would somehow strengthen their resistance and sustain life. Even laughter became part of resisting, and of defending the city. In fact, all desires in that moment appeared part of the struggle to protect life and its little pleasures.

As Alawiyya stood waiting for their turn, she noticed that people were unusually considerate towards one another. The line proceeded in order, and people stood patiently, seemingly unconcerned with the Israeli bombing.

They returned like conquerors to the apartment, and were met with raucous cheers and applause. They drank, sang and indulged. But they burst into laughter when before them was placed the orphan loaf of bread, a paltry offering that might satisfy twenty eyes but not ten mouths.

When Ibtisam arrived home, she found on the kitchen table a lone bottle of water standing on the beige and white plastic table cover. She picked it up and walked to the bathroom. 'Careful with that water, ya Ibtisam,' shouted her mother from her bedroom, 'it has to last. There's no more water left.'

Ibtisam took her clothes off, stood in the tub and closed the flowery pink curtain behind her. She dampened the sponge with a few drops of water, just enough to get the lather moist, then scrubbed her body. She dripped the water carefully first on her shoulders and back, then used what had remained to wash away the traces of soap left on her body.

She was coming out of the bathroom with the towel wrapped around her breasts when she heard the phone ringing. It was Kareem. 'Kareem, is that really you?' she yelled, as soon as she heard his voice. 'When did you come and how did you get here? Where are you? Since when? Is it really you? I can't believe it. Where are you?'

'I'm here in Beirut.'

'When did you come? The airport is closed.'

'I've been here a few days but your phone had no tone.'

'Liar. Don't use the dial-tone-excuse with me. If you wanted to talk to me, you could have called or come to my house.'

'Anyway, I want to see you.'

'When?'

'Now.'

'Now? Are you crazy?' and she laughed.

'Yes, now. I want you. I need a woman, but not any woman. I want you.'

She fell silent for a moment, then said, 'All right, but how am I supposed to get out right now? Don't you hear the shelling? And what am I supposed to tell my parents?'

'You'll think of something.'

She laughed again and said, 'Fine. I'll be in front of the building. Pick me up in half an hour.'

It was almost midnight and the city was like a broken necklace whose beads had fragmented in all directions under the Israeli mortars. Ibtisam got into the car, next to Kareem, and he drove away calmly, unconcerned with the shrapnel that fell in front of or behind them. Neither cared. Life began to quiver again inside her and suddenly Beirut, despite all its darkness and cruelty, became a turquoise ring whose azure hue could not be subdued.

Their fingers intertwined and she forgot to reprimand him. She began kissing his fingers one by one, and her kisses climbed from each fingertip to his wrist. Then she continued to his shoulder, his neck, his face, unconcerned with the ambulances or jeeps of gunmen racing past. When they reached Mar Elias, they went up to a flat owned by a friend of Kareem's who had just fled to Paris through Syria.

They found their way to the flat by the glow of a cigarette lighter, and, once inside, Kareem went into the kitchen and returned with several lighted candles which he placed scattered from the entrance to the various rooms of the flat. In the dim light of the living room, black-and-white posters of foreign and Egyptian actors could be seen, covering the walls.

Kareem pushed the coffee table away from the centre of the living room and sat in its place on the carpet, with his back to a wooden wardrobe that stretched along the length of the wall. He motioned to Ibtisam to join him on the floor, tapping the floor with one outstretched hand, as if urging a child to take her first step. As soon as her hand touched his, he pulled her to his lap and she wrapped her arms around his neck, hiding her face in his chest and kissing him with an old hunger, as he kissed her hair. They began twisting and turning like two waves merging their rhythms and waters. Then without pause, he laid her on the floor beneath him and pressed his chest to hers. He split her legs with his and soon her thighs were pressing on his sides. Swiftly, he unbuttoned her shirt, unclasped her bra and took her nipples into the hollow of his mouth. Then he lifted his head over her face, with the sweat dripping from his chin, and said, 'Why don't you take off your clothes?'

'It's hot, isn't it?'

'It's very hot.'

He climbed off and sat beside her while she took off her shirt and lay down again on the floor. He slid her bra aside and said, 'That's much better.' As he lay on top of her again, he started unbuttoning her trousers, 'Take them off,' he said, kissing her, and together they started pulling them down from her waist.

Later that day, Ibtisam did not understand why Kareem laughed afterwards, as he tapped her cheeks with his fingers and said, 'So, you're still a virgin?'

They had never discussed it. She had not had to tell him, because he had never asked. He must have understood why she avoided being alone with him throughout their relationship which never went beyond kisses and caresses.

'How can this be, you being a revolutionary and all?' he chuckled. But his tone of voice hurt her. 'What's with you, ya Kareem? What's your point? I can't be a virgin and a revolutionary? Besides, you've always known very well that you are the first real love in my life, and that the ones I had before you were just childish affairs, people I'd get infatuated with and then get bored with right away. If I'd wanted to sleep with somebody, it would have been you.'

'All right, fine. But why now? Why not then?'

'I don't know. I know that you're being silly with these useless questions. Just like you felt that you wanted me now, I felt that I wanted you too. What, are you angry or something because I slept with you?'

'Not at all. On the contrary, I'm very happy. I think we should have done it a long time ago.'

'Then why are you interrogating me?'

'No, not at all. Are you crazy? You're my sweetheart. Of course I'm not interrogating, and I'm very happy with you.'

She laughed, as he lay on top of her again, trying to forget her annoyance with his questions. With his fingers, he combed her hair carefully along the sides of her face, then buried his nose into the hollow of her neck and breathed deeply in it.

'You know, when I'm on top of you like this, I feel that you are totally under my control, that you're in the palms of my hands.'

'How's that?' she chuckled.

'I don't know. Maybe when one has a woman under him after he's been inside her, he feels that she's become his, that he owns her.'

'Really?'

'Maybe.'

'So what? It doesn't bother me to feel that you are on top of me and in control of me. It makes me happy.'

She slipped her body from underneath him and sat next to him on the floor where he now lay silent with his eyes closed. She knelt over him and started kissing his forehead, his cheeks, his chest and his stomach until she reached the very tip of the feet, kissing every toe after she pressed it to her chest. Then she stood up straight, raised her arms and started shouting, 'I love you! I love you!'

When he took her home before sunrise, the darkness still cast its shadows, and the city sky was patrolled by the carrion-eaters whose ominous cries were followed by shots fired towards them from the residential areas. Ibtisam rolled down her window, stuck her head out in the air, and screamed into the unforgiving city night. 'I love you!' she cried, 'I love you!'

'Keep your voice down. You're going to scandalize us,' he said with amusement and pulled her back into the car.

'I love you in spite of Israel, and the planes, and the sieges, and the hunger, and the thirst, and everything! They can all go to hell!'

'All right, my love. Keep it down now. I love you too.'

She kissed him on the cheek before she left the car, and when he kissed her back, he said, 'Bye. I'll see you tomorrow.'

Whenever he was away in Saudi, Ibtisam's concentration would start wandering. She would scream her love to him over the phone, and he would laugh and say, 'Me too.'

*

But he was not smiling when, one day, he said to her: 'I love you, but I can't marry you. We have to stop seeing each other.'

That day she had walked to the cafe to see him; she had leapt along the streets, like a bird just released from a locked cage. She had just found out that he'd been released after a kidnapping and a detention—a second time—that had lasted two weeks. Earlier, he had called her from Saudi before leaving, to tell her that he was going to be in Lebanon for two weeks, and that he would be going from the airport straight to the north to see his mother. After visiting his mother, he would come to Beirut to see her. He said that his mother had called him and cried over the phone: 'I need to see you,' she had said, 'my heart is melting.'

He took a taxi from the airport directly to his village, crossing all the checkpoints safely until he reached Madfoun where the militiamen took him out of his car after scrutinizing his papers. They had noticed his family name which was known for its Leftist leanings. And so Kareem disappeared again, and the calls and negotiations continued for two weeks, this time with a rival party, before he was finally released.

His parents had to prove that he lived and worked in Saudi and that he had no ties to any militia. But Kareem's tongue did not loosen up after he was released. After the incident, Kareem began to stutter, as if the spaces between his words and sentences were trying to communicate the empty spaces in his head.

He did not answer Ibtisam's questions when she went to see him. Did they humiliate him, did they beat him, what did they say to him?

How did they interrogate him, where did they take him? Why did they take him when he had never carried a gun, and never hurt anybody? He would not tell her what had happened to him during the second kidnapping, just as he never told her what had happened during the first.

It was as if his dignity kept him from talking. He turned away, changed the subject. His kind, honey-tinted eyes had yellowed, and his olive skin, once lit by a fleshy smile under his moustache, had paled irrevocably.

He would not say anything about what had happened; instead he described to her at length the pain caused by a certain vein that seemed to have swelled since his release. He put his hand on the left side of his neck, tilting his head sideways while he explained about that pain that had stretched from his neck to his shoulder.

He said the vein was speaking to him and saying, 'Marry, ya Kareem.' And as he spoke, he yawned repeatedly.

That day, he told her that he loved her but that the vein was telling him to marry another woman from his own sect and family. It was up to the vein, not his heart, to dictate whom he married, for the vein was at his core and so could not be contradicted. That is what he told her, and after he said it, he became even more convinced. She looked at him with wide incredulous eyes and a gaping mouth that was unable to articulate a reply.

She did not utter a word when he told her about the vein and wished her a happy marriage with a man who deserved her. He was going to marry as the vein had ordained. She wished he would give her a thousand real reasons for leaving her, because she wanted to understand. She was no longer listening when he said that the vein has finally awakened after a long time of lying asleep. She heard him well, however, when he said that he loved her but that this love was impossible.

She stared at him and sensed the falling of all things—dreams, ideals, cities, loves and her heart. Everything was sliding into a void.

She walked away from him, leaving him behind at the table they had often shared under the dim lights in the May Flower coffee house on Hamra Street. Sometimes, he would put a pistachio nut in her mouth, wrap his arm around her shoulders and glance at the silver chain around the sensitive skin of her neck. The little vein at the bottom of her neck excited him so intensely that he would look away to the edge of the sofa and smoke as he stared at the wall. Then he would turn to her again and put his finger there, pressing gently and smiling. Primitive societies, he once told her at that table, thought that the spirit dwelt right there in that little spot.

She would smile shyly and whisper into his ear something she could have said without drawing close to him. She took any excuse to draw closer to him, to take in his smell and let him take in hers. He loved smelling her, especially when she had her period. She would bite her lips, inviting more playfulness, but when he would bury his head in her armpits and speak to her of erotic things that would set them both on fire, she would push him away and fold her arms across her chest, warning him that she did not wish to listen any more. Then she would relax her arms to her sides and surrender again to his words.

This time, she did not surrender. 'I love you,' he said, 'believe me, I inhale you with every pore of my body. I've transformed into nothing more than *you*, and when I talk to other people, their names become muddled to me. I feel that I am always talking to you, because I no longer know how to talk to anybody but you. You are the only one who knows me as I am, ya Ibtisam. You accept me with my weaknesses, my angers and my tears when they fall. You engulf me.'

The vein had decreed that he would marry a relative who lived in Brazil and spoke a few words of Arabic. Her parents had brought her to the village to spend the summer when they heard that the war had ended in Lebanon. They did not know enough to realize that the war always ended just in order to begin again. In any case, they brought her to Lebanon to introduce her to her own country and family, and to find her a suitable groom from her native village. Arrangements were made hastily, and Kareem's face lit up with a smile whenever his bride called him 'habibi' in her foreign accent.

Ibtisam's mother said to her, 'At least you've managed to tease out the vein of insanity from your brain. Go look after your own life, what are you still waiting for? You insisted on a Christian, and we said fine, we'll take him, as long as you love him and he loves you. We said we're all the children of Adam and Eve after all. But where is he now? He went off and got married, so what are you waiting for?'

Ibtisam had no answer.

She lay in her bed for many days, covering her head and body with a heavy blanket, sobbing as tears streamed from her eyes down to the base of her neck. She kept her curtains closed, the lights switched off and her eyes shut.

When she opened her bedroom door to me, I turned on the lights, rolled up the shutter and let the sunlight bathe the room all the way to the middle of her bed. I drew the blanket away from her and helped her sit upright. She squinted with her swollen eyes, like a prisoner seeing the light after years of deprivation.

'Ya Ibtisam, you've always reprimanded me for being weak. How can you be doing this to yourself?' I said, combing her hair with my fingers. I brought her a glass of lemonade, so she could wet her lips, but she stared at me and asked, 'Where does love go, ya Maryam? Why does it end? Where does it go? What happens after it dies and leaves us?'

*

When she asked me to meet her at Café Modca years later, to tell me about her decision to marry Jalal, she asked me the same questions and new ones; but again, I did not have answers. After taking the last sip of her drink, she said, 'When we're young, we expect that there will be a day when we'll wake up to find the world as we want it, the way we dreamt it would be before we went to sleep. Then the days roll like marbles, and we wake up to find that we are the ones changed while the world has stayed the same.'

Then she said that she was decided, and would marry Jalal. Jalal and her parents agreed to wait until the end of the month of Muharram because marriages were believed to be ill-fated during that month. Her mother asked for a fifty-thousand-dollar dowry and he consented, as did Ibtisam.

At her wedding, Ibtisam stood like a dove in her white dress, a white veil covering her face and her gaze lowered to the ground before the Sheikh. Her aunt called out, 'Cover up, women and girls, the Sheikh is here,' and those who could not cover their heads and bare shoulders disappeared from sight, making way for the Sheikh who strode in to conduct the ceremony.

The Sheikh repeated the question three times: 'If she consents to be the wife of Jalal for a dowry of said amount, she should say, "I appoint you as my proxy."' Ibtisam did not answer the first or the second time, just as her mother had instructed her.

'Be careful not to answer until the third time, or else people will think you are desperate to marry. Wait until the third time. Do you hear me?'

'Yes, I hear you.'

And so she waited. The Sheikh asked the question twice, and each time the women would study her face to hear if she would answer. Silence was the answer the first two times, until she said 'I appoint you as my proxy' on the third instance.

At my sisters' weddings, things were done differently. Mother and my aunts would take turns answering the Sheikh the first and second time. The first time, Mother would slap one hand on the other and rolling her eyes she would say, 'She went to the seamstress!' and the second time, my aunt would answer, saying, 'She left to go to the bathroom to relieve herself.' Then the third time, the bride would speak up and say, 'I appoint you as my proxy.' Like my sisters,

Ibtisam answered the third time, and her mother and aunts filled the air with ululations. His work done, the Sheikh would lift his robe slightly off the ground and walk out, whispering his congratulations, 'Mabrouk, mabrouk.'

In her college years, Ibtisam would always tease Kareem about their wedding. 'When you marry me, I want exactly one quarter of a Lebanese pound for my dowry, do you hear me? Understood, my love?' She would tell him, and lift her delicate brown finger to his face so he could see their silver engagement band. I could not tell whether Ibtisam was saddened by the realization that she was worth money.

I was surprised when I saw Ibtisam's mother dancing at the wedding, because it was the same as Mother's dance at my brother's funeral. The only difference was the tears—the difference between tears of happiness and tears of mourning. Ibtisam's mother proclaimed, 'Cheers to the bride' whereas Mother had said, 'Cheers to the groom.' Mother had tied a black strip around her forehead while Ibtisam's mother decorated her hair with a red flower. Otherwise, the dance was identical. Arms uplifted, one higher than the other, neck tilted to the side of the higher arm, face slightly downwards and steps moving rhythmically backwards, then forwards.

Ibtisam's mother dried her tears, yet they still reminded me of my mother's tears which would flow for months, each time one of her daughters married and left the house in a white dress. Mother resented all her sons-in-law for taking away her daughters and, after each of the weddings, would tie a white scarf around her forehead and tighten it from the back in order to kill the crying pain. Her tears and lamentations would fill the house: 'My daughters are gone—they took them away from me. I raised them with the tears of my eyes for those strangers to come and take them from me, one after another. They're gone, and I have no say in their lives. The house is empty without my girls.'

Father would scold and curse her, 'Be quiet you owlface, you face of unhappiness. Instead of being joyful for them, you want to jinx their marriages? Pray to God that they be happy.'

'I pray from my heart that God gives them happiness. But the one whose hand is in the fire does not feel the same as the one whose hand is outside it. They have left my heart's side, and who knows, maybe one of them will turn out to have married an evil man who will make her miserable. And he may even forbid her from coming to the house of her father who raised her. Who can say no to the husband? The law tells her to do what her husband says. She can't say no to anything he wants.'

My heart would ache at the sight of Mother's tears. I would approach her, wipe them with my hands and try to soothe her.

'That's enough, Mother, why are you crying?'

'I am crying because a girl is victimed.'

'What do you mean "victimed"?'

She would stop her crying and push me away. 'Get out of my sight. You want to make fun of me? You don't know what "victimed" means? Didn't you get into schools and study? What a waste those degrees are that you've got.'

'You mean she is victimized?'

'Yes, she is victimed means she is a victim. Do I need to explain to you these things after I raised you to be a lawyer?'

'What does that have to do with marriage? You should be happy that your daughter is married.'

'I am happy, but a mother cries anyway. You don't understand. A daughter leaving is the hardest thing to endure in the whole world. The mother knows the misery awaiting her daughter. A man has no mercy and is demanding. The mother knows how she will be victimed in pregnancy and labour and late nights—that she will have no say in her life or her body or her time. She is at the disposal of her children and her husband, and everybody can make demands on her.'

Ibtisam's mother, on the other hand, dried her tears and said, 'This is life, my child. Each one has to raise children and give them to life, to others.'

We rode with Ibtisam, her mother and I, in Jalal's Mercedes decorated with flowers and white ribbons. We made the rounds of the bride, along with the other cars, cheering and sounding our horns. All the while, my eyes remained fixed on Ibtisam as I tried to penetrate her silent restless gaze. She was enveloping the city with her new eyes while I did the same to her with mine.

6

I am Maryam, the last grape hanging at the end of the bunch. My family started as a collection of little young berries when we first migrated to Beirut, only to ripen and scatter all around, until each grape matured and gave seed to a new cluster.

Lu-lu-lu-lu-lu-lu-leesh . . .

My mother Fatima, daughter of Najib, mother of Ahmad, and wife of Hassan—son of Ali and father of Ahmad, filled the air with her ululations, cursing harvest, farming, misery and hunger, the day Abu Ahmad arrived from Beirut. After a week in Beirut, he entered our house wearing slacks and shirt in place of his old village trousers, and a triumphant smile on his face. He sat down to rest from the trials of the road, and Mother ran to the kitchen to fetch him a cup of dark tea with lots of sugar to restore his energy. As he took a long slurp from the hot tea, Mother squatted in front of him and searched his face. She could not wait any longer to hear about the fruits of his journey to the capital. She said, 'Come on now, Abu Ahmad, tell me what happened. Good news, is it?'

'Get yourself and the children ready. I found myself a job in Beirut, working for the trains.'

'You don't say!'

'You bet, Um Ahmad.'

And after exhausting her tongue, her eyes continued the ululations. She slept soundly that night, shutting her eyes after staring for a long time at the sand walls that she and Father had built with their own hands, and at the wooden ceiling that they had extended together over bamboo stalks topped with a mixture of pressed sand and straw so the rain water would not seep through it.

She slept and dreamt of Beirut, even though she had never set eyes on it. Earlier in the evening, she had asked her husband:

'What's Beirut like?'

'Beirut is a city, it's not like the village.'

'What do you mean? How?'

'I mean big stone buildings with many floors and huge open lots with trees and cactuses. The important thing is that there's work there. You'll see.'

So, that night, she dreamt of the moonlight flooding her sight, and in the morning she was scared of her dream because seeing the moon in her dream always forecast the arrival of a new child in her belly.

She was confused because her youngest daughter, number five, was still nursing. Her heart calmed and her fears left her when she remembered that she was moving to Beirut. Perhaps the moon forecast the birth of a new life for the whole family there. She told Father of her dream, as she did every morning.

'God willing, it'll be for the best,' he said, 'from your lips to God's ears.'

But the best did not come overnight.

*

The bus shipped her, Father and the children, along with many large canvas bags full of provisions—lentils, bulgur, chickpeas, thyme, rose tea and fava beans and everything else that she could fit. They threw the bags onto the bus, leaving behind the cows and the chickens in the courtyard, in Uncle's care. In those days, the yard had not yet been enclosed with a cement wall.

Mother wore her brand-new flowery dress in honour of the journey, but on the road the dress soon started reeking of the children's vomit.

My brothers' and sisters' eyes bulged when the bus swerved at the village of Zrayriyya, leaving them facing the vast ocean which spread along the coastline for as far as their eyes could see. They gasped, and my oldest sister, Zainab, said, 'What in God's name is that?'

'It's the sea.'

'The sea? Why, it's so big and all filled with water. Where does all the water come from? God save us when it empties out. Where would they fill it up from, Father?'

Mother was struggling to stay conscious in spite of her headache, so Father turned to her and said, 'See why I don't let you ride behind me on the camel? This is why I didn't take you with me to the Tayba for the Bey's funeral. You're vomiting now just the way you did when I let you ride behind me once on the camel all the way to Tyre.'

Mother did not respond. The pain drummed at her brain, and the blazing sun burnt her to the core as she sat there in the sun's gaze, all the way from the village to the heart of Beirut. When the bus arrived, the passengers gathered their things and divided themselves among the various carriages parked on the sides of the road. The carriages went to Ashrafiyya, Lower Basta, Zuqaq al-Blat, Khandaq al-Ghamiq and all the areas where families from southern villages were settling, along with their furniture, their hustle and bustle and their way of life.

Father led the way to our carriage and pointed the driver to Sayyufi in Ashrafiyya where he had rented a piece of land. Then he loaded our bags of provisions—food, clothes, blankets, a small gas stove, sleeping mats stuffed with canvas and bedcovers that Mother had patched up out of rags. Everything was hauled into the large wooden crate at the back of the little carriage pulled by two horses. Mother walked behind the carriage, and my brothers and sisters behind her, for Father forbade her from walking beside him at the front because his image as a 'man' might come into question if his cousins, who had gone before him to Sayyufi, saw his wife walking beside him.

'Walk behind me with the children,' he said to her, 'or would you rather have my cousins see you walking next to me, and say that Abu Ahmad lets his wife walk beside him?'

So Mother walked behind him, accompanied by her headache that always came after she used any means of transportation. Half a century later, she would still vomit every time she was driven by car inside Beirut.

Suddenly, my sister Zainab let out a shriek that startled Mother, Father, the carriage driver and the rest of us. When a black car sped in their direction and blasted its horn, she screamed at the top of her lungs, clutched the back of Mother's dress, and hid herself in it. 'Oh Mother,' she screamed. 'The hyena has come to get us. Where should we hide? He saw us, Mother. Did you see his wide jaws and black coat? Hide me, please.'

Zainab had never seen a hyena in her life. But she knew that the village stories reached their climax of horror when hyenas attacked people. It seemed to her that what she'd heard, over and over again, about the hyena had finally materialized in front of her eyes, in the form of this astonishing creature who shot towards them without flinching or hesitating. After the car passed, Father had to try everything to get her to calm down.

*

But Mother's worries did not go away after moving to Beirut.

She moved from a life of ploughing to a life of work in strangers' houses and hospitals. Father lost his job. He was dismissed by the railways and could not work for many hours as a porter because of his limp and the shoulder he injured a long time ago when he fell off a camel. Mother struggled for four years before the Bey set Father up with a job at the harbour. Until then, the family lived off the little money that Father made whenever he could find work lugging light merchandise, and from Mother's sweat, cleaning houses or washing towels for the Hotel Dieu Hospital. She would bring back the dirty towels every day from the hospital and return them clean the next day, the smell of fresh soap enveloping them. She would let the breeze sway them on the clothes lines that Father had put up in the back-yard, for the sun to sanitize them. There were towels for as far as your eyes could see. Mother would sit on the floor with the basin between her legs, and rinse the towels with water and soap until her hands dried up and the skin cracked from all the rinsing. Her hands were still chapped in her last days.

The family survived Father's unemployment only by the cracking of Mother's hands and the little salary of my sister Zainab who, at thirteen, worked as a maid in a house in Ashrafiyya. My brothers Ahmad and Mahmoud also worked; they were ten and nine years old then. At first, they worked as office boys in the harbour's Depart-ment of Duty, but soon they learnt how to apply stamps to transac-tions and got promoted to clerks. The family's difficult situation meant that they could not attend schools once we moved to Beirut, even after they had learnt to read and write under the tutelage of the Sheikh Fadel in the village and completed the reading of the Koran.

As for the other daughters, who later rolled out of Mother's belly like thread off a spool, they had the good fortune to go to school. And so, a brother would raise a sister, and a sister would raise another, and no sooner would Mother's belly flatten than swell again, until we became like a family of chickens: two sons and eight daugh-ters, not counting the ones she aborted and the 'four bellies' who died in the loneliness of her womb.

But she grieved less for the babies who had died in her womb than the little lump that appeared one day on Father's spine, which the doctor could not explain. But Mother was certain she knew what had caused it, and she told everyone, as she slammed a palm for emphasis on the other, 'It's his suffering. Men, they can't handle grief the way women can. Who knows why, but a woman can carry a heart full of misery. But a man, he'll wither and become paralysed.'

Nevertheless, this time the matter passed as merely a pimple and no paralysis, and so she thanked God.

She also thanked Him for what she had learnt working at the house of the Metni's. Besides sweeping, washing floors and cleaning, she had learnt how to spread sheets elegantly on beds, how to set a table and how to arrange the plates on it. Soon, she could not help comparing the sheets and blankets at the Metni's to the ones she had at home. She said to Zainab, 'Ya Zainab, can those be blankets if the ones we have are called blankets?'

The blankets at our house changed after my sister Zainab married a military man from among our relatives. We soon had military blankets and other better things when the Bey Al-Asaad went personally to the harbour to arrange a job with a decent salary for Father. But Mother never stopped working, of course. Whenever the income increased, the number of mouths also grew, as did the pains of her labour.

*

Once again, the moon lit her dreams. And when it returned, it was full and resplendent in a vision that came to her 'as if the light lifted its face'. That day, when she opened her eyes and looked through the window into the Beirut sky, she saw nothing but the dawn's glow making its way to her eyes. She sat up cross-legged in her bed, waiting for Father to wake up so she could give him the happy news. For this time, the moon she had glimpsed was not the same moon. She must be pregnant, with a boy!

For this child, it was the sure hands of Harfas, the Armenian midwife, that welcomed her offspring into the world. This time, she was far from the gaze of Sayyed Rida who in the past had sat 'over her head' and recited verses from the Koran to ease her delivery while two women kept her open legs covered by a sheet, to conceal what was forbidden to his eyes. The full moon materialized as a girl. Perhaps it was because Sayyed Rida, whose charms cured people from their maladies and lovers from the heart's damnations, had not blessed the delivery this time. He joined heads under the blessings of the law, turned poison into water for those who had been stung and counted with his rosary the years and days that the villagers would live. Mother, even after she crossed the age of sixty, could not believe that she wasn't dead yet, for Sayyed Rida had counted her years when she was fifteen.

She had asked him, 'Ya Sayyed, how many years do you think I've got?'

'Be patient, ya Um Ahmad.'

'I've been patient for a whole hour.'

'May God bring longevity to this soul,' he grumbled.

'Well, that's reassuring. So my soul has a long life? Will I live to see my children and children's children until my sixties?'

Once she finally turned sixty, she did not give it a rest. At fifteen, sixty sounded far off; it would take aeons to get there. But when she did, each day she would wake up, open her eyes and look at the light and the things around her, to make sure that she had not yet died. She did that every day until the age of sixty-three.

Two months before she died, she said to me while I sat next to her bed, 'Where are you, my girl?'

'Here, Mother, I'm sitting next to you.'

'Sayyed Rida was right when he said that I would die at sixty.'

'But you are sixty-three now, still alive, and may you live for all time. This proves him wrong. Shoo his words from your head.'

'They're true. His words are true and more than true. In the last three years, I've been dead and not alive. Or did you think that a sick person tied to their bed could be counted among the living? No, these years can't go on the tally.'

She fell silent for a little, then said, 'To be a bird is flying, the bird must fly, but if he sits still, he may as well be a stone. Maybe . . .

Maybe, in the end, it's better to be above the ground than under it, my girl.'

Despite her deep fear of death, Mother had prepared the shroud that would clothe her corpse, with the Verse of the Throne inscribed on it in green ink. She had asked one of her relatives travelling to Iraq to buy it there, where they were available in the widest selection of sizes. This way it cost less, and was more flattering than had she asked the seamstress Asmahan to make it.

Asmahan, who had packed away her sewing machine for lack of customers, brought it out of storage with the start of the war, to sew the shrouds of the neighbourhood women who marched, all laughs and embraces, to the fabric stores in the Watwat neighbourhood to purchase the cloth. The women were having coffee at Um Talal's house when their hostess told them about the shroud that her sister in South Beirut had sewn her out of linen to her exact size. After they all remarked on the increasing deaths in the country, they agreed on both death's justness and on the necessity to visit Asmahan to request that she sew their shrouds at a price of ten pounds per piece. This was how much each of them would save their family, since burial expenses had become so costly. And so it was that they had their shrouds sewn in anticipation of the just day.

Mother collected her shroud, the glass etched with Koranic verses, and the bottle of Zamzam water to be sprinkled over her corpse. She put them all in a nylon bag, which she stored in the corner of the closet, in order not to see it and be reminded that she was going to die. But when she asked the Sheikh at the neighbouring Husseiniyya, 'Isn't it desirable to prepare death's clothing, our Sheikh?'

'Desirable and more than desirable. Death is just.'

'And is it desirable as well to hide it from my sight?'

'You can put it away as long as it is clean and sanitized.'

'And shouldn't I try it on every once in a while, in order not to pay an expiation?'

'Why not? That too would be desirable to God.'

'Are you sure, our Sheikh?'

'Of course it's desirable. Death is just.'

I almost lost my mind when I entered the house one day to find Mother lying on her bed in her burial clothing, trying to wrap the shroud around her body without covering her face with it or tying it around her neck.

My veins burnt with horror and the curses shot from my mouth like thunderbolts, without regard for whom they hit—Mother, the sheikh or whoever it was who bought her the shroud. If Sayyed, who had predicted her death at sixty, were still alive, he would not have given her such advice. He would always say that death was just and that his breast did not fear its coming. Sayyed smiled at the mention of death. He would spread his arms and say: 'He is most welcome— most welcome.' But he also opened his arms to life and said, 'She is most welcome—most welcome.' He considered the world, and everything in it, to be ephemeral, except for the face of God. He never forgot the world or stopped smiling at it with his small glittery eyes etched over wrinkled cheeks. When he spread his lips to smile, he revealed a formidable set of youthful white teeth, and always boasted that he'd never pulled out a tooth in his life.

The moon of Mother's dreams proved sweeter than cream. After reaching the end, with the blossoming of the last grape in the bunch, the family started inching its way slowly towards the middle of the scale.

I know that I was born in the 50s, and I know where, but I don't know exactly when. Our birth certificates, anything from exact, make the oldest younger and the youngest older. I can't remember Mother ever giving me a firm answer about which day I was born, the season, or which part of the day, let alone the hour.

She said I was born 'as the light lifted its face'.

'What light?'

'What do I know? Leave me alone. Most people are born, and die, as the light is lifting its face. But no, your sister Amina . . . or was it one of the others . . . maybe Ahmad or Mahmoud . . . Definitely, with light's face.'

'Mother, try to remember, please.'

She would pause then say something like, 'I think that day I had just come back tired from the harvest and I felt that I was going to give birth, so I did. No. That wasn't you. You, I had in Ashrafiyya. We'd been in Beirut for a while. It must be your sister Hasna I'm thinking of. By God, she made me suffer. And if it hadn't been for Sayyed Rida who was reciting verses over my head every day after staying up all those nights of watching over her, I would have died. She was a daughter of dogs. All your sisters and brothers were calmed by holy recitations. All but you, you daughter of dogs. All of them together cried less than you alone. Until you turned one, you kept crying.'

'Fine, but when was I born?'

'Maybe when your sister Samiyya gave birth to her son Radwan . . . Or no . . . Or was she still pregnant with him, or had she already delivered and was pregnant with her son Bassam?'

'And when did she give birth to Radwan and Bassam?' I asked.

'My cousin Badia had just moved to Beirut, and it was raining a lot. When she got to our house, she was dripping with water, and she got sick for four or five days, and came close to dying.'

'And when was it that Badia came to Beirut, Mother? When did you have me?'

After pausing a little, she said, 'Yes,' excitedly, as if she had finally discovered when it was, 'I know when it was. It was a few days after the Abu-Deebs fulfilled their oath of revenge by killing Um Khalil's son. They waited for him on the street, and he had nothing to do with any of it, the poor kid. He was a budding young boy when they killed him. Later, they said one of their youngsters had done it, because he was underage and wouldn't get a life sentence.'

'And when did the killing happen, Mother?'

'Can you leave me alone, and shut your mouth? You've made me talk so much that my heart is drained. I can't remember everything, you know. It's the truth, and you can make fun of me as much as you want. By God, the saying is true: It's not enough that they come out of your own ass, they have to cry boohoo on top of it! By God, "Beware first of your own dog biting your side."'

Mother doesn't remember. She forgets dates but she doesn't forget the unforgettable, or the things she doesn't want to forget. When she would remember her labour pains from the days we were born, Father would grumble. He would fix his little hazelnut eyes on her, and say with a wave of the hand, 'Don't you listen to her. She used to lay you like eggs. One of you would come out while she was working in the field or in the house, and she'd feel nothing. The next thing you know, she'd be up and about like the devils.'

'Beware of God, you tyrant. By God, by our God, there's no devil but you.'

She would lift her arms to the sky and speak to her God, 'Where are you, God, in all of this? Do you have your ears open to hear me well? You hear and see everything, and you know very well who suffers and who causes the suffering.'

* * *

On the land that Father rented in Beirut, my parents built a shack made not of wood but of soil. They would dampen the soil, pour it into wooden moulds, and leave it in the sun and air to harden and solidify. That way, they produced identical smooth bricks that insulated cold air in the summer and warm air in the winter. Since the roof consisted of tin boards, it would often be blown far away by the winter storms, sending Father running after them while the shack filled with the rainwater.

Mother built a cage for her chickens and their chicks, and they grew so numerous that they almost made up a full-scale farm. Mother took such good care of the chicks that they became 'big as a lamb' as she used to say, smiling proudly and showing with her hands the size of the birds.

And when she noticed that her neighbours from Biqa, who had rented the nearby strip of land, were taking advantage of the land's generosity by growing mallow, okra, parsley and mint, she followed their example and exploited every little patch of land for some kind of vegetal or animal product.

In the evening, the sounds of a fiddle would rise at the neighbours', and Father's relatives who lived in the same neighbourhood would join the crowd for a long night of merriment, swinging their shoulders, clapping and nodding to the beat. They joined hands, stamped their feet and let the beat of the Dabka resound in the evening air. The residents of Ashrafiyya would look out of their windows and peer down from their balconies, and think that they must have been transported to a dusty village square in the south or to the dry air of the Biqa valley. Sometimes, they would come down to watch the Dabka more closely, the dancers stepping rhythmically to the music of the fiddle. And as the dancers' feet stamped on the ground, Ashrafiyya would shake with the beat of the folklore that had put down roofs in their neighbourhood.

In those days, the world was blessed a thousand times.

The neighbour had no peace of mind if he didn't send his neighbour a plate of his meal. All of us, Muslims and Christians, worked as a single hand. The world still had one mother, until the mothers and fathers multiplied tenfold during the war, as did the 'bastards'. Then, anyone who married your mother would call you 'my nephew', and from there, things fell apart.

The only thing Mother would not give up for the neighbours was one of the chickens that ran about in the den to become 'big as a lamb' and whose eggs she hoarded. Only once did she send two eggs to her Durzi neighbour who taught her how to knit a sweater from yarn. For years, or for all her life, she talked about her generosity for giving her neighbour those two eggs. The sacrifice of two fresh home-farmed eggs is not the same as a bowl of stew. But, her neighbour was worth it because when Mr Metni's wife gave Mother an old wool sweater that she didn't like, it was she who told Mother, 'Ya Um Ahmad, unravel the sweater, wash the yarn and hang it on the line. When it dries, gather it into a ball, and I'll teach you what to do.'

'And she taught me, God bless her, and the sweater came out beautiful, burgundy dappled with beige, of that thick woven wool that kills the cold like murder.'

Mother would always remember her neighbours in Ashrafiyya. She would never forget their names or stop telling us their stories, in spite of all the time that had passed since the ties were broken as my parents left Ashrafiyya for Burj Hammoud, following the incidents of '58, a few years after my birth. And even then, she kept visiting her neighbour, Um Ibrahim, in her dreams, just like she managed to see her childhood friends, some of whom had died, and others whom she hadn't seen since she left the village.

Mother lived her friendships and her past in her dreams until her memory became nothing but a dream. This dream replaced an impossible life, memories became the past of days, the absent present and murky future. Loves, conflicts, jealousies . . . none of these had any place in her daily life, and could awaken only in her dreams. As for the eyes that stayed open during the day, they merely witnessed the distance between time and life, living and the world. And so, those who had left the world or travelled away from her life became the protagonists of her sleep. They conversed with her slumbering tongue and whispered into ears that had shut to the night.

As the light lifted its face, they gathered before her, just before she opened her eyes. She hesitated to open them lest she should lose the image in the day's light, and be cast back to a world without pleasures. These were not the same dreams that transported her to the past, and of which she spoke to Father in the morning.

The ones who visited her most often were her neighbours Um Ibrahim from Ashrafiyya and Um Ibrahim from Baalbek.

She told us many times her story with Um Ibrahim Al-Masri, how her heart danced to Um Ibrahim's ululations after the murder of the French agent responsible for her brother's death during the French occupation. Um Ibrahim's brother fought in the Biqa alongside Abu Milhem Qasim's men in the popular resistance. With them, he ambushed a squad of French horsemen passing through a side road, killing an Adjudant-Chef with an old FM rifle.

The French went mad as a result; they spoilt the harvest and set fire to the fields, and announced that whoever killed Um Ibrahim's brother would be admitted into the army and given a salary—kill him or turn him in, it made no difference.

One of the villagers was tempted by the prospect of entering the French army, so he decided to kill the resistance fighter. He watched the man's house, soon to discover that he visited his pregnant wife. One night, he followed the wanted man from his house to the wilderness where he discovered his hiding place.

A few days later, he visited the fighter in his hiding place. The man sat on a rock, his rifle gleaming beside him under the moonlight. The fighter greeted him like a friend, 'Welcome. You must have killed a Frenchman too. Be patient, my friend, you are strong and honourable.'

The spy looked at the man and said nothing. He just stared at him with anxiety and fear.

'Why're you looking at me like that?' asked the man. 'Sit down and tell me your story.'

But instead of sitting, he snatched the rifle from the fighter's side and shot him in the chest. Then he fled to Shwaifat where he worked and lived in fear of revenge.

The son, born after his father's murder, grew up and began to ask questions about his father. When he asked his aunt Um Ibrahim, she told him the story of his father's murder and of the one who murdered him. And when the boy matured into a young sixteen-year-old man, he asked everyone in the village until he discovered the hiding place of his father's assassin in Shwaifat. The boy watched him calmly, for several days, until he learnt the times at which the man left his house and returned, where he went and for what purpose. Then one day the boy stood in the face of his enemy who recognized him on account of the curly hair, deep wide eyes and broad figure he had inherited from his father.

The assassin looked the boy in the face and said, 'Did you come to kill me? Your father did not scare me, so you think you're going to?'

The boy pulled out a gun from his pocket and emptied 14 bullets in the head of the traitor, leaving him and a quickly growing pool of blood around him on the street.

That day, Um Ibrahim filled the air with her ululations; the avenger had declared the vengeance done, despite the delay, and was sentenced to only six months in jail. After the boy served his time and was released, Um Ibrahim ululated again.

And Mother ululated by her side, on both occasions.

She ululated almost as passionately as when the Bey arranged a job for Father at the harbour, and Father received thirty thousand Lebanese pounds in one payment for several months' work. She said the moon had told her that my face was to bode well for them, and so it did, as our circumstances changed, and Mother foresaw good fortune in Father's purchase of a piece of land in Ashrafiyya, and in her being able to stay close to Um Ibrahim and her neighbours. But Father refused.

'Listen. Look around. Let's buy a piece of land right here with this money. There's a Durzi going back to the mountains who's selling his land for nothing.'

But Father flatly refused.

That was after the sectarian conflicts of '58. Father wanted to follow his cousins and fellow villagers to Burj Hammoud where they were crowding in neighbourhoods that resembled tightly arranged sardine cans.

He said to Mother, 'Let's go live with our own people. We could be driven out of here one day.'

And so, the family bought a one-level house in Burj Hammoud, and Mother built a chicken shed in its little garden to nourish each and every chick all over again until it became as big as a small—feathered—lamb. The tiny one floor house later grew into a three-level building, where we lived until the Lebanese war broke out in '75. The chicken shed was moved to the roof, and those of us born in Beirut went to schools and learnt English and French. Mother boasted about our degrees and hung them on nails high on the living room walls—my sisters' primary school certificates, then their middle school certificates and, finally, my sister Maha's baccalaureate. On the walls, our degrees shared the stage with a picture of Thul Fiqar's sword, various Koranic verses, famous sayings like 'Patience is the key to success,' the Verse of the Crown or 'In God I trust.' Mother bragged the most about my university degree; she walked around the room with it cradled in her arms before hanging it on the wall, and nodded her head at me, saying, 'Who'd have thought you'd come up with this'—then smiled broadly.

Many years earlier, in the village, she had been so proud when my brothers Ahmad and Mahmoud finished reading the Koran that she put her hand over her upper lip and ululated from the joy. Father danced the Dabka in the courtyard in his shirwal and tarboosh and tears sparkled in his eyes. Then, Mother too danced in the square, for the first time. As she stepped forwards then backwards, her eyes roamed and her shoulders shook from side to side, and her handkerchief waved high in the air as she moved among the dancers, men and women with shoulders pressed against one another. The sweat poured from her body, and the happiness from her eyes. That day, for the first time, it appeared to her that she had married the handsomest of men. She did not care about his small limp or his slightly crooked shoulder.

That night, tears fell from his eyes when they returned home. It was the first time she had seen tears in her husband's eyes, and she felt that he was a 'man'. She slept with him like he was a king, and he told her, for the first time, 'You are the lady of ladies, ya Um Ahmad.' After wiping his tears with her scarf, she told him, 'You are my man, and the crown on my head. Why are you ashamed of your tears? A man's tears can burn down cities, and who told you a man does not become more of a man when he cries?'

She wiped his tears from his cheek, then slept with him.

7

The moon was Mother's portent, but the city moon was different from the village moon. In the city, she considered the moon an interloper, a passer-by peeping without anyone to care about him. He was lonely in the sky far above the buildings; nobody talked to him or looked his way. He almost wept in his loneliness. Like a beautiful woman, he had no presence unless others contemplated him and fell under his spell.

In the village, the sky and the mountains conversed with him and he would respond with a smile, that smile which started as a narrow thread to become wider as he grew and blossomed into fullness. But in the city he appeared, disappeared, grew and diminished—without anybody noticing.

Mother's moon remained the same, that moon which came to her in the hour of darkness, and waxed and waned in step with her dreams. He told her everything in her dreams.

It was the moon who told Mother, less than six months after her father's death, that her mother was going to remarry. Mother was nine when her mother was seduced by a man and eloped with him. She saw the moon pale and sad in the sky and slept with tears burning her eyes.

'Better a maiden for life than a widow for a month,' said the village women when Grandmother left her other children in the care of Mother and ran away—driven by her obsession with sex—with the man she loved, leaving Mother as easy prey. From that day on, sex was the bogeyman that haunted Mother—throughout her life.

Mother was not easy to tame, she who had been named *Sharaa* for all the arguing she did. It was easier to subdue her desires, to erase them with the lash of discipline. And it was possible to domesticate her tongue only when her father died and it became stuck in a knot.

My grandfather was one of those who threw themselves in the ocean that stretched to America to flee the oppression of the Turks at the turn of the century. When he came back, he brought with him a tin full of gold coins. After only four years of travelling, he built the first house of white stone in the village, with balconies perched on tall columns etched at the crown and base.

Grandfather told the secret of the tin—full of gold—to the villagers in two versions, both of which were widely believed. Each time, he would tell the story in the same entrancing style, stiffening his neck, motioning with his hands, his wide green eyes shining in his sun-warmed face. He never forgot to examine the impressions he left on the faces of his listeners and the responses he provoked, to make certain they were believing him.

Perhaps for fear of him, they believed both stories. When he stood to perform, his gigantic frame, his strong torso and wide shoulders spoke of the enormity of his strength. His bulk and aspect reminded them of the camel he had won in his story.

And so, nobody could figure out which of Grandfather's stories about the tin of gold was true. He himself was lost between the two tales and could no longer place the truth of the tin's secret after telling them so many times, each time changing nothing but the protagonists' roles.

In the first version, he arrived in America and started working at a bakery owned by a man of American origins. He worked alongside another worker who was of Jewish origins and constantly cheated the owner. Then, at one point of time, the Jew made the owner start paying him a large cut of the profits. And when the Jew started acting as if he was the owner of the bakery and the owner his employee, the American started thinking about how to dispense with him for good. He tried to dismiss him several times but the Jew would not go away. In the end, the American found no other way to get rid of the worker than to offer Grandfather a little fortune to do the dirty work for him.

The owner said to Grandfather: 'How am I to deal with this problem? Can you help me get rid of this man? You look strong and seem capable of finding a way.'

'I'm at your service. You order and I'll execute.'

'If you rid me of him, I'll give you as a reward a tin of gold.'

'Don't worry about it. I'll find a sure way to get rid of him.'

The next morning, the American left the bakery to Grandfather so he could put an end to the problem with the Jewish worker. No sooner did the worker try to confront Grandfather than he lifted him like a loaf of dough and threw him inside the oven to burn. Grandfather's payment was a tin of gold, because after the end of the Jew, the bakery would bring its owner much more gold. For the American, sacrificing a tin of gold today was tolerable in view of the many tins to be filled tomorrow.

As for the other version Grandfather told, the story in essence did not change, but the owner of the bakery was the Jew and the worker the American, to the same conclusion. Again, Grandfather threw the insubordinate worker into the oven and took as his bounty a tin of gold from the Jew. And his audience believed both stories without any objection.

But when he returned to his village home, Grandfather did not expect to find his fifteen-year-old daughter pregnant and unmarried. The girl did not confess to her mother who had fooled and assaulted her. Her silence might've been caused by fear of the one responsible, who may have threatened to kill her if she mentioned his name, or by the possibility that no one would believe her if she said who it was.

Her mother, in spite of being anguished, did not really want to know the answer for fear of the answer itself. She suspected her nephew, for she smelt the scent of a confused glare in the girl's face whenever she laid eyes on the boy. She also suspected the girl's uncle but dreaded her own suspicion, for when she beat the girl, an awkward memory flashed before her, of her brother's dreamy eyes when she walked into the house one day to find him lying beside the girl on the bed. She also suspected one of the families that took an oath of revenge against them, and she had seen their son hovering around the house several times. But she didn't want to find the answer to her confusion even when she grabbed the girl's hair and hit her head against the wall until she bruised the smooth forehead and broke the already bleeding little nose.

At times, she even made her put her hands on the hot baking tin on which she had baked bread. She grabbed the girl's wrists and pressed the trembling palms onto the sheet over the burning fire, so that the flesh and skin stuck to the metal and the house filled up with the smell of burning. Even after the girl fainted from the pain, the mother did not relent. As soon as the girl came to, the mother brought out scissors and threatened to cut off her tongue if she didn't speak. The girl stared at her mother, her eyes dripping with smoky tears, like two charred logs drying over embers.

The girl's uncle stood watching his sister, saying to her fervently, 'Burn her more, burn her, like she burnt our honour. Burn her heart and eyes because her sex is evil and lets the devil play with the mind and ruin households. Burn her, may God kill her and rid you of her. Your daughter deserves nothing but death.'

Because the mother was torn between wanting to know the answer and not wanting to, she was reassured that the girl would not say a word.

For wells are the only places for throwing secrets.

A few days after Grandfather returned from America, he found out about his daughter, looked at her burnt hands and understood from his wife the reason the little one was lying in bed and hallucinating in pain. The girl slept like a little burnt tear, with a burnt heart. He did not try to ask her about the secret. He took revenge on his wife by divorcing her and marrying Grandmother Ghaliya, Mother's mother, to look after his older daughters, Samiyya and Naziha, after he had drowned his youngest daughter, Rawda, in the well.

He killed her without asking her a single question; even if he had asked her, she would have been unable to answer. The silent tear moaned and raved in bed, as drops of cold sweat fell from her because of high fever. He lifted the tear and carried it in his hands, hiding his own tear that burnt deep within him for the daughter he loved so much. He went shrouded in black, cold sweat glistening on his face, and the heat of the daughter he had always pampered now scorching his hands. He walked away from the village houses towards the farthest well. He threw her and her pain in the emptiness, and the teardrop transformed into tiny bubbles frothing her little mouth until her hollow filled with the well water and a motionless form floated silently on the water's surface.

Grandfather, before he died of tuberculosis, would take Mother—his little Fatima—along with my aunts Samiyya and Naziha to the wheat fields, to help him with the harvesting, sowing and ploughing. He would make them walk barefoot in front of him to take his revenge on all girls, after his own little girl had caused him so much pain. He walked behind them mightily, hiding his tears, as he watched their little feet crack and bleed in front of his eyes. But he did not hide his tears when he returned home in the evening for dinner. Grandmother Ghaliya would hurry in with the copper bowl and put it on the tray in front of him on the floor. He would not eat except from my Mother's young hands. He would open his mouth widely and Mother would press the morsel with her fingers into his mouth. He would close his mouth on her hands and she would pull them out, finger by finger, as he licked them clean and wiped the traces of food left on them with his lips and tongue. Then he would unfold her palms and kiss them, and wipe them over his face and cry. He would never eat pounded beef except from her hands. She would sit in front of the meat mortar, lift the big wooden pestle in her lean arms and pound. He loved eating Fraaki dipped in olive oil prepared by her, and his tears fell as he kissed her hand, finger by finger, after eating. Mother would wipe his tears with her hands without knowing why he was crying or kissing her hands. She believed that whenever fathers ate from their daughters' hands, they cried.

When Grandfather died, Mother sobbed uncontrollably. She opened her hands while she bawled and stared at her fingers for a long time, thinking that her father could not sup in his grave without her.

After Grandmother Ghaliya eloped, Mother cried and said, 'I want my mother.' Uncle Akhil took the two older girls and raised them in his home until they married while Father married Mother in order to raise her as well as my uncle Daoud and my aunts Tuffaha and Narjis. And so, the sisters and brother split between the uncle and the new husband of the ten-year-old daughter.

* * *

The village was a handful of houses on a mountain slope, below which the plains, hills and valleys stretched under the low sky. At its centre, amid the houses, there was a square and a mosque made from the same soil as the rest of the houses in the village. Only later would it become a building made of stone. The muezzin's voice reached nearby villages just as their muezzin was heard by the people of our village. At the beginning, large tiles had been placed at the edges of the square to serve as benches, and only later was a sitting space set in concrete. The villagers would gather there at night to dance the Dabka or celebrate weddings.

The vast empty area surrounding the village houses was, according to the villagers, the dwelling of jinns and fiends who had claimed a territory much larger than the village. However, the jinn territory narrowed as human territory expanded, so they could no longer fit in isolated areas, cemeteries, wells and valleys. Or, as Mother put it, humans took over the realm of the jinns when they themselves became jinns. In the end, the spirits moved into houses, thrived in corners and sometimes nested on human heads. They came to make humans friends, lovers and foes.

Whenever Mother heard the whistle of air in the winter or the sound of breaking plates or glasses that had fallen off the wooden stand where they'd been set to dry in the sun, she would ask them, 'What have I ever done to hurt you? If I've never hurt you, why do you want to hurt me? By God, tell me.' She was even more surprised by their mischief when she'd wake up to find the clothes line cut and the clothes she had worn herself out rinsing and churning thrown into the mud, needing another wash.

She always complained about the nuisance caused by the jinns whenever one of them would get married and have a wedding through the night, just like humans—with dancing, singing and beating drums. Mother always remembered the threats of her 'double' to wreck her house over her head if she did not surrender her oldest son, Ahmad. Mother was so overjoyed with Ahmad when he was born that she slept clutching him close to her chest, for fear that the jinn would come and take him from her, especially when she touched his forehead and found him hot with fever. Mother would tell the story of how she saw with her eyes and heard with her ears the lady jinn, warning her that if she did not hand over the baby she would wreck her house. The jinn said this in a blink and disappeared. But Mother held him tight despite the jinn's threat and brought down his fever with daubs of cold water from the well. That night, a storm almost uprooted the house. After it broke the roof made of cane, straw and soil, the muddy water drowned the blankets, sheets and sleeping bodies.

In the morning, Mother found the way to banish the jinn. She went to Sayyed Rida and asked him to write her an incantation to keep the evil power of her double away from her children, Ahmad and Zainab. She was fifteen at the time. Later, the roof and the walls would be rebuilt with stone, and the house would be enhanced with a porch and a small garden in the front.

Mother's position towards Grandmother changed with time but she never forgave her. Sometimes, Grandmother visited us during the winter for a few weeks in Beirut, fleeing the cold of the village, outside of which she never learnt, or wished, to live. I would never forget Mother's sharp looks at Grandmother on those visits. Grandmother would sit on the couch in front of the television to watch Egyptian soaps. She would be overjoyed when the hero confessed to the heroine that he loved her. Her eyes would glitter above her flushed cheeks and she'd sit up and perk up her ears for the talk of love that had become permissible in public. A dreamy look would wash over her wrinkled face as she listened to the words of romance that she worshipped—that had driven her to abandon her children. Mother would watch her nervously, and Grandmother, after immersing herself in the love scene, would suddenly become alert and correct her posture and expression. She would look away from the screen and tell Mother, pointing to the television: 'This man is a liar, a son of liars.'

'Why is he a liar, Grandma?' asked one of my sisters.

'Look at me, ya Fatima,' she told Mother, 'you see this man telling the girl in front of him "I love you"? I just saw him looking at your daughter Suhaila sitting there with her hair and thighs uncovered. Tell your daughter to cover up!'

*

My sister Suhaila was a calm and romantic one, an ocean that hid the tides of desire under her serenity. At times, the clear gemstones of her eyes would betray their secret when she fixed them on a screen to not miss a word from a romantic encounter, looking away only for a second to tear a thread from the needle of the sewing machine.

Mother was more comfortable with the placid Suhaila than with any of us because Suhaila, as the saying goes, had 'a mouth that eats but does not speak.' Suhaila's maternal affection towards me as a child made me think that she did not share the same feelings as the rest of us girls. I thought of her as a second mother to the extent that her marriage came as a bitter shock to me. Suddenly I realized that she was a candidate for marriage, like any other girl, unlike mothers whose lives we considered our indisputable possession and who in our eyes had few ties with femininity—their bodies void of any trace of female sexuality.

After Suhaila left, I cried for a long time when Mother would try to bathe me the way my sister always had. She would undress me impatiently while I whined and said to her: 'I don't want you, you hurt me.'

'Do you see your sister anywhere, you daughter of dogs?' Mother would swear, 'Your sister is gone. So sit down and glue yourself to that spot—or else . . . Not half a word, or I'll pull your ears.'

So I would sit stone-still as she scrubbed my body without tenderness with one hand and gripped my shoulder firmly with the other—to keep me from slipping. Mother scrubbed vigorously and would not yield until I left the bathroom 'clean and light'.

Not much changed in my sister Suhaila's life after her marriage, except that she became a real mother. She still sat for long hours behind the sewing machine, her eyes stale with exhaustion while her hands spun gold to support her family as she once helped to support ours. Her roaming eyes, hungry for passion like her Grandmother's, remained untethered after marriage. Night and day, she would doze off, then wake with a start in her chair at the sewing machine, weaving love stories—in her imagination—of romantic trysts adapted from the films and soaps she imbibed daily. Her eyes would snap open and the sleep flutter away, when she heard the words 'I love you' in an Arabic soap or deciphered them from the familiar tones in a foreign movie. At that moment, the hero's flirtation seemed directed at her, or so she dreamt. And so, she would yearn and burn, delight and exalt, strain and burst—silently in front of the screen.

So great was her appetite for emotion that she convinced herself that she had fallen in love with her husband, a relative of ours who had returned from Brazil in the 60s. He had saved 'a few pennies' to open up a falafel restaurant in Sin el Fil and wanted to settle down with a wife. For his bride, his mother chose him my sister because she had a reputation for having 'a mouth that ate and did not speak,' and because her hands dripped gold from her sewing while her manners oozed courtesy and obedience. He visited our house for two weeks before the engagement, and marriage was announced jointly, for it was not in our habit to let a strange man enter our home without being married to one of the daughters. A man could easily jinx the house with a bad reputation.

But on his several visits, Suhaila's fiancé rarely spoke to her except to greet her on his way in and out of the house. But Suhaila, who experienced love neither before nor after marriage and who had no way of encountering it, convinced herself that she had married for love. Moreover, she conjured stories in which she, the heroine, and her husband, the hero, struggled and suffered before they could finally be together. Every time she'd see a film or soap about the difficulties, obstacles and conspiracies plotted against two lovers, she would point her finger at the screen and tell her children: 'This is exactly what happened with me and your father. God, did we suffer before we could be together.' Her chest would freeze when a plot against two lovers would be uncovered, because in her mind each one of these events spoke to her personally, about her story with her husband.

Her husband spoke little, and if he talked, it was only to call her, 'You donkey. You ass.' But she never answered him or rarely even heard or she was certain that she'd misheard and that he was talking to someone else. And sometimes she would pause and say: 'I can't hear you.'

She told each of her customers how her husband wooed her, and insisted that all the conspiracies spun against all the lovers in Mexican movies 'would not compare to half our pain, Maher's and mine, before we could marry.'

My composed sister, whom I'd never seen lose temper and who had never shouted at me, raised her voice at me and howled like a winter wind, on my last visit to her house with Mother. That was after the famous incident at the Ghandoul and my break-up with Mustafa. I said to Suhaila that day while she worked calmly behind her machine, 'Do you know, Sister, it was better in your days when there was no love and no nonsense. Look at you and your husband, all happy together, and you never even fell in love with him nor he with you.'

It was then that a voice I could not even recognize as hers roared at me, 'Oh, yes, we did. There was love between me and Maher, and much more, from the moment we met.'

'You were in love with him? When was that? He saw you barely fifteen days before the wedding, and you hardly spoke half a word to each other, not that Mother would have allowed it anyway.'

'Yes, there was love, and a strong one too.'

'Strong how?'

She glared at me, and this time her answer came in the classical register, 'It was written in our glances.'

I laughed but Mother didn't, as usual. She lifted her eyes and said to Suhaila, 'I know you, you snake hiding in the grass. You worthless dreamer, just like your grandmother. I can't believe I've always said you were the most modest among your sisters. I spit on you, you daughter of dogs. And you say it in front of your sister that there was love, and written in glances too? Aren't you ashamed of yourself? By God, it's true what they say about "The cunning that hides under the guise of wistfulness!"'

But my wistful sister was far from cunning. When the date for her husband's retirement approached, she began to regard him narrowly and talked back at him on every occasion. Suddenly, she had 'a mouth that spoke'—not because her husband no longer made money but because he was about to stay home with her and upset the perfect balance she had devised between sewing, housework and television. His presence would also force her to admit that her love story with him did not exist—never had existed. He would destroy what she spent a lifetime building.

When I told her, 'Come on. He is the heart of your heart whom you've loved all your life, first by glances and then by more. Here he is, at last, retiring to grow old at your side.'

'No,' she said angrily and raised her eyebrows in a way I had never seen before.

'What do you mean No? Your husband is retiring and that's what you've always wanted—having him closer to you.'

'No, men are not for homes. If he wants to retire, he can go live in the house at the village and I'll stay here. And if he wants to stay here, I'll go there.'

'Why do you say this? Your Maher is a good man, and you love him.'

'No man is good, and no one could be more annoying than him. By God, Sister, he is unbearable.'

'And what if he married another woman in the village?'

'May he marry and God never return him to me. Or did you think I'd rather have his face in mine all day and let him make my days miserable?'

* * *

Mother too made Father's days miserable, by dreaming as she did of daughters who did not stay at home. She never allowed Father to enjoy the feeling of satisfaction. She who had endured hunger would not endure his decision to deprive her daughters of an education. She stood with arms akimbo in front of him for a brief moment before shrinking from his blow. 'Whether you like it or not,' she said defiantly, 'I will give my daughters an education. Or do you want them to end up like me who can't unknot a letter?'

'You want to teach your worthless daughters how to write, so they can write love letters to men?'

'My daughters will write to nobody. They're not sly. I will send them to school whether you like it or not. And my daughters are not worthless,' she answered defiantly.

But that is not to say that she herself would not call us worthless. 'May the path away be clear and the return road closed. Worthless all of you!' she would say, before slamming the door behind us on our way out to school.

Even though Mother mourned the departure of each one of her daughters when they left for the bridal homes, tying a bandana around her forehead to alleviate the headache caused by nostalgia, the symphony of curses on our sex remained one of her favourite refrains.

'May God take the fathers of girls and those who bore them and may He do away with your whole evil sex.'

Her lips stretched effortlessly around the letters of the word as if her tongue were licking each honey-dipped symbol, savouring every flavour of its sounds.

Her curses almost had me convinced that Mother did not share our sex, that mothers did not belong to the same sex as girls. In my mind, mothers belonged to a third sex that was sexless. Just as when boys grow up, they can speak like men, she had come to hate girls because she no longer belonged to the same sex.

Mother did not believe in pleasure, let alone the pleasure of her body. She would not even admit the pleasure of eating. When I asked, 'What's for lunch? Anything good?' 'What do you mean "good"?' she would say. 'Where do you get these ideas from? Good or not, one has to eat, and it's all food.'

On the few occasions when she wore her gold bracelets, she'd be ashamed of herself and the rest of us. She did not believe in her right to wear jewellery or to adorn her bare wrists. The moment we'd notice them on her hands and smile, she would say nervously, 'You know, I wore them because the Sheikh said I should wear them every now and then, so I wouldn't be guilty of hoarding them. I don't like gold at all and the only reason I bought them in the first place was to sell them one day if we need the money.'

Mother never admitted to her pleasures or to her sex, or that father, the Good Hassan, was her mate. She'd forgotten many things but she never forgot that she was raped. Most of her life, she looked upon him as an odd and wretched cripple, with the exception of a few particular moments.

Each time she gave birth to a boy, she would chatter incessantly about Father's handsomeness and rank him with the best of men. The day he finished building our village house, one of the first stone houses in the village, he walked straight as a die in her eyes. She had a sheep slaughtered on the threshold of the house, and as Abu Ahmad—her Good Hassan—stepped over the offering, she said to him, 'May God guard you and keep you over us, you crown of my head.' She made certain to ask the builder to etch the Verse of the Throne above the gate, and she asked Sayyed Rida to compose an incantation for him—the crown of her head. 'By God,' she said, 'how he walks like a spear!'

As a young man, my Father had walked like his father, carrying his upper torso erect as if he were riding a camel. But when he saw the Bey, Kamel Al-Asaad, in the village square during the election campaign, he took to walking like him. He grew the same moustache and twisted it upwards at the ends. In those days, Mother liked his look and posture. But to spite him she said, 'Not all who walk on the Dabka floor can dance.'

Father walked behind his father who walked like the Bey but only in the Bey's absence. In the Bey's presence, all shoulders bent lower than his. Father's shoulders straightened and became erect the day Mother let him enter her in the way of a man.

Father entered Grandfather's house for the first time when he came looking for a small room to rent. Or more correctly, when he rented a room in Grandmother Ghaliya's house after her husband died. The room had a door with a round opening to match the dome-shaped ceiling. Hassan moved in with his sister, the only family member to survive the plague. He had lost his other four sisters to sickness, then his mother to hunger and finally his father to sorrow.

Hassan had nothing but the memories of death and a donkey and two beasts on which he moved goods to support himself and his sister. The only piece of land he inherited from his mother went to his aunt when he exchanged it for four Ottoman silver coins. He surrendered the land to buy barley that he could soak in water and eat with his sister in the days of hunger under the Turks. His aunt took over the land and said to him, 'Soon, I will give you your land back, when you return my money.' But he never could pay her back, not in those days.

'May you not live to see such days,' Mother said of those times. People would unstitch the pillows that they slept on, remove some dry chaff and eat it. That is why Mother always felt comforted by the sacks of rice, bulgur, sugar and other grains piled up in the attic, as if they promised to lift the nightmares of hunger she suffered during the World War.

Father never felt safe again after the death of most of his family. The world had taught him to be a man since boyhood, and he believed that men could have no childhood. When one day I asked him about his own, he said, closing his left eye the way he always did, 'What childhood? Listen to this one talk. Where do you get these ideas? Do you learn them in school? Childhood is for women and girls. Your father has been a man since he was little.'

The world had taught Hassan how to be a man. Smallpox had spread as had 'the yellow air' epidemic. I had heard women cursing their enemies by saying, 'May the yellow air swallow him,' and would imagine a yellow air blowing on a person and making him deathly ill, until I realized that it was the yellow fever.

Many villagers would go to the fields to plough or harvest and never return. They would eat their lunch at noon and go to sleep, never to wake up again. They died instantly and nobody knew why— whether by a sunstroke or by a gust of yellow, red or black air.

My father's two older sisters had caught smallpox in Beirut where they had moved to find work, and when they returned to the village, they died while harvesting the wheat field. Then his four younger sisters died too, one after another, and each of their little bodies was dusted in calcium before their burials to keep the disease from spreading.

Grandmother Um Hassan spent a year wailing and mourning the death of her daughters, until she died of her sorrow for them. Her blood dried, and so did the whites of her eyes, until she would cry without shedding a single tear. Grandfather Ahmad Abu Hassan entered the house and found her lying on the floor behind the door. He approached her and asked, 'Ya Um Hassan, ya Zainab, why are you sleeping here at the door?'

She did not respond.

He shook her, then turned her over, to find her body, dry and solid while the tear on her cheek was moist and dewy. 'Finally, your tear has fallen, ya Zainab,' he said and cried like a child as he sat beside her on the floor. 'Why don't you answer me? Answer me, ya Zainab,' he insisted. When his son Hassan walked in at that moment, his little thin body shuddered at the sight of his father sobbing and imploring his dead mother.

Father would always remember the way his father kept repeating, 'Where are you going, ya Zainab, and leaving me here? You think this is the right thing to do, following your daughters? You want it this way, ya Zainab, but I don't. You've broken my back, ya Zainab, you who never broke your word in your life. Why did you betray me like this in the end, you who were the strength of my years?' Grandmother did not answer him. Her closed eyes had finally found rest in the two tears that haunted Father his whole life.

Her death broke Grandfather's back and his love for her broke his heart. When he would return home in the evening, his stomach tortured by hunger, one look at her would be enough to fill him like the tide. He would embrace her with his eyes during the day, and at night his strong arms would engulf her bony frame. He could not bear how much he desired her, how she had stolen his heart, he who had been helpless to the curves of the flesh in a woman's breast or bottom. After Grandmother Zainab died, he chose a plump wife, but every time he would embrace her soft flesh and wrap himself around her, he would imagine his Zainab's lean body between his hands and have to fight back tears.

His love for Grandmother Zainab extinguished his lust and made him miserable with his second wife. His sorrow for Zainab and his daughters overwhelmed him and he died two years later, after the birth of his son Hamza, our Uncle Abu Ismail. And while Grandfather's corpse lay in its shroud, his new wife began to reprimand him just as he had done to Zainab. She rocked her body from left to right, her head hanging over her chest: 'What did I do to you? What did I do for you to not love me? Tell me. Answer me now. What did I do to you? Come on, answer me, or do you just want to follow Zainab?'

This time, Grandfather did not answer.

His wife told the villagers how he would leave her asleep and go to the graveyard before dawn, after his ablutions and prayer, to read her the *Fatiha* and talk to her under the silence of the trees. He sang to her with the birds in the morning, mourned her with poetry, and wailed his family's fate, then washed the grave with his tears and water he had carried from the well.

And so my Father was left all alone after his sister Saada married. But his circumstances did not stay unchanged.

The camel became two camels, the donkey two donkeys, the cow two cows, the goat two goats and the chicken many chickens. All of that happened after he married my mother and became father to a flock of children; or more correctly, after they married him to her; or even more correctly, after her family married him to her.

They sealed her contract when she was ten. Father had rented the room to get a roof over himself, his donkey and camel. At that time, Grandmother had just eloped with her lover, leaving Mother and her little siblings.

'Fatima is pretty and young, a kitten with eyes still shut, so you can raise her the way you like, as you prefer.'

Father agreed and the issue was settled in the presence of Mother's uncles and Sayyed Rida who, however, became unsettled when he looked at the little girl. 'Marrying her is against religion,' he said to her uncle. 'She is still a child. This is forbidden.'

Mother was encouraged by Sayyed Rida's protests, so she ran to his lap, looked up into his eyes and said, 'Please our Sayyed, I don't want to get married. Please.'

When her uncle, sitting nearby, heard her say this to the Sayyed, he grabbed her, stood her in front of him and hit her so hard on the face that she dropped to the floor. 'Shut your mouth,' he said, 'not half a word. I know you, you want to follow your mother and do what she did, you daughter of a whore.'

Mother's eyes and knees shook at the anger thrusting at her from the bulging eyeballs. Her uncle would have the same bulging stare for the rest of his life, especially when he later became blind.

'God is great,' she would say to him afterwards, 'This is your punishment for marrying me by force, Uncle. God does not cast stones but He finds other ways,' she would say to him whenever he called her from his room in Grandfather's house to clean, feed, serve him. The window separating the two rooms, which Father had closed with wooden boards and nails after they got married, had to be opened again when her uncle went blind and had to live within her earshot. He would cry out to her so loud that his calls reached the street, not just her room. 'Ya Fatima, come here my niece. Please, run!'

Mother would set down her children or housework, run out of the house and into his room. She would find him sitting in his bed with his pants down, ready to urinate. Quickly, Fatima would grab the bucket with one hand and his penis with the other. She kept a firm hold on both until he was done, so he didn't sprinkle all over his bed, clothes or floor. His bulging eyes which now naturally turned upwards reminded her of the day he had married her off. She would dry his penis with an old cloth that she'd left aside for that purpose, pulling down hard on it as if she wanted to take revenge by tearing it from between his legs.

'Akh! Why are you pulling on my pigeon, ya Fatima?'

'I will pull today and every day, if I want to.'

'Please, ya Fatima, you daughter of virtue.'

'So now I am a daughter of virtue, not a daughter of a whore?'

He'd stay quiet and not answer.

'Now you see that you have nobody other than me to serve you, to feed you, clean you, even help you take a piss! I am pulling because you damned me the day you married me off by force. Can you see now, you who are blind and can't see? See what God did to you, how He avenged me? He blinded you because you married me when I was a child and damned me for life.'

'What have I got to do with any of that?'

'What do you mean, what *you* got to do with it? Who was the one who slapped me and made them marry me off? *You* are the one who wronged me, no one else.'

'No. It's your mother who wronged you and the rest of her children when she ran off and abandoned you.'

*

Mother couldn't remember the exact date or year, or wished not to remember, when Father had first entered her. All that time she lived with him and kept him at arm's length while he raised her and her sisters and waited for her puberty with utmost patience. He watched her chest turn from a flat cage with breasts the size of sesame seeds to a set of round and stiff pomegranates. He would often wonder about their shape under her loose nightgown while singing verses of poetry in his head as he swayed his shoulders to the tunes of the fiddle and stamped his feet to the Dabka.

During the day she would go to work in the fields, sowing the harvest for the landowners, and in the evening she returned to play with her sisters. In the meantime, he used his camel and donkey to transport provisions back and forth to neighbouring villages, making just enough money to satisfy his hunger and Mother's, and to feed her sisters and brother. In the evenings, she looked for rags that nobody needed and sewed them into dresses for her doll. Sometimes Father would take away her doll and scold her, 'You are the bride now, not her.' 'No, not me. She's the bride,' she would sob.

In those days, she still spoke to her doll. But the day her hymen was torn, she pinched the doll between her thighs and tore the doll and the rags into pieces.

*

Father was twenty-three years old when he married Mother, still a child. At first, he did not beat her when he entered the house and she fled from him, nor did he beat her when he'd approach her, taking off his clothes, and she would start wailing and shouting as she saw nothing but her uncle's eyes and his little face.

He would pull up his trousers quickly and tighten his belt, 'Don't scandalize us, you girl of virtue,' he would plead. And she would not stop crying until he put his head on the pillow to sleep. 'The kitten's eyes are still shut,' he would think as he closed his own eyes for the night.

Though she might have preferred not to, Mother remembered well that whenever she saw him taking off his trousers, she would steal away from him and flee the house. One time, she blocked the house door before he returned in the evening by putting the heavy wooden box—in which she stored her clothes—against it from the inside, and on top of the box, all the mattresses, blankets and pillows. That night Father went mad, and he became even angrier the time she escaped from him to the roof by scrambling up the wooden ladder. It was tied to the edge of the roof on both sides with a rope, but she quickly undid the knot with her little teeth so the ladder dropped to the ground and he couldn't reach her. In spite of the dark, she was not afraid of falling because her fear of Father was much greater than the darkness that spread around her. The night was stark and its calm was interrupted only by her exchange with Father, 'Don't scandalize us, woman,' he shouted, but the little girl who was not yet a woman chose to scandalize him anyway.

After that incident, Father began tying her every evening with a long rope to the steel windowsill over the mattress where she slept. In the morning, he would untie her so she could go to work in the fields. And so, she learnt from him the technique of roping hands to the windowsill and started tying up her sisters and brother whenever they misbehaved, giving them the punishment she got from him.

In the end, Father succeeded in domesticating her.

He went to her uncles and complained of the frustration she was causing him, and they told him: 'Things are not right between you and her—we know that she's stubborn. You have to discipline her so she won't defy your word.'

'How am I to discipline her?' he asked.

'You have to beat her—let her know that you're a man. Make her fear you. If a woman doesn't fear her man, she'll control him.'

*

And so Father learnt from my great-uncles how to enter her like a man. But he did not enter her or become a man overnight.

Hassan found out that he couldn't enter her, even after he tied her hands one night to the windowsill, raised and opened her legs, and managed to fix them right and left with his knees. When he undid his belt and took off his trousers, she saw his member and screamed. 'Don't scandalize us, woman. It's just a stick. I'll do it for you and it'll be over!'—but in her mind's eye, the stick was for her beating.

He took off her undergarments and touched what was between her legs in preparation for 'making a stick for her,' but since he had never seen a woman's intimate parts before, as soon as he set eyes on what was between her legs, his member went to sleep. And around them the night lay quiet in the room, barely stirred by the feeble light of the lantern.

Father tried again, half-crazed with lust until he saw his member shrink a second time from her screaming. His sweat had mixed with the fluids beneath her belly when he covered her mouth with his hand and said, 'Don't scandalize us, woman. May God open your eyes. Look how you've broken my will.'

But Fatima's will was also broken, and by the end she could neither scream nor tug with her hands to undo the rope. Her desperate movements had wrung the sweat out of her little body, the pain from her little heart, and streaks of blood from her little wrists. Her body dripped a new kind of sweat, unlike the sweat that bathed her while ploughing in the fields or working around the house. This sweat which had now soaked the rope smelt rotten. She sobbed and sobbed, but Father could think only of his member. When he lost his will at the sight of her naked body, he realized that someone must have cast a spell on him.

'It looks like I won't be able to make a stick for you, ya Fatima,' he said.

He fell silent and stood there drowning in his sweat. He sat by her side at the edge of the bed, tilted his head to one side and sighed. He covered his member by folding his arms over his knees, and looked at the sweat of his body and hers on the white sheet with which he had covered the bed. It looked all wrinkled and chewed, and there was no red streak shining on it to certify her excellence in virtue or to attest to his graduation from youth. In the dark, he tried to spread the sheets on the bed and fold them under the edges. With his hands, he felt the dampness of the sweat that had replaced the blood, reminding him that he had failed.

Disconsolate, he cried, put on his trousers and untied her. He embraced her, and sobbing, he said, 'Forgive me, ya Fatima, for failing,' and kissed her hands as if he were her father. She didn't understand why he was crying, just as she didn't understand when her father used to kiss her hands.

'Please don't beat me,' she answered, 'and don't make the stick for me. And don't tie my hands, may God bless you and watch over you.'

Being a child, she did not understand what had happened and was in no position to forgive or not forgive him. For the sleeping kitten, even if she had opened her eyes to some things about her body and what was around it, she kept her eyes shut as the Good Hassan wrapped it, folded it, spread it and lifted it whenever he came to her in the night, opened her legs and the dark thickened between them. That was how he made her belly swell time and again, until she became a woman who was determined to keep him 'tied' by misery in order to take her revenge.

'I won't beat you,' Father said, 'I can't. But be quiet and don't tell anybody what happened, or I'll make the stick for you and hit you with it too.'

But Mother did not keep quiet. She told her uncles about what happened even though she did not know what it meant, and both of them responded by beating her to teach her not to tell her husband's secrets. When her uncle finished hitting her with a long stick, he said, 'A good woman, one who knows proper behaviour and her duties towards her husband, would herself bring him his shoe every morning and say, "Hit me." That's how a good woman behaves. Otherwise you're going to end up throwing your sisters and brother on the street without a man to look after them, and you'll be just like your mother.'

Mother became scared that Father would throw out her sisters and brother and that her uncle would beat her if she complained again. She kept quiet without understanding exactly what had happened and why he started sleeping in the barn with the cows.

The Good Hassan slept in the barn for a week while peaceful slumber filled Mother's eyes. She slept deeply and hugged her sisters and her doll after she put out the lamp. Little did she know about the secret of Father's decision to sleep with the cows, and the reason he came back every morning with the smell of hay and cow hair stuck on his clothes.

*

Father began doubting himself after a lifetime of certainty about being a man, and more. He had discovered his manhood with animals, as had the Effendi Abu Talal—with Qut al-Qulub, the whore in the red district on Al-Mutanabi Street—after moving to Beirut in the late 40s.

Father was thirteen when his bodily transformation signalled his entry to the world of men, that is, when it sprang between his legs one spring morning amid wide pastures of wild flowers and green grass stretched out against an infinite sky. A cool breeze filled his chest, and suddenly he enjoyed a feeling of newly won freedom. He walked behind his goats and sheep with a joyful lightness that he had never experienced before, a weightlessness that enabled him to move in musical waves. His mouth started singing for the first time the songs that until then he had only heard the men in the village sing. His mouth sang like a bird, the birds fluttering in his body, while the birds in the sky sang across the silence of the meadows. One day, he passed by a house on the village outskirts and saw a middle-aged woman with a checkered red-and-blue dress bending over to wash her laundry in a basin between her legs, lifting her undergarments high above her knees. He imagined himself stepping in front of her, lifting her until she stood facing him, taking off her dress, kneeling before her and lowering her undergarments. He wanted to kiss her on her belly and thighs, and then nuzzle his face between them until he felt the warmness that emanated from that place which he knew existed but could not imagine because he had not seen it before. He imagined himself laying her on the wet grass in the middle of the silent wilderness and lying on top of her. But then he was confused again when he tried to imagine her breasts and bottom and complexion, he who had never seen a woman naked before. He wondered whether her breasts resembled those of a cow or a sheep. Did her bottom have the warmth he felt when he lifted the sheep's fat and felt his erection inside it? The sheep that excited him the most was the one that indulged him, like an obedient woman, with her calm and quiet, and who did not kick him when he stood behind, as the other animals did.

But he did not conjure the woman again after he came to puberty in the fields. The woman's image vanished from his imagination as his body became light like the gentle waft of air that touched it. It was one transparent breeze caressing another, there yet not there, a light penetrating all his silent parts, showing itself only between his legs, standing and announcing its coming. The contented numbness between his legs after he held his erection with his hand and became wet with his new fluid was unlike anything he had known before.

That day, the nanny goat ran away from him after he took off his trousers and tried to enter her from behind. In spite of his knowledge and surveillance of all his animals' body parts, he had forgotten that the male goat's member is much smaller than that of a donkey or a bull. He also forgot his pity for the male goat whose member expanded no more than a little finger's length when he got excited, and who left no sooner than he had entered his partner.

Desperately, he ran after her with his member in his hand until she disappeared from sight. He looked at his erect member to see if it was pointing leftwards like those of the animals when they were excited, trying to determine whose member resembled his the most. He wished his could extend as long as the bull's until it became an arm's length, or the horse's whose member was half the length of the bull's but thicker and when excited, would become three quarters the length of the bull's.

The Good Hassan's knowledge and wisdom were not limited to his animals' sexual parts. It extended to all their body parts, skins and fluids, in all their ages and stages. He knew at a glance when an animal was excited and, like the males among them, he could smell the desire of the females. Since he was a young boy his eyes would sparkle and widen when he saw the bull's member and testicles; he would touch himself between his legs and wish the bull's member were his own, tickled by the sight of the bull raising his front legs to mount the cow's back and almost breaking it after catching her smell. Hassan would watch the bull jump and fix the cow's body on both sides with his legs until she could no longer move. He noticed that the bull's movement triggered the cow's instincts, because after that she sat still and surrendered to him; and when he entered her, she made a sound that Mother never made, a sound that mixed pain with pleasure.

Others who raised animals would often come to the Good Hassan when they needed to castrate their stock, when their bulls, constantly excited by the whiff of a cow's desire, could not work the fields as they walked behind their females. With sheep, Hassan castrated the male as soon as it was born. He would stretch an elastic band around the testicles and leave it there, pressing on the root until they dried out and fell off on their own. Hassan also removed the horns of sheep so they would not butt. When it was still two or three months old and its horns still soft, he would perform on the lamb an operation that resembled tattooing. He would prick little holes around the horn, dip needles in ink and plant them into the roots just as the village women tattooed their hands, chests and faces. Soon after the ink was injected into the roots of the horns, they dried and fell off.

Most of all the Good Hassan would enjoy castrating the calf, perhaps out of envy for the bull who could single-handedly master a hundred cows. In those times, the villagers were confused about whom to slaughter, the cow or the bull. They could not slaughter the cow because she bore calves and made milk, nor could they slaughter the bull because he was rare and much needed for ploughing and impregnating the cows.

The law of the French army penalized anyone who used a cow to plough his field. Ploughing was the bull's task, too tiring for the cow. In spite of that, the villagers used the cow, even when she was pregnant. One villager would stand on the hill to warn them if French horsemen were on their way to inspect the peasants. As soon as a French soldier appeared from far away, the watchman would shout 'Let's go' and they would scatter for fear of the penalty and the anger of the French soldier who would scold them, 'You know no humanity. How can you work the cow who gives you her milk? What's the bull for? What's the bull's job? Can't you understand that the bull is for ploughing and the cow for nothing?'

*

Father would watch closely when the sheep or the cow gave birth. Two days before he reached puberty, he had watched his sheep give birth and noticed that she recognized her lamb from its smell which Father smelt too. The sheep dragged her young by his front feet away from the blood that had drained from her. The newborn knew his mother by instinct; he stood awkwardly on his feet after a few bad attempts, then put his mouth around her nipple and nursed.

But Father didn't know Mother's body as well as he knew his animals'. When he later found out that her body and reproductive organs were exactly like those of a cow, the discovery astonished him even though he had discovered his own body by comparing it to theirs.

The day he entered her and tore her hymen, he saw in his mind's eye the bull penetrating his female from the back four or five times.

But Mother did not hemorrhage, not like Um Talal did on her wedding night. When her husband tore her hymen and the tender flesh around it, Abu Talal had to take her to a clinic in Ashrafiyya administered by the French troops. That day, in spite of Abu Talal's sorrow for his wife, and the French doctor's scolding, his eyes watered and his breast inflated with pride when the doctor told him, 'Are you a donkey or a bull?' So he knew his was superior to other men's members.

Before the Good Hassan could enter Fatima the child, to make her a woman, he had to reckon with his conviction that he was tied and only the cow could untie him. In the end, it was the cow who healed him of the spell that had tied his member.

The cow, about whom he knew everything—and whose sexual parts he happily discovered to match Mother's—had a uterus, a vagina and labia just like a woman's. This reassured him. He knew that the labia received the male's member, that the vagina gathered the semen, and from there they travelled upwards through the uterus to where the egg awaited fertilization into a foetus.

He noticed the similarities between the breasts of a woman and those of a cow. When the cow was young, she got excited when her breasts were touched; they were soft like milk, pink in colour. And as she grew older, her breasts grew and became flabby, the nipples hardened and became darker in colour, as did Fatima's breasts after all those years nursing several children. Father continued to crave grilled or fried nipples of cows for years—he would crave the sensation of crushing them between his teeth. 'How good it tastes! Soft like milk,' he would say. He was not the first to notice such similarities. To describe the large breasts of a young woman, the villagers would say, 'She has a cow's udders,' and if they were small, they'd say, 'She has a sheep's udders.'

The Good Hassan took good care of his cows' nipples whose gradations of colour he knew by heart, from the lightest shade of pink to the darkest shade of black. He would wash them with warm water to keep them from becoming infected or cracked, just as women do when nursing. The cow, however, could contract her muscles to conserve milk for her young even when her owner tried to milk her, but Mother had no control over the flow of her milk which dried up several times under the influence of a shock or some source of trouble.

Father also noticed later on the similarities between a cow's mood during pregnancy or after delivering and Mother's mood during a pregnancy and after she gave birth to one of their children. Both would start eating less a few weeks before delivering; they would grow tired and prefer isolation and quiet, each entering the layers of her private universe, away from the external world.

He noticed the cow's love of security during those times and her confusion when her place was changed or her routine upset in any way. She would look with wide eyes at her owner whenever he tried to move her, as if asking him for his justification for the nuisance. Father was aware of all these similarities between the cow, whom he knew well, and Mother, whom he knew barely.

*

Fatima floated on a serene ocean of sleep after Father started spending his nights in the cow barn. Her body forgot, for a little while, the smells it produced when Father tried to bed her as she lay tied with a rope to the metal windowsill. When Father told him about his failure with Mother, Sayyed Rida said: 'It must be that you're tied. The girl who made you the incantation has cast a spell on you tying your will to hers. And a man whose will is tied cannot enter his wife until the spell is undone.'

He prepared for Father a counter-incantation, attached it to his wrist, and told him that it would not take full effect until he had slept among the cows for a week. Since the jinns were afraid of cows, they would stay away from him. The cow, with her wide eyes, was the only animal who could see the jinns even in the dark.

Father slept with the cows until the spell left him. As soon as night crept in and lowered the veil of darkness on the village, Father walked into the barn. The shadows wrapped their silence around the cow lying beside him, drawing her into obscurity except the white gleam of her sleep-filled eyes and the soft sheen of her pink nipples. The pink light would remind Father of Fatima's small nipples, and as he glanced at the cow's belly and genital parts, he imagined them looking the same in Fatima. He let his thoughts slide down Fatima's smooth belly, anticipating the moment when he would make it swell like that of a cow. When he inhaled the tangled smells of the cow, hay and body fluids, the need grew inside him, little by little, as though the music of desire must start with a gentle melody before exploding in a strident anthem.

He touched his mouth as he imagined himself drawing closer to suck the cow's breast, his soul suckling at a pleasure that had been unknown to him. He closed his mouth on the soft flesh and ran his tongue about it, as if he were licking the milky fluid that dripped from the soft nipples. He let the milk wet his lips, tasting her honey on his tongue. Little by little, he made his heart and eyes tremble, his shoulders shake and his body shudder like a green leaf, before the numbness rushed in. His member quivered between his hands, like the slaughtered bird bathing for those few last seconds in its own blood. His milky fluid had wet his trousers as he imagined entering the cow whose opening must look exactly like that of Fatima.

It was dawn when he ran from the barn to the house, to Fatima. He banged at the door with his fist when he found it locked from the inside. 'Open up, ya Fatima, quickly. Open quickly, I said.'

When Fatima opened the door, the urge fell on him like a water-fall pouring inside his body—to suck Fatima's pink nipples and drip his milky fluid between her legs.

'It stood like a stick, ya Fatima,' he said while he tied her hands with the rope and laid her on the bed without taking the time to put on the sheet. He held up his stick between his legs and said, 'I am going to make a stick for you. Don't be afraid.'

Fatima screamed with fear as he lifted her dress up to her neck. This time, when he looked at her genital parts, he saw them exactly like the cow's. He sucked on her breast exactly as he had sucked the nipples of the cow's breast, but milk did not drip into his mouth, nor did he get the same taste. Instead, he felt the bones of her thin chest pressed beneath him as though they were about to break; but his milk soon poured inside her, softening his stick of flesh.

*

The daylight was budding, as were her breasts—from a sheep chest, young and firm, to a cow chest, soft and relaxed after the work of years. Her belly was smooth, the skin clinging tight towards her back, before it bulged and swelled like the cow's belly. Her milk flowed for one child after the other, and Abu Ahmad kept sucking the milk out of her breasts, and making his own milk flow between her legs, until the child Fatima became a woman identical to the cow. Her body, her breasts, her milk, her fear of the loss of peace or a fixed place, and like the cow, she would kick Father whenever he would try to come up to her from behind.

* * *

Her belly knew no peace.

It carried eighteen times, ten who lived and eight who died either in her belly or after birth. Although she used to boast about her children and their children to her last days and until her living children and grandchildren numbered more than a hundred, she always mourned those who had died.

'If they had lived, I wouldn't have a thing to worry about. At least then I wouldn't have felt alone in this world.'

'Alone, ya Hajji?' asked our neighbour who had come to wish her a happy Eid after the house finally became empty of the noise of my sisters and brothers and their children.

'Of course I am alone. Maybe if there'd been more of them, I wouldn't have felt all alone.'

'But your family is large. May God keep them all safe.'

'And how did you make it out to be *large*? There are barely nine or ten children of mine—touch wood. And you say the family's big? I don't see that bigness around me!'

'Yes, they're many. Your kinfolk have lots of kids.'

Mother fixed her eyes on the neighbour and threw the edge of her veil to the back, 'Stop envying us. Because of envy, our kids are falling dead and dying in the streets. If we didn't have all these children, we would've ended a long time ago. In spite of the devil's will, we will give birth to all of them who have died.'

Then Mother remembered that the neighbour's family was not small and said, 'And you people don't have a lot of children? You're entitled to it and others aren't? How many kids do you have?'

'Eight altogether.'

'There you go. It doesn't seem to me that you have yours sealed with concrete or red wax. So why should we?' Then she pointed between her legs and said, 'Besides, what use is this for? It's for peeing and having children. Otherwise, it'll rust and sag.'

'Why, the Hajj doesn't give you pleasure there? It's only for peeing and children?' the neighbour asked, laughing.

'May a sharp pain plug your mouth for good. May your face and his pleasure be buried. What for? Filth? Me, I don't enjoy anything. Nothing can please me. You see me running after happiness, silliness and debauchery?'

'No, ya Hajji. That's not what I meant. I'm just saying there's a better chance of it rusting if we don't feel pleasure.' the neighbour said, and roared again with laughter.

'Spit on you and your pleasure. Is it pleasure when the man dirties the woman, or when he makes her heart rot? I wish I didn't have the thing in the first place. What for? I wish God made me with just a mouth to eat and nothing else. What for?'

*

Most of Mother's offspring were girls.

First she had my sister Zainab, then my brothers Ahmad and Mahmoud, and then a line of girls rolled until the bunch of grapes ended with me.

One girl after another; round belly after round belly. And as the saying goes, each child brings its sustenance with it. God provides what is necessary, for He is great. A girl is a boon, her wings are broken, so God commanded that she be cared for; and the Prophet, God's blessings be upon him, said that raising a girl was a benefaction.

Mother told all this to Father more than once, always concluding with the wisdom that a girl is a boon to her parents. She would tell herself the same when she lifted her head after a delivery to see if it was a boy or a girl. She would raise her head and interrupt the baby's screaming with her own, 'What? Another girl?' Then her voice would fail and her pain subside as she fainted from the world. She loved girls but feared Father's treatment of her after a girl was born.

After she gave birth to my brother Mahmoud, Father was elated that two boys had come into the world—'one head following the other'—and expected the rest to be the same. In her fourth pregnancy, he made her work less during the harvest, and during her sixth month, he bought her a piece of flowery fabric whose colours lifted the spirit. He said to her, 'Take this. Have it tailored and wear it. You deserve all the best, ya Um Ahmad. A third boy is on his way, so look after your health.'

Fatima was pleased with his gift, the second dress she had made for herself since her marriage. It made every day like a holiday for her. She was so happy that she fell asleep hugging the fabric. She lay down on her back with a hand resting on her forehead, and fell asleep with the colours pressed against her chest. She dreamt of a beautiful long dress, tapered at the waist, and flowing all the way down to her feet. As she glided across the meadow in it under the moonlight, its colours lit up the darkness of the night and the dimness of her life.

Just then, as the light shone its brightest in her dream, she awoke to the wailing of my brother Mahmoud who wanted to nurse. She opened her eyes, the dress and moonlight still filling her eyes, and said as she turned to him and lifted her breast to feed him, 'My son, couldn't you wait a little? I was going to get up and feed you at some point. Or did you think the world was going anywhere, my heart? Neither the world nor these breasts are going anywhere. How could you break my beautiful dream, you little dream of mine?'

The dream didn't fade either, for it never left her throughout her life. She continued the dream after she gave him her breast, and the next morning she woke up overjoyed with the dress and the visions in her sleep. But as soon as she became aware of her happiness, her eyes widened with fear and her pupils hardened like glass. 'God help me,' she thought to herself, 'what could this happiness be about?' For her, moments of absolute happiness forecast future tears—even if a vision is given by the moon. In fact, she lived all her rosy dreams under his light. Under his gaze, she lived that impossibly beautiful life she could not have with her eyes open.

Her heart froze as soon as she became conscious of her joy. She narrowed her eyes and thought hard, trying to conjure the moon's image and remember whether the light that had shone all night in her eyes had covered the sky completely or only partially. But the image had been lost.

She had won herself a dress but not another boy.

The moonlit dreams followed, as did a string of girls, after she gave birth to Suhaila. The bunch became heavy with eight daughters, one after the other: Zainab, Suhaila, Samiyya, Jamila, Hasna, Amina, Maha and finally me—Maryam—the final grape.

'A girl is a boon,' she would say to Father, and after a few days of bearing his complaints, all was well again. In the end, he would agree with Um Ahmad that a girl is a boon and that raising her is a benefaction.

But in her fifth pregnancy, he looked at her belly during the ninth month and said, 'What do you think, ya Um Ahmad? You want to get another useless one of those? Who's going to raise all these girls?'

'What have I got to do with it? They're all from God. How can I know what I'm having? Fear God, man, so he will keep Ahmad and Mahmoud safe for us. If there were a light inside my belly and I could look up my hole, I would check for you if it's a boy or a girl and let you know!'

Abu Ahmad did not complain the night she had the girl. He asked God's forgiveness, and slapping one hand over the other he relented, 'There is no will or strength save in God. There is no will or strength save in God.' Although Abu Ahmad did not complain, Ahmad and Mahmoud cried after the girl was born. Mother turned to Ahmad and asked him, in spite of her pain, 'Why are you crying, my son? You are making Mahmoud cry.'

'Why do you think? All the kids laugh at me and say your mother can only have girls. I'm ashamed of them.'

'Why should you be ashamed, you dog? Do you see your mother with each leg on a mountain? Do you see her being immodest? Get out of my sight! May you be buried. Damn your father and those who bore you.'

And when he started crying again, she lowered her voice and said, 'My son, you are ashamed of me because I have daughters? By God, son, you and your brother light up my whole life. Fine, tell me what I should do to not have girls. May God forgive me! I accept your blessing, oh God, and girls are a blessing from you. Do you see anybody questioning God, other than you and your brother and your father? Go wash your face and ask God's forgiveness.'

Whenever Mother became pregnant with a baby boy, she would either miscarry or he would die in her belly a few months into the pregnancy. After three dead boys, she became convinced of what

Sayyed Rida had told her, that she had a 'twin' among the jinns, who would not allow her boys to live. She knew it for a fact because she had seen her 'twin' after delivering Mahmoud.

She was nursing him, lying on her side and leaning on him to give him her breast. Sometimes, she would sit him in her lap and rock him left and right with her legs until he calmed down and went to sleep. But on that day, she was exhausted and started nodding off. As the baby nursed from her, the desire to sleep tugged insistently on her eyes. The house was quiet; Zainab and Father had left the house, and Ahmad was sleeping next to Mahmoud on the little bed. The sunlight from the window cut the room in two. So Mother knew it was five in the evening—she knew the time from the movement of the sun and the length of objects' shadows in the house and in the fields.

There was silence except for the baby's suckling at her breast. Mother lay suspended between drowsiness and sleep, losing herself in that sweet sound, when she heard footsteps in the house. The footsteps advanced towards her bed until they stopped the sound of Mahmoud's nursing. Mother thought them to be the footsteps of a thief. A couple of days earlier, the soldiers had captured two thieves in the night, stealing chicken from one of the dens in the village. She woke with a start and the milk dried up instantly in her breasts. Mahmoud did not nurse from her breasts ever again after that day. A woman had suddenly appeared standing before her, with a large head, thick black kinky hair and eyes big like lights. Her terrifying proximity to tiny Mahmoud made Mother clutch the child and scream in the intruder's face. 'What do you want? Why are you here inside my house?'

'I want the boy,' said her twin.

'May you be buried. Which boy? The boys you already took are not enough, you also want my son Mahmoud?'

'I want the boy, whether you say yes or no.'

'Get out! This is *my* son. You want him as well? Be reasonable. You are a virtuous woman. Would you let me take your son?'

Mother covered Mahmoud's body with hers, and would've almost cut off his breathing if she hadn't come to at that moment and glimpsed at her twin's back as she left the room.

'Just like that, I threw her out.'

That's what Mother said.

She kept Mahmoud in a tight embrace for several days, worrying and crying for him. But she was reassured when Father took her to Sayyed Rida who read verses for her and the boy, and made her incantations to dispel her twin's spells.

After that, the twin disappeared, Mother rested and Mahmoud lived. Until he died of cancer . . . 'The twin took him,' said Mother, 'she took him in the end.'

*

But Mother did not dream of the moon being lonely in the sky when my sister Samiyya was born. When she had Samiyya, she still hadn't moved to Beirut. She dreamt of a small white bird streaked with the blue of a cloudless sky, flying all alone in the evening under the moonlight, dipping and soaring to touch the moon itself. The bird sang a lovely tune throughout the dream.

She rose in the morning, put her veil on her head, tied it around her neck and went to visit Um Ibrahim, her neighbour in Ashrafiyya. After telling her about the dream, Mother put her hand on her mouth and asked, 'So, what do you think, ya Um Ibrahim? A boy or a girl?'

'I think it's a boy. I believe a bird in a dream is a boy but only God knows for sure.'

The other neighbours at Um Ibrahim's house winked at each other; one stood behind Mother and sprinkled salt on her veil. Mother shook the salt off her head, then scratched her face when some grains fell on it. The women shouted, 'It's a boy! By God, it's a boy!'

That day, Mother told Father what had happened and he bought her a new piece of cloth to make a dress. Again, she dreamt of wearing it under the moonlight. But in her ninth month, the moon disappeared from her dreams; doubts started nagging her and the nightmares rushed in. She would wake up tired, her whole body sore the way it felt after the Good Hassan hit her. In the same month, the skin of her belly became a swollen wall of flesh, through which she tried to eavesdrop with her hands on every movement of her foetus, to better understand 'him'. Normally, at that stage, she and her foetus would reach an agreement: that he would get ready to come down and she would wait for him patiently. Although she would start waiting from as early as the fourth month when he would knock on the wall of her uterus, a soft knock that resembled a heartbeat, clutching then relaxing, until he would start flicking inside her stomach in all directions with his head and legs and hands, like breaking waves, making her belly rise and fall like the sea. Most of all, she felt his head when he moved it to the right and pressed it down, making her run to the bathroom to pee, only to discover that he was playing with her.

*

Mother thought the foetus was playing, especially when she was young. After all, she was thirteen when she became pregnant with Zainab. She would talk to her unborn child, especially when she was sad, complaining about her worries and fears as she had once done with her doll when she was angry with Father. She would always address her foetus in the masculine, asking 'him' about his shape, skin and the colour of his eyes. And whom did he look like, her or his father? And whom would he love more, her or his father?

She would ask him, 'If the answer is yes, kick two times, and if it's no, kick once. You send me an answer and I'll be waiting.' Then she would put her hand on her belly and wait for the reply, and if she didn't like the answer, she would ask, 'What, why?'

Every time Mother would get pregnant, she would draw back into her body and lock the world out. She would sever all ties except the one uniting her with that soul that made her whole body into something unlike a body—a soft breeze or a thin fog rising from the earth and the dull details of living. It became more like a thin, transparent soul wrapped around another soul that grew within it. She dedicated herself to an inner world where her body became no more than the tenderness of lettuce leaves wrapped around a tiny creature that grew within them. She went about her housework mechanically, unthinking, unconcerned, and never let the work spoil her seclusion.

The day she miscarried, she was alone in the house. She fell to the ground and her body clenched relentlessly against itself as her water broke between her legs. She managed to reach the gate and screamed for the neighbourhood women who quickly rushed to her aid. Some women ran to call the midwife who quickly got to work. When the foetus left her body and the cord was torn, the women were boiling water over the fire and the Sayyed stood as usual over Mother's head, reciting the verses from the surah of Our Lady Mary. The baby girl cried out, announcing her entry into the world amid the acrid odour of Mother's sweat. Mother cried, not because it was a girl but because she brought her into the world without a 'drain pipe' from the bottom. The baby lived for a day, then died. Mother mourned her and composed poetry in her memory, likening her beauty to that of the moon. Abu Ahmad also cried. He had left the house after he heard that the child was a girl, and when he returned the next day, she was dead. He cried and told Mother, 'Forgive me, Um Ahmad. I have been blasphemous, because a girl is a blessing. Ask Him to forgive me, I beg you.'

And so, Abu Ahmad raised Um Ahmad, and Um Ahmad raised her sisters, brother and children. But Abu Ahmad never learnt his lesson, even after asking his wife to ask God to forgive him the day the girl died.

When she was carrying me, the 'boy' she had in her stomach was supposed to be the last grape in the bunch. She had become pregnant while still nursing my sister Maha, so when she gave birth to me her body was exhausted from the long series of consecutive pregnancies and our endless wailing. Although her nipple was in my mouth day and night, I never quieted. The pains in my stomach were constant; neither chamomile nor any other remedy could make me feel better. When Sayyed Rida visited us from the village, Mother's eyes were red and half-shut with exhaustion and lack of sleep after she had stayed up all night to feed me.

She asked him the news of the village but my crying spoilt the joy of listening to the stories. She hit the bed with her leg in frustration, making it fall, and I fell to the ground. 'May you live to see a funeral,' she said.

'No, ya Fatima,' said the Sayyed.

She looked at him and said, 'And a thousand funerals too.'

'No, no, no, ya Fatima. Don't curse her. If your curses are heard and the girl dies, you'll be judged for it. All children are birds in Heaven, angels. If your curse is heard, she will judge you. Take it from me. What if Heaven's gates were open at this moment, and God heard your curses? It's not right. Ask God for forgiveness, ya Fatima.'

Mother answered in a feeble voice, fearing that Heaven's gates might indeed had been open and that God had overheard her. She said, 'I didn't know about all that. How was I supposed to know? She was torturing me. I cursed with my tongue, not my heart. God must know that.'

She hoped with all her heart that Heaven's gates were shut to her curses, for it was bad enough that she was accountable in life for deliveries, housework and everything else on this earth. Was she to be held accountable for more in the afterlife?

Father held her accountable when he found out that she was pregnant again after I was born. He threatened that if she didn't get rid of it, he'd show her.

'Another useless girl? A ninth one? No . . . no, ya Um Ahmad. By God, I will bury you and all your daughters. You hear me?'

She did all she could to get rid of the baby. She drank medicines, moved all of the furniture of the house including the closet full of clothes. She even lifted it off the floor. And finally, after she did all that, the neighbours said she had succeeded.

She hemorrhaged, then lost consciousness—as had happened to her once when she lost a baby in the seventh month at Hotel Dieu. But this time she was in her fourth month. Abu Ahmad took her to the hospital; she almost died in his hands on the way. The doctors told him that the foetus had died in her womb. The boy died because of all that she had done to kill him.

That day Abu Ahmad went crazy. He forgot that he was the one who had threatened her and insisted that she get rid of the pregnancy for fear of a ninth girl. He cursed her at the hospital and cursed her friends who showed her a thousand ways to kill the child, as if none of it was his fault. 'You are a blasphemous woman,' he said, and almost fainting she said, 'What could I have done to prevent it, ya Abu Ahmad? It's my twin. She won't let us keep any of the boys.'

8

Everything changes, and nothing changes.

A human being forgets that he has been murdered, and so the murdered must learn how to become a murderer. Many things had been put to death inside Mother, and even so she tried to kill the rest in order to forget that she was alive. The kitten opened her eyes to some things and kept them shut to many others. But one day she could not keep them closed any more to the humiliation.

Father had a cow called 'bride' whom Grandmother Ghaliya had given him to plough the land alongside the donkey he owned. One day, the cow wandered away from him and went to graze at the green wheat stalks in a nearby field.

'How was the cow to know?' said Mother when she told me the story. Father called her from a distance, 'Ya Fatima, keep the cow away from the wheat.' At first, she didn't hear him since he was standing at a distance. So, Father shouted louder. 'I said, you daughter of a whore, keep the cow away from the wheat.'

His voice resounded throughout the valley for all the peasants to hear in nearby plots of land. Mother answered for the first time, 'Your sisters are the whores, not my mother.'

Among those who had overheard was Father's aunt who was picking corn nearby, so she shouted in her loudest voice to her nephew the Good Hassan, 'Will you stand for that, ya Abu Ahmad? Your wife is saying that we are all whores.'

Father crossed the distance separating him from Mother in a blink. He pulled her by the long hair under her scarf and began to beat her with a switch that he had picked up from the field.

She hurt so much from the beating that she fought back taking hold of him with all the strength in her arms and pushing him onto the ground. He tripped on a big stone and fell, and the villagers who had hurried to a cliff overlooking the field to watch the fight started laughing and giggling. Among them was a man called Naeem Yihya who was tall and 'beautiful like the moon' as Mother described him to me—his face tanned and his eyes green and 'this big' she'd say, showing me with her fingers.

That day, Naeem Yihya smiled at her and she smiled secretly when she thought of Naeem Yihya watching her push her husband and throw him onto the ground, as if she were a champion among champions.

She smiled again as she told me the story.

But Father did not smile that day. He set about her again, this time with his sister, and they beat her together. Her uncle too did not smile when he heard about it from Father. But before her uncle could subject her to more beating, she started hitting herself, slapping herself until her fingers marked her face for days to come. She punished herself in order not to be punished by him, for her cheeks preferred to take her own slaps than those of her uncle.

God bless his soul, and the souls of all believers.

'But he wronged me and I'll never forgive him,' Mother said. 'Forced marriage is the greatest wrong. They'll get no pardon from God for it—neither him nor my other uncle. Even if I were to pardon them, God wouldn't, neither in life nor after death. Marriage is blessed—but to force a child to marry? That's a sin.'

Those were Mother's words.

Mother, who had mastered the ways of survival from the lessons of her life and misfortunes—she, who had learnt to deny in speech what she approved in her heart or approve in speech what she denied in her heart—she, who sang and danced the Dabka with that pure pleasure of one singing solely to herself. Many years later, in Beirut, she would still hum that song:

To the aubergine, to the aubergine,
I love him with all my heart,
Though I'll deny it with my tongue . . .

That was the only song I heard her sing when she wasn't cursing while she laboured over our laundry or dirty dishes. Mother sang after her life had become a vast distance between the tongue and the heart.

* * *

Father did not like to upset Mother's sisters Tuffaha and Runjus. They were Mother's sisters, from her father and mother, but he was the one to raise them after her uncle found a husband for her step-sister Samiyya, and her other sister Naziha fled from the village without leaving a trace. Naziha would reappear twenty-five years later, at the beginning of the Lebanese war.

My aunt Tuffaha's apple-like form lived up to her name. Very early, the little girl became a woman; her mouth blossomed into a red rose and her breasts grew from two sesame seeds (like those of her sister Fatima when Father had married her) to two budding flowers under her dress—'God's glory' as the villagers said. Luckily, her sister, my mother, knew the meaning of a forced marriage and her brother-in-law, my father, was a kind father to her.

Tuffaha's eyes were meadow-green and her skin tanned by the days behind the plough. When she moved, her body spoke its own language, and when she slept, she curled up on one side of the bed that Father had made for her with his own hands. He sawed the base and legs from some lumber and joined the pieces together firmly with iron nails. Mother sewed a thin mattress for the bed and stuffed it generously, then made pillows out of all the colours of flowers and scattered them over the mattress. She put the bed in the living room and Tuffaha would sit on it, resting her back against one of the pillows, her breasts protruding and her smooth belly tucked in. She would gaze up at the sky, sighing and daydreaming, while the breeze tickled her face playfully and cooled her from the constant heat.

Unlike Mother, Aunt Tuffaha was conscious of her body and took pride in it. She would rest her hands on her waist and let her hair fall along her back below her veil, often flipping the veil backwards with an unconscious movement of her hand. When Father was not home, she even reached under her dress and into her underpants to touch her legs.

Tuffaha liked to pamper herself, especially the crimson mouth, with the dripping lower lip, and her thick chestnut hair. Mother became her mother while her real mother lived in another man's house. When Tuffaha would sometimes run into her real mother, she would greet her and run to embrace her but Mother would pull her back by her dress and say, 'Let her go. She threw us on the street like dogs, all for a husband. I know her . . . She melts like butter in front of a man. It's a good thing we didn't turn out like her.' Tuffaha, whose real mother had abandoned her to mine when she was six months old, would hold the tear prisoner in her eyes while Mother held it in her heart and never let it gleam in her eyes. Grandmother Ghaliya's new husband did not pamper her as Grandfather had. Yet, Father pampered Tuffaha and she, her own body. She would boil sugar to remove her leg hair, and one time she even boiled honey instead of sugar. Mother pulled her by her hair and said, 'This is blasphemy! We would have fed the honey to Ahmad or Mahmoud.' After Tuffaha cried for her hair, Mother embraced her and said, 'I did not mean to make you cry, Sister. But how can you do this, waste the honey, when we barely have bread to eat?'

When the matchmakers started flooding the house, Mother began to dream of marrying her sister, the apple-shaped Tuffaha, to a catch whom all would envy.

'Your beauty would be wasted, Sister, on a poor man. Don't you marry a poor man, or your beauty will go for nothing. It's enough that I married poor.' Mother would caution Tuffaha as she combed her sister's silky curls. Tuffaha would smile and say, 'God willing. Pray for me. But I swear by God, Sister, that my brother-in-law is kind-hearted and good. He raised us all. Be kind to him, Sister, and you'll win him over that way.'

'May the devil be kind to him. I've tasted the juice of bitter olives with him. He may be good to you and to others, but not to me. The way they forced him on me, I'll never forget.'

One day, a woman from the village came to the house to ask for Tuffaha's hand for her son. She came with a woman called Zakiyya who had blue eyes and gapped teeth. All the village women feared Zakiyya's presence in their houses like that of the devil himself. That combination of 'gapped teeth and blue eyes' could send one to the sick bed in a blink.

When she entered the house, Tuffaha had just woken up, and 'God's glory,' exclaimed Zakiyya. Tuffaha's sleepy green eyes left a magic hue on her cheeks. Zakiyya eyed her from head to toe and repeated, 'May God's name protect her. May God's name protect her.' Zakiyya drew closer and tried to pull up her nightgown to see her legs, pretending she wanted a closer look at the fabric. But she couldn't see anything because Tuffaha slept with drawers on under her nightgown.

'God protect her from the evil eye,' said Mother in her heart.

When the two women left, Tuffaha was told that the woman wanted her for her son, and she heard Mother tell Father, 'Why not? Her son is good, and he has a big piece of land for planting tobacco.' Tuffaha fell sick right at that moment.

'It's all the work of that blue-eyed woman,' said Mother about Tuffaha's sickness. 'She touched my sister with her evil eye,' she said while Tuffaha lay with fever.

Father said to Mother, 'What if the girl doesn't want to get married and is just keeping to her bed as an excuse?'

'Do you know what I think? I think you must hate me and my sisters. I'm telling you, the girl's been touched by the evil eye. Are you blind or what? The girl's going to die while you stand there like a wall!'

But Father was not standing like a wall; he was boiling. He loved the girl much more than he ever loved Runjus, and he had scolded her more than once when he noticed her looking at the French soldier who visited the village with her brother Daoud who had become a soldier in the French army. Father said, 'You should be ashamed of yourself, girl, looking at foreigners like that.'

When Father told her uncle about it, she got a beating. 'It seems that the girl loves the Frenchman,' Father told him. 'Maybe he loves her too. He's been coming to the village to see her.'

When my aunt Tuffaha ran into the Frenchman and he saw her swollen eyes blue from the beating, his eyes filled with tears and he pressed into her hand a bouquet of flowers that he had gathered from the sides of the road to the village. She took the flowers, crying. She did not know how to talk to him in French but his tearful eyes spoke to her, clearly saying, 'I love you.' Later, as she lay hallucinating in her bed, she kept repeating the one sentence he had taught her, 'Je t'aime.'

Mother, who did not understand the words, cried and beseeched Tuffaha, 'Who? Who's come to you, my sister? "Tem" who? Is that a jinn? Answer me, say something.'

'Je t'aime.'

Mother brought a bullet, put it in a large pot and boiled it until it exploded. It took some time because the eye that had touched Tuffaha would not leave her easily. Mother tried boiling several different bullets until one finally burst in the pot. As she poured the liquid in search of the culprit's figure or features, some drops splashed on her face and hands, causing tiny burns that became inflamed under the sun while she worked in the field, leaving marks that dotted her face until she died. 'It's all worth it, for you,' Mother said. 'My skin is yours. Take my soul too if you want. Just be well—stop torturing me. Put my mind to peace—I have to raise my own children too.'

'Come look at this bullet,' Mother cried out to everyone. 'It's Zakiyya with her eyes and nose and cheeks. Or do you think that I've no eyes and can't see? That's her exactly.' The women gathered around the bullet and agreed that it was her. 'It's Zakiyya's face, her flesh and fat, all in the bullet,' Mother told everybody who passed by the house, but Father begged her, 'Don't scandalize us, woman! You will cause me problems in the village that are bigger than me. Put off this talk for another time.'

'Put what off? My sister's sickness? The girl is crying and wailing in her sleep. The bullet does not lie. They're Zakiyya's eyes, I tell you. Everybody who saw the bullet said it was her. Are you blasphemous that you don't believe it?'

Mother took Tuffaha to Sayyed Rida's house, and he read verses for her and made her incantations. But the girl stayed sick for many months before she recovered and calmed Mother's heart. Mother's mind did not calm though. She wanted to raise Tuffaha's status in everybody's eyes since the whole village had started talking about her. They said that she loved the Frenchman, and that the jinn visited her for her beauty. And they also said that no one would want to marry her now that she'd gone mad.

When the son of the woman who had come with Zakiyya got married, Mother insisted on dancing the Dabka at his wedding. She danced to demonstrate her indifference to him, his mother, his whole family and the village at large. She insisted on regaining her family's respect and celebrating Tuffaha's recovery. She danced all wedding long in a new dress, and Father, dressed like the rest of the men in the village—in embroidered trousers made of charmeuse, danced with her out of relief for Tuffaha. Mother danced and sang:

'It will rain two days and a night
Until the charmeuse trousers get lost in the flood;

You wait on me, just two days and a night
And you'll see with your eyes who asks for us.'

Mother's mind found peace after she sang and danced, making it clear to everyone that she and her sister were above pity. But then she was worried again when the rumour began to circulate that Tuffaha loved the Frenchman who had accompanied her brother Daoud to the village. The mayor's daughter was the one who started the rumour after she saw the two of them exchange passionate glances and gestures in one of the village alleys. To the mayor's daughter, the look Tuffaha gave the officer was unforgettable.

'May God see that he suffers, whoever made the girl lose her mind,' said Mother as she watched her sister Tuffaha tossing and turning in her bed all night, moaning constantly. 'The girl was like spring water, drinkable even with mud in it.'

Mother could not be pacified. She woke up in the middle of the night, after sleep had abandoned her eyes, and poked Father's shoulder. 'Get up, man.'

'What do you want, ya Um Ahmad? What in God's name? Why do you poke me when you know that I'm exhausted and need to sleep? You bring nothing but worries.'

'Get up. I need to talk to you.'

'What?' he said, sitting up in bed.

'You must find a proper groom for Tuffaha. I don't know why the men who were courting her disappeared after Zakiyya touched her with the eye. What, they think the girl is crazy? If that's what they think, then they're crazy.'

'You talk as if the groom is knocking at the door and I'm not letting him in.'

'Just come up with something. I'm telling you, the girl is not right. And now none of the men in the village is asking for her hand. May God make him suffer whoever brought this upon her.'

Mother decided to reproach the mayor's daughter. She woke up early in the morning, covered her head with her veil and went straight to the mayor's house, near the square. She pushed the door open and said, 'No good mornings.' In front of the mayor and his wife, she looked at the daughter and said, 'You should know I have no qualms about committing a murder on people who have no conscience or religion.'

To silence the villagers' tongues, Tuffaha accepted, as her groom, a young man who proposed to her from a nearby village in Palestine. He was on a short visit to the village when he glimpsed her in the square and was immediately taken by her magic. Father did the impossible to make the wedding a success and the Dabka continued for seven days and nights. Tuffaha made the wedding dress herself, made another dress for Mother and a pair of new trousers for Father. Father danced in his new trousers and his happiness danced in his heart where Tuffaha had a special place. When Father would try to hit Mother, and Tuffaha would stand between them, he would stop for fear that a blow would fall on Tuffaha. She always obeyed his word and never contradicted it. When he said, 'This is a good man and you won't find another like him,' she answered, 'Whatever you want, Brother-in-law.' He was always crazy about her, he who had raised her since she was a nursing baby. He would get up in the night and, fearing she would get a cold, cover her when she kicked off the blanket.

Mother was overjoyed when the groom told her that he worked in Palestine at a restaurant whose owner was Jewish. She concluded that he must make good money.

Or so she thought.

The groom, for his part, did nothing to correct her impression. All the way from Bint Jubayl to Palestine in the sedan seat, he described to Tuffaha the beautiful house that he owned and the luxurious bed in which he slept. Tuffaha listened and her cheeks flushed beside her crimson lips. Luckily, her sad gaze of farewell to the mountains and valleys did not catch the groom's eye, nor did he discover their secret. .

When the sedan reached Palestine, he helped her step down on the ground, and she soon found herself in a little room shared with four other men who had also emigrated from South Lebanon to Palestine in search of work. This was in the times before the calamity of '48 when most workers would go south to Palestine instead of going north to Beirut—because it was closer—and would share a room to save money for food.

The room was empty except for a few blankets spread on the floor. The groom had split the space between himself and the rest of the 'lodgers' with a sheet that he had nailed across the room from wall to wall. He had also hammered some extra nails for hanging clothes.

The groom put Tuffaha's bundle of clothes in a corner he had designated for her, then he turned to her and said, 'We are going to sleep here for now, and we'll go home tomorrow.'

'When will we go to our house?' she asked.

'Tomorrow, God willing, or the day after.'

Tuffaha started crying, so the groom locked the door from the inside and tried to appease her. 'It's just temporary, ya Tuffaha,' he reassured her. Earlier, he had asked his friends to stay out late that night, so he could enter her. Before she would give herself to him, he said, 'It's temporary, I promise you. If you want, we'll move out tomorrow.' But the act was not enough to calm her. It did not make her forget the mountains and valleys she had left only hours before. She also remembered well the bouquet of flowers she had been given in a dream, the hand that offered it, the eyes that looked at her expectantly and whispered love in incomprehensible soft words, 'Je t'aime.'

Tomorrow never came.

Every day he would say 'tomorrow' until Tuffaha discovered his lie. Her Palestinian neighbour told her that he had been renting the same room with his friends for two years and that he always returned from his job in the evening to sleep in the same room, and the neighbour knew nothing of him owning another house.

Tuffaha found that she had to reconcile herself to reality and stop living in the dreams of tomorrow. But the dream of the bouquet did not leave her, nor did the tender voice.

'Je t'aime.'

'Je t'aime,' answered her eyes and the green smile in them. In her eyes, she began to weave dreams of love, and with her hands, she sewed dresses for the Palestinian and Jewish women of the neighbourhood. The owner of the room spread the word that the Lebanese bride was a handy seamstress and soon she had enough clients so she could live off her sewing. Not only did she satisfy the hunger in her belly, she also moved into a private room with her husband once they could afford to pay the rent on their own.

But the groom could not satisfy her other hunger. Tuffaha told her Palestinian neighbour how, when night fell, her husband would lie down beside her and lift her dress, take off her drawers and fondle her with his hands until her body heat up and all its flowers blossomed. He would watch the dew of love dampen her body in the night but then his face would change, grow pale and his eyes would shrink and wither as if he had put on a new face. He would leave her and walk out of the room to the shed behind the house. At first, she did not know what he did there. Sometimes he would hurry back, holding together the loosened waist strap of his trousers and enter her quickly as if he was afraid of coming before getting inside her. At other times, he would come back calm and relaxed, put his head on the pillow and leave her body boiling after his hands had set them on fire.

She did not understand until she followed him out of the room one night. She peeked into the shed to find him standing with his face to the wall and his back towards her. He loosened his trousers and started playing with himself. So it was that Tuffaha discovered that he left her to masturbate. She left him and ran back into the room.

Her husband continued with his habit for months, and when he ceased, she would not let him touch her. For ten years, she kept him at arm's length, and Mother would say, 'Her husband was so patient with her—for ten years she didn't let him near her.'

Tuffaha would scream whenever he came near her, with or without his trouser belt. The secret was in the jinn who fell in love with her, Mother said. He was the one who prohibited the husband from coming near her, for the love of a jinn for a human is far stronger than that of a human for a human, and so is the jealousy.

One evening, Tuffaha went to urinate near the shed after her husband went to sleep. On the way back, she remembered what her husband used to do when he went in there, and she went inside. She lifted her dress above her chest and touched herself in the dark, then caressed what was between her thighs while imagining that the French soldier was touching her. From that day on, she did not let her husband come near her.

Mother was convinced that it was the jinn. That night, Tuffaha's apple-shaped body shone in the dark. She was fair, her skin pure like snow, and her beauty indescribable. As soon as she lifted her dress, the jinn noticed her and 'marked her for himself'. For that very reason, Mother would caution us a hundred times ever since we were children not to take off our clothes anywhere; she would say, 'Nakedness is not desirable at all, even if the woman is by herself, because the jinn can see and desire, especially if the girl is pretty and her body is fair.'

And so it was that the jinn fell for Tuffaha and the beauty of her white body. Every time he would enter her, she would squeeze her legs together and her limbs would start thrusting and coiling. The jinn would make her scream, moan and arch her back. Sometimes she would even make a hissing sound, and by the end, her hair would cover her face, sweat dripping from her. He was so hot, she said, that she felt a fire burning and scorching her from the inside.

'Help me! There's fire burning between my legs,' she said when her Palestinian neighbour found her on her bed, shuddering.

'It's burning,' she told Mother, after her husband took her back to the village, hoping that the jinn would not follow her there. But the jinn knew no borders and would have followed his beloved's body to the end of the world.

The affair continued, her husband fondling himself while the jinn fondled her, until a day came, ten years later, when she suddenly announced to him that the jinn had died.

The French had left Lebanon, marking ten years of sex with the jinn. Finally, all the villagers knew that Tuffaha was no longer burning for the hot member of the jinn. She proclaimed his death, and only then did she get rest from his flames, and put to rest her heart's fire.

'But not all jinns are evil,' said Mother.

When Mother was a girl, she loved to eat hemp seeds. But there was no way of getting them in 'those days of poverty and misery'. Later, she found out that a jinn had learnt of the craving she shared with the rest of the people in this world. So she began, whenever she felt like crushing the little seeds between her teeth, to go up the wooden ladder to the roof and sit on the edge waiting for him. She would close her eyes and open her little hands so the jinn could come and sprinkle the seeds in her hands. She would eat them in her sleep in order not to see his face, and to make things easy for her he would always wait for her to tire and fall asleep before throwing the seeds into the palms of her hands. He brought her the seeds and fed them to her because he knew that she wanted to taste it but could not afford it.

That jinn who watched over her neither fell in love with her nor hurt her in any way, unlike that lady jinn who gave Father that 'kink in his step', as the villagers said, or 'made him limp', as Mother said.

*

Mother's story of how Father got his limp, of course, was not the same as his version. Mother said that he forgot the facts and he said that Mother had become 'distracted'. According to Mother, his limp started when he was nine or ten years old. His father, Ahmad, had rented a piece of land from one of the landowners so far from the village houses that one had to cross the mountain to reach it. Grandfather had decided to grow lentils there, for the pilaf made of bulgur red lentils from that red soil had an aroma and taste that could not be resisted.

One day, Ahmad said to his son, 'Ya Hassan, I'm tired and won't be able to harvest the lentils today. You go without me, Son, and may God protect you. Go and take the cow with you.'

Hassan, my father, good as he was, set out with the cow and kept his eyes open. It was noon or a little after; memory failed Mother on those details. But the timing need not be accurate; more important was the accuracy of the story. He headed towards the field and dragged the cow behind him. There, after the Good Hassan crossed a long distance under the sun, he started to feel tired, numb and sleepy, and his feeble boyish body could not hold up to the exhaustion. He tied the cow with a long rope to his wrist, to let her graze freely around the lentils while he fell asleep, the kind of deep sleep that Father loved and which forever remained 'his totem and religion' as Mother used to say.

He did not wake until sunset and found it was completely dark. He was somewhere different from where he had fallen asleep, a distant place he did not recognize. The cow had loosened the rope from his wrist before wandering off, probably going mad with loneliness in an unfamiliar place. She had given birth to a calf only a few days earlier, and when hours passed while Father slept, she had become afraid that her newborn would die of hunger.

So she started making her way home, dragging Father behind her by the rope but, all the while, he remained in such a deep sleep that the rope slipped from his wrist sooner than the sleep left his eyes. He had not sensed what was happening to him while he was sleeping, until he opened his eyes to the pitch darkness and his knees started shaking. He was overcome by fear when he found himself in a place he did not know. He walked and walked, trying desperately to find his way out of Ayn al-Tina, a place haunted by jinns and filled with caves and rocks of all sizes.

The Good Hassan ran and ran, and the jinns ran lightly behind him amid a silence broken only by the cackles of hyenas. Somehow he managed to cross half the distance to the village safely but, before long, an enormous figure appeared before him in the dark, blocking his way. He was a towering genie whose head reached the sky while his feet rested firmly on the ground. The Good Hassan shrieked so loud that his voice filled the silence and the dark. Then he took off in a panic, his legs tripping over each other, as he pleaded, 'Dear legs, save me!' As he drew closer to the outskirts of the village, he heard the sound of singing and dancing, and realized from the noises that reached his ears that it was a wedding of the jinns.

By the time he reached his house near the square, he had fallen ill. He lay in bed for more than a month, suffering from the pains of fear and a broken leg which the village doctor did not know how to fix. His leg never healed completely and he walked with a slight limp ever since.

I almost believed Mother's version after Father endorsed it. But then he contradicted her on the ending.

'Don't listen to your mother, she's grown dim and forgets things. Why, she can barely remember her name! It wasn't then that I got the kink. After that accident, my leg had healed and I walked normally again. It happened when I fell on the same leg again.'

'Don't believe him, Daughter. He's the one growing dim and he's the last one to tell the facts the way they are. All his life, he's muddled things. It's true that he fell on the same leg later but he was already limping when I married him.'

The cause of Father's second accident was a lady jinn who fell in love with him and demanded that he have sex with her. But when Father refused, she made him fall on the same leg and break it again.

According to Father, Mother was at the end of her pregnancy with my sister Zainab, the first candle to light our home, as Mother used to say. It was one of those burning nights in August. She asked Father to go to the well, fill the urns with water and bring them back on the sides of the donkey.

Father went, but when he stretched out his arm in the dark and could no longer see his hand, the void of light became filled with his uncontrollable fear. He hurried along the cemetery road that led from the village houses down to the well. But the fear in his heart grew in the soundless night. He could sense a presence riding behind him on the donkey and wrapping her arms around him from the rear.

Instantly Father realized that the presence was a lady jinn and he continued quietly on his path, careful not to look right or left, or to utter a single word. With each step forward, the jinn's legs would extend, becoming longer and longer until they touched the ground and began dragging behind the donkey. Then she reached back and threw her long black hair, black as the night itself, over his face. Father could no longer see anything besides the dark surrounding him, only the edges of her feet dragging on the ground whenever he would steal a glance backwards.

Her arms, still wrapped around his waist, began pressing more tightly and her hot breath seared his neck as she panted her desire on the side of his face. He heard her whisper that she wanted him. She wanted him to stop his donkey, turn to her, take her in his arms and kiss her, to make love to her as they rode along.

Father screamed in protest, 'Even if you'd kill me, I would never do it.' Not much time had passed since he got rid of the jinns at the stable. He was afraid that if he had sex with her, she would prohibit him from approaching his wife again. He couldn't get himself back into the same bind, not after he had finally got rid of them.

His refusal infuriated the lady jinn. She slapped him on the back and nudged the donkey with her long legs until the terrified beast darted away. Father flew off the donkey and fell on his back on an old grave. He injured his head and broke his leg a second time, all because he rejected the lady jinn.

*

Mother disappointed him the day he told me the story.

She interrupted him more than once, lifting her finger to his face. 'Stop lying. You've been limping since the first time you fell. Come off now with all this talk. Who's going to fancy *you*—humans or jinns! What's there to fancy? Your height, your looks or that leg of yours that has always limped?'

Her insults shot forth fast and regularly as if from the muzzle of a gun. She spoke and scrambled past him, holding her veil to her head with one hand and the edge of her long, wide dress with the other. When she had escaped and he realized that he would not be able to catch her, he spat in her direction and said, 'Tfeee on you and your evil sex. By God, no house could keep or tolerate you.'

They fought constantly over the truth of their stories and they uttered the words 'lady jinn', 'jinns' and 'genies' many times without saying 'In the name of God the Good and Merciful,' as Sayyed Rida had advised. They fought so viciously that they forgot the warnings of Sayyed Rida who knew everything there was to know about the jinns. And because he knew everything about how to divide and reconcile the jinns, they were aware of his knowledge and feared him. The Sayyed said that whenever one mentioned fiends and jinns, one should beseech God to keep the speaker from being beset by those whose names had been mentioned. Their fear and humility towards him were confirmed after the incident involving his nephew's bride. The family had built a cottage for the bride and groom's honeymoon in the orchard owned by the groom's father. The bride was sleeping with her groom in the cottage. One night, the bride left her husband asleep and went out to relieve herself. She climbed down the wooden ladder and as soon as her foot touched the ground, she by accident stepped on a jinn who had assumed the shape of a cat. The animal cried out in pain and flew away with the bride to the jinns' kingdom where he hoped to try and punish her. For jinns too, like humans, have a kingdom, a king, rulers and rules of law.

But when he arrived with her and presented her to the judges, they demanded fearfully: 'You had to pick Sayyed Rida's relative of all humans? Come on. Get up now and take her back to earth. We can't get mixed up in his affairs.'

The cat returned her in an instant, as quickly as he had taken her away, after the judges instructed him to deliver her safely to the cottage or face being burnt.

The bride told her husband what happened, that the jinns did not harm or touch her and that the whole journey took less than a minute. Her groom did not notice exactly how long she had been gone or when the jinn took and returned her. He did not find out about it until the next morning when he woke up and she told him what had happened to her during the night.

Such are the tales, woven and spun on the tongues of the people in my village. Everybody believed these tales and slapped hands together incredulously. 'God save us from them,' they said. As for Mother, when she used to enjoy eating the little seeds thrown into her hands by the kind jinn, little did she know that one day the jinn's wife would hurt her, when Slow Aunt Runjus would fall on the lady jinn's child.

*

Everything in Aunt Runjus' face was round, perpetually fixed into an expression of exclamation. Her cheeks were two balls always ready for the tears that rolled easily on them from her sad, misty eyes. Her voice rose from her throat, dripping wet, as if it had been bathing in a pond of tears. She was always on the verge of sobbing, even when she spoke of little things; her words always infused with a faint sob, even when she laughed. Everything about her moved in a mournful rhythm as if she belonged to the genus of reptiles. She did not move her head right and left unless she was at a mourning session and it was her task to wail to the sad story of the Prophet's family. At those times, she became 'Runjus the wailer' who was so good at her job that she made tears rise in bulbous drops from women's hearts. She read the stories in a sad sonorous tone; her voice seemed born to guide her in the occupation of crying and drawing out the tears of others.

Slow Aunt Runjus made Mother's heart burn with annoyance when she asked her to go with her to the wilderness to gather the stems of the wild iris which burst forth in the fields with the coming of spring. Wild iris started off as weed, then grew longer and its stems extended to become like trees. When it blossomed, the bees sucked its nectar just like thyme, primrose, hoarhound or any other wild flower that grew far away from the village houses and the grazing cattle. Mother needed those stems to finish the bed at the two-level shack that was being built in the field, where they slept in the summer— away from the insects and reptiles.

My aunt did not reply when Mother asked her to go with her, saying neither 'yes' nor 'no'. Mother asked again and again, 'What, Sister, you're not answering me. Will you come with me or not?'

Still no answer.

'Good child, bad child! Get up and help me get the wild iris!'

Mother asked her again and again until finally my slow aunt said, 'I don't want to go,' with a wave of the hand.

'Get up, I said!'

'I said I don't want to.'

Mother reached out and poked her in the head, saying: 'By God, are you slow!'

But as soon as she said that, Aunt Runjus bit her hand abruptly, sprang from the floor and ran away for fear of Mother's blows.

'You daughter of dogs, you bit me? What a waste it's been, raising you.'

Mother picked up the stalk of pomegranate lying nearby on the floor and flung it in her direction, making Aunt Runjus trip and fall as it fell between her legs.

Her leg swelled without bleeding the way my sister Zainab's leg bled when she fell at the edge of the well. But Aunt Runjus went mad. As if no longer from the genus of reptiles, she ran to the corner of the room and hid inside the chimney.

For several days, she stayed and slept in the chimney.

That day, my uncle said to Mother, 'God punish you, ya Fatima. What did you do to your sister? It's a good thing there's no rain or cold or we would have had to light the chimney and she would have burnt and died.'

'I swear to God that I didn't do anything. She was the one who bit me so hard that her teeth sunk into my flesh. I just tossed the stalk of pomegranate at her and she tripped.'

Later, after Aunt Runjus recovered, Mother said to her, 'Come here, you slow one. Why did you run away to the chimney of all places? Tell me the story.'

'If only you knew, Sister, whom I tripped on.'

'Who?'

'I fell on the daughter of the jinn who used to feed you the hemp seeds when you were little. He used to drop them in your hands, remember?'

'You wretched soul! What made you trip on her? Couldn't you pick someone else's child to trip on? Is this his reward, you slow one?'

But before she could beat her out of sadness for the jinn's daughter, my slow aunt reassured her that the jinn's child had also healed.

'How do you know she's healed?'

'Her Mother, the lady jinn in the chimney, called out to me, Sister, and she said to me, "Come here, Runjus girl. You fell on our daughter and I'll tell you the solution: If our daughter heals, you'll heal—and if she dies, you must die."'

Mother rejoiced in her sister's recovery, and even more for the recovery of the jinn's daughter. She would never have hurt the jinn's daughter intentionally. In spite of her father's affection for her as a child, no one other than the kind jinn had given her the tasty hemp seeds she cherished.

After that incident, Mother repented. Once she watched Aunt Runjus' mind slip away and then back into place; so, whenever she would run after one of my sisters to hit them, she would say in her heart: 'May God, the Prophet and the angels guard you. May God's name protect you,' so they would not be hurt.

She thanked God for Aunt Runjus' recovery, just as she had done for Zainab when she hit her head on the edge of the well and her head bled until she lost her senses. Uncle Daoud was away when it happened. In those days, he worked for the French army and was on duty that day, or he would have gone mad with all his love for Zainab. Uncle Daoud spoilt Zainab more than he would spoil his own daughters later on. When he was at home, Zainab would not fall asleep except in his lap. He would sit her on his lap and tell her stories about the jinn, the Wazir Salem, the Good Hassan and many others.

'Stop spoiling her, Brother,' Mother would complain, 'if you keep this up, I won't be able to handle her any more. She never listens and always does what she wants.'

She thanked her God he was not at home that day, just like when she entered the house one day and found him sitting there with Zainab on his lap, telling him what she had done that day.

Mother had been worried for a long time about her brother. She worried about him day and night, whether she was in the fields, at the house or lying sleepless in her bed. As soon as dawn broke and Father rose to pray, she said to him, 'Ya Hassan, my heart is telling me that today Daoud is going to show up.'

'God willing, may your feeling come true. I too am worried about him.'

She prayed and fed the children, then left the house, cursing wars and armies and everything that caused them. But years later, in the mid-80s, when he died during the Lebanese war, she would curse the day Daoud left the French army before the soldiers left Lebanon. 'I wish he hadn't quit the French army,' she would say. 'What possessed him? He could have kept collecting pay cheques like Abu Akram who stayed in the army until the French withdrew. They gave him a passport and to this day he goes to the Embassy every month and gets paid a salary. At the least, his kids would have seen his pension.'

Mother was sad that her brother left the army, but she was just as sad when he was a soldier and she constantly feared for his life. She also lamented the French withdrawal from the southern villages, mountains and farmlands. After that, Abu Djaj, as they had nicknamed Uncle Daoud, started stealing chickens from the dens around the village houses without fearing the military patrols who could have imprisoned him. She always told the story of her sorrow when the French troops departed, passing by the villagers and their women and children like silent, broken stars.

*

That morning, her heart ached for her brother. She had a feeling that she would see him soon, as she told Father. So, she went to fill the urn at the valley spring where the water restored the soul and lightened the burdens of the body. She would put the urn's mouth at the source and when it became full, she would lift it lightly with her strong arms, as if she were lifting a bird's feather to carry it on her shoulder.

For the way back, she chose a lesser path off the main road, which was shorter but windy and steep. No one would think to take that road carrying a water urn except somebody with Mother's strength and stubbornness. The descent was trying, down the course that resembled a vertical pole. She was midway when she received the news from a village girl of her brother's arrival, after many months without news of him, what road he was taking or on what side he was fighting.

She threw the urn off her shoulder and dropped to the ground to realize that she could no longer walk or move. Her back had been hurt as a result of the shock and her sonorous voice which could send an 'O-o-f' travelling effortlessly from the valley to the mountains near the village was now failing her as she tried to scream, 'My brother, my darling.' She had to crawl to the house on her knees after the joy had softened her limbs. For all she knew after such a long absence, he could have been dead and abandoned somewhere on the war fronts without anyone to identify his corpse.

When she arrived, Uncle Daoud was sitting on the floor, in his French uniform, with Zainab in his lap. 'Yes, sweetheart. Tell me more,' he said as he stroked her long wavy hair with his thick, cracked hands. 'Who else beat you? Go on, tell me all about it.'

Mother threw herself in his arms, stumbling over Zainab. She hugged him and could not stop sobbing. She sniffled him all over his head, shoulders, neck and hands, and kissed him all over to make sure that he was actually in front of her, in the flesh.

Then she sat on the floor in front of him, took his feet in her lap and began undoing his shoes. She cried again when she found his socks stuck to his flesh and to the military boots he hadn't taken off for two months.

The smell of his feet filled the room and it filled her nose as she sniffled his toes, kissed them and rubbed them on her face. Then she brought the brass basin, filled it with warm water and soaked his feet in it. She washed them with her tears, then dried them with a towel, and kissed the new smell.

He too cried and kissed her hands, 'I can't take it any more, Sister. This is too much—you're spoiling me rotten!'

She calmed him after her heart quieted; his legs stretched out on the floor and his feet tucked against her belly. Finally, after the long absence, her mind settled—she who never knew calm, whether from work, hunger or sorrow.

Her sadness deepened for the Bey when she was denied a ride to his funeral.

She complained about it to her brother, just like her daughter complained to him about her. Mother told him how her heart darkened and became like the black mourning cloth Father had hung outside the main door, after news of the Bey's death arrived at the villages. She told him that all the women of the village went to his 'death' to express their condolences. All the women went, except her.

Father owned two camels whom he covered with sheets in preparation for the journey to Tayba, the Bey's native village. Each camel carried four women lounging comfortably in a wooden sedan.

The whole village went—women, men, the very young, the very old; even dogs went. All but her, she told Uncle. Father refused to take her; at first with the excuse that the children could not be left alone, but eventually he 'popped the pebble' and said, 'It's bad for my business. We need to feed the children.'

'All I know is that I am going, and they can all starve for all I care. There! Suit yourself.'

When the sedan moved, Mother moved stubbornly behind it. But soon, she turned back out of fear of Father while her neighbour walked the entire distance even after her husband had refused to take her, for exactly the same reason Father would not take Mother.

Mother's neighbour Badriyya had just given birth. When the women in the sedan noticed her, they told her husband, 'Look, your wife is walking behind us.'

When he looked back and saw her, he said, 'You stubborn woman! So you came anyway. Fine, climb up with us.'

'I don't want to. I'm going, but not with you.'

'Come on.'

'I said no. I don't want to,' said Badriyya and she did not ride with him. Mother, though, got scared and went home. She never forgave Father, but nor did she forgive herself for not going on foot like Badriyya.

She felt even more distressed when Badriyya returned and told her about the funeral. Until then, like Mother, Badriyya had never left the village. Her universe did not extend beyond the space of the village or the rhythm of the harvest—of fields to plough, water to heave and children to bear.

Mother listened with remorse and envy as Badriyya described what she had seen, 'There were people as far as eyes could see.' She described the speeches and the poems delivered at the funeral, most of which she did not understand. 'But it was men's talk, ya Um Ahmad,' she said. 'You don't have to understand it to know that it's important. Anyway, it's not for us women to understand the talk of men.'

*

The mourners came from seventy or more villages, and from the Seven Villages. Badriyya saw the men with their horses and bayonets, and the women with their tears and ululations. She said one group of men called out, 'Hula has come! Pave the way for Kamel Bey.'

'They slaughtered offerings as far as your eyes could see, ya Um Ahmad. They left them whole, simmered the rice in the large copper cauldrons and spread it on the sugarcane mats in the salons. They would spread out the mat, soap it and rinse it with water flowing from hoses until they shone, then throw the rice over it. Now those were *mats*, not like ours. They were braided properly out of that long cane, the kind you get from Palestine and the Golan. How can I describe it all to you!'

Badriyya talked and Mother choked as she listened to her descriptions of the offerings and rice and the Bey's 'real *mats*'. Mother herself wove mats out of cane by hand for an extra wage, in addition to her work in the fields. Every day, she and my siblings would weave at least a dozen, for a penny each.

But it wasn't the Bey's mats that interested her. She cared more about the funeral and the sight of the crowds. She cried because her eyes had not savoured the scene nor had her tongue tasted the rice cooked in the cauldrons while Badriyya had her fill and recorded it in her memory for ever. She had every right to tell it for the rest of her life whereas Mother, if she ever talked about the event, could only say, 'That's what they told me but I can't say that I saw for myself, with my own eyes.'

Badriyya, like most of the village women, had been 'naughty' with the Bey in her dreams. The women would almost faint when the Bey appeared during his visits to the village. They were spellbound by his large glittering eyes and the aura of power that surrounded him, which no one—woman or man, young or old—could deny.

'What does that mean, they were "naughty" with him?' I once asked Mother.

'It means that they were naughty with him in their dreams. You don't know how?'

'How?'

'Shut up and get out of my face.'

'I swear I don't understand what you mean.'

'I mean that she did dirty things with him in the dream, like Hajji Tamima and all the women.'

'Who told you about this?'

'When they used to get together, they would talk about who had the best fun with him in their dreams. I heard Badriyya say once that she would wake content the morning after being naughty with him in her dream. She would feel that the whole world was made of happiness—his magic, his strength and his beautiful eyes . . . And, you know, a man starts from the thigh downwards.'

When Badriyya insisted on going to the Bey's funeral, it was by choice that she walked to Tayba. As she walked, she thought of her encounter with the Bey in her dream on the night she got pregnant with her child. Badriyya was confused about the child's true father. Was it her husband or the Bey? But as she walked towards the Tayba, she felt strongly that she was walking to the funeral of her child's father. She was so sure of the feeling that she refused, again, to ride her husband's sedan on the way back from the funeral. When he said, 'Get behind me on the camel, woman. Have mercy on yourself. You will die. You have just given birth.'

'I don't want to,' she said.

'Have mercy, woman.'

'Leave me alone! The Bey's memory is worth the walk back.'

But she did climb behind him in the end, when the distance seemed too long. But as she rode sleepily in the sedan and the cool breeze caressed her cheeks, the reveries of her naughtiness with the Bey tickled her imagination.

* * *

Mother told me all the stories, including the stories of each one of my aunts.

Slow Aunt Runjus, the wailer, packed her suitcases at the age of seventy and hurried up the steps of an aeroplane leaving Lebanon for America. She abandoned her country without even considering the possibility of a return or pausing to lament the grave she had secured for herself as the final resting place.

Aunt Naziha, the prostitute, moved in the opposite direction. After vanishing thirty years earlier, she suddenly reappeared in the village, in her seventies. She rushed to the Civil Records Department to fulfil her dream of obtaining an identification card which would prove that she was still alive and well, and here in Lebanon.

Thus, the wailer hastily fled, the prostitute suddenly returned, and my apple-shaped Aunt Tuffaha lived her final years pursuing her ambition of becoming Adam's mermaid or his apple in Heaven. Aunt Tuffaha, who returned from Brazil towards the end of her sixth decade to die among her relatives, died alone in a dark corner of the big house she built for herself in the village.

Aunt Tuffaha had emigrated from Palestine in the late 40s, a little before the Nakba. Her husband took her to Brazil after she let him sleep with her again, and aboard an ocean streamer, they fled from hunger and the jinns.

That's how she told it to me on the balcony of her village house.

She tried to recall, in broken Arabic, old scenes still drifting in her memory. And as she spoke, she measured the coffee in my cup, worried should I ask for more.

'After a month's trip of vomiting and seasickness,' she said, 'more vomiting than Fatima did on our first bus trip to Beirut, I thought my eyes and intestines would pop. Then we arrived in Brazil and I found myself like the deaf person at the wedding, understanding nobody and understood by no one. I had neither language nor profession, except for the little sewing that I'd learnt here and in Palestine.'

'What did you do after that?'

'I learnt the Brazilian language quickly. I enrolled in a school and learnt to read and write Brazilian. But, to this day, I can't write or read Arabic.'

'How did you live and work?'

'I lived off the dough.'

'What dough?'

'The sugar-dough!' she cried, kneading an imaginary ball of dough between her fingers. 'I would boil the sugar, lemon juice and water, then remove women's hair over there with it. With money from the dough, I opened a salon, and later the salon became a cosmetic institute.'

'How did you think up the idea?'

'My Brazilian neighbour suggested it. She walked into my house one day and found me boiling the sugar. The beautiful aroma filling the house flooded her heart and nose. "What is this?" she asked. So I explained to her how we remove our body hair with the boiled sugar, and demonstrated it in front of her on my leg, then on hers. She went crazy for it. Her body started shining and became soft like silk. On that day, she said to me, "Ya Tuffaha, why don't you do this for a living? I'll tell all my relatives and friends about you." And that's how it started. My beloved, my dear God said: "Take."'

When Aunt Tuffaha returned in her seventies, she looked at her house and wished she'd had 'even a limping girl' to lessen her loneliness. After dyeing her hair gold throughout her stay in Brazil, she covered her gray hair with a scarf and pinned it in place on the right side. She also covered her neck and chest after all the obstinate surgeries that failed to tighten her sagging skin. Finally, the white tint of her skin returned, after the Brazilian sun had toasted it for so many years of wearing bikini on the beach, even in her sixties.

She returned after the years had dimmed the glimmer in her eyes and cooled her rosy cheeks to an earthy tone. Her lips would tremble whenever she saw a young girl flaunting her beauty. 'It's not proper,' she would say in a broken accent, 'it's not proper for a woman to show her body. This is filth and blasphemy. It's not in our religion.'

'Then why did you dress like this until you were sixty-five?'

'I repented when God gave me the gift of sense. By God, how He can give you a gift when He wills it. He gave it to me, and I pass it on to you. And he who shares a gift is rewarded in Heaven.'

'Leave these innocent girls alone. What do you want with them? Just like God gave you the gift of modesty when you became old, He will give it to them when they are old like you.'

'What kind of talk is this? This kind of joking is not proper, my child—just useless mockery.'

She would not leave her house for fear that she might sin and be barred from Heaven should her eyes fall on somebody or should she wander even in her thoughts. Her eyes might sin if they saw something, or her tongue err if it said something. She would only wear her perfume on Thursdays before going to bed, just for the angels to smell on the eve of Friday.

She returned to the village to build a grand house. She furnished it after several trips to Tripoli, famous for its affordable French *stile* furniture sets, made of golden-coated carved wood. She bought three full sets of furniture. It was '*stile* and more *stile*' whichever way you turned—oversized chairs arranged in clusters around gigantic coffee tables so that there was barely any space to pass between them. The contrast was striking. Inside, the overflowing showroom housed suffocated places separated by protruding shapes and colours; and outside, the vast distances between the mountains and the fields, joined by endless grapevines, long groves of fig tress and infinite olive orchards. When outside, one could finally take a deep breath.

In any case, the salons were strictly for display.

The visitor was to enter, look, then say, 'Congratulations! May God give you the years to enjoy it. You've toiled away for forty years and now you've reaped the fruits of your work.'

But Hajji Tuffaha took pleasure neither in her house nor her bed. All she thought about was her end. She had the house key tucked safely in her pocket while the key to Heaven's gate lay in her repeated visits to the Hajj and the Najaf. She did not enjoy the fruits of her toil for fear that the overuse would wear them out.

'My beloved, my God!' she would say passionately, walking alone in her house. 'I don't want anybody else. I beseech You, God.'

She would hug herself and let her ample breasts spill over her arms. Wiping drops of sweat from above her upper lip and around her eyebrows, she would lift her eyes to the sky and say, 'I beseech You, oh God. For me, there's only You. Nobody will ever come close to replacing You, my darling. Never, never.'

If she received any guests, she would seat them on the old sofa that she put at the entrance of her personal palace to receive guests after their tour of the four-storey building.

'Why do you receive your guests at the entrance, Aunt Tuffaha?' I asked. She answered, 'The tiles will get dirty from the stepping, and the fabric wear out. Besides, my child, I am a praying woman. Shoes will bring in dirt and defile the floors. Or did you think praying was a light matter? Prayer has its rules. What else did you think? So, I set aside the entrance, for stepping and wearing out.' She said this and threw her grey robe over the layers of flesh which now replaced what once was a thin, strutting waist. Dreams of death and Heaven had cast yellow shadows on those meadow-green eyes, emptying them of life and spring.

But Aunt Tuffaha was not the only one who did not dare enjoy the fruits of a lifetime's toil.

*

'The living room is for stepping and wearing out,' Mother would say.

Aunt Tuffaha's salons, their emptiness and coldness, reminded me of our salon in Burj Hammoud. Entrance was strictly forbidden in spite of the apartment's small size: a bedroom, a living room and the closed-off salon. Our furniture were smaller and made of plain wood. I remember well the frail wooden legs, the yellow and brown velvet upholstery. Mother would protect the chairs with covers sewn out of white raw linen by my sister Suhaila, designed to cover the seats and cloak the wooden arms. I still remember how, as a child, I was terrified of entering the salon, especially at night when the covers looked like cold tombstones in an empty cemetery.

Although the room was rarely used, Mother would wash the white covers weekly and iron them vigorously, relishing every whiff of steam leaving the iron. I still remember how she smoothed every wrinkle of the linen with her fingertips after spreading it evenly over the sofa and tucking the edges into the fold at each end.

As for the bedroom, nobody was allowed to sleep or sit on the beds during the day lest the covers get dirty or she be forced to replace the mattress cases every year. So, we would always be huddled against each other like ants in the living room.

When I would make the mistake of saying to Mother, 'I am going to go study in the salon,' she would snap at me, 'Go study on the roof or in the kitchen. I've told you a thousand times to leave the salon in peace. I will break the legs of anybody who goes in there. The salon is there for looking good when we have visitors of respect.'

But no visitors ever came.

Which visitors of respect were she anticipating?

During the twenty years I lived in Burj Hammoud, I don't remember any visitor entering the salon, except occasional relatives during the holidays. When the doors would be opened in the morning, I knew that the men of the family were going to visit us that day, and that we were going to enter the salon, one after the other, to greet them.

I would wait on the kitchen balcony for their arrival, to watch them walk along the street like a tribal regiment, with a senior delegation at the front and the rest following. I could see the pride on the faces of the boys who, finally permitted to don suits in order to join the delegation, quickly adapted their gaze, stride and manner, becoming miniature models of the adult men.

'Come on girls, go in and greet your relatives,' Father would insist.

We would all enter and shake hands with everybody. Even the old religious men shook our hands in those days, before the men of today discovered the error in the custom. Some of my sisters, those from the middle of the bunch, had started wearing scarves tied at the back of their necks. Father would tilt his tarboosh forward and settle regally in his chair in the middle of the salon to boast the marks of his superlative daughters. Mother would watch resentfully, swallowing her spit and grumbling under her breath. 'Oh yes, go ahead and take the credit, when I'm educating them against your will.'

Then the salon doors would be shut again and reopen only for a suitor who had come to propose to one of my sisters. Or it would be turned into an exhibit showcasing every single item in the bride's trousseau. The panties, bras, nightgowns, evening dresses and suits would be displayed hanging on a wire, stretched from one window to the other.

And for every visitor, the display ritual would start all over again.

Mother would explain to each one of them, in detail, how each item had been purchased or sewn, the uniqueness of the fabric and colours, what was negotiated between her, the bride and the groom's parents before all agreed on the most appropriate style or the best-matching shoes. The visitors would scrutinize the fabric before curling their lower lip in approval. Then they would nod their heads in admiration for the dexterity of the bride and her mother. 'May God give her the days to enjoy them,' they would say.

'May the needy be given the same,' would be Mother's proud answer. She never forgot to sprinkle charms under the seat cushions to ward off the evil power of envious eyes.

After each daughter's wedding, Mother would reopen the salon to receive congratulations. She would place the white towel with my sister's virginity streak on a tray and go around the salon, showing every visitor the evidence of the bride's honour, so each would sign the certificate of modesty with their eyes.

Mother kept the proof of virginity of each of her daughters in her closet, in a wooden box, just in case somebody ever decided to question a daughter's purity. I remember how, after we fled Burj Hammoud, Mother cried more over those 'certificates' than she did for the dozens of unused plates and glasses, blankets and mattresses that we left behind.

One day, she cried so much that I couldn't tolerate it. 'Stop it already! The linens and the glassware, yes, but you're crying for rags stained with spots of dry blood?'

'How can I not cry? Everything can be replaced but not the marks of your sisters' honour—from where am I supposed to get those?'

'My sisters are almost old women, their children's children are getting married. What use is it to certify them now? Everybody knew when they got married that they were decent and pure.'

'No, still . . . what if one day an enemy insulted one of their children with a lie that they'd invented? If we have her mark in our hands, we can rub it in their faces if they make up lies. Who can know the future?'

'But wouldn't one's husband know? Their husbands are all alive and they know.'

'Nobody can be trusted. If a man loves you he dirties you, and if he hates you he shames you. The world is not safe for women, especially from men.'

Mother felt secure, and walked with an upright neck and square shoulders whenever she stood before a visitor to display the proof of my sisters' virginity.

'May God protect your daughters' honour and keep their heads raised high.'

'Aameen,' repeated the consort of guardians and witnesses.

After the visitors left the salon, the couches would be moved outside and the walls would be scrubbed with soap and rinsed with water flowing from a hose. The floor would be washed, the windows shined and the water would run from the salon floor to the rest of the house—through the main door, down the stairs and to the street.

Mother's happiness on those days, when she poured water into the house from the hose, cannot be described. The more she saw the water ebbing and flowing on the room floors, running in a stream, the more delighted she became. As she scrubbed the walls, windows and doors, she would press firmly on the opening of the hose with her thumb, making the water rise until it reached the ceiling. She would knot her eyebrows as she held the hose as far up as her arm could reach; her mouth half-open in concentration, exposing the crooked teeth she inherited from her family. At those moments, her joy was unequalled and her happiness, unmatched. Her hair would become soaked with water and the water would run down her sleeves in streamlets to her underarms, waist and thighs, and her dress would become wet in the front. She looked as if she had just walked out of the ocean.

Whether there was a visitor or not, the cleaning would happen every Saturday. The beds, couches and every other furniture in the house would be moved to the balcony, to empty the rooms completely in preparation for the flood.

The cleaning party that was a weekly pleasure for her was a weekly punishment for us. Saturday was an extended romantic rendezvous between Mother and sanitation. We knew that, after the walls drank the water, the humidity would gnaw at our bones that night. We the children would host a coughing party that lasted through the night.

I hated all Saturdays and all mothers on Saturdays. I wished we never had any guests or relatives, so the cleaning would stop. I did not understand the secret of Mother's obsession with cleanliness. Was it because she was proud that finally she had the walls and a house to clean, or did she think that cleaning the dust and dirt would forever preserve her hard-earned home? Did the distraction lend an escape from her life? Or could it be that she was scouring her memory to remove something in her past or her flesh?

I don't know.

Today, all empty places, like Aunt Tuffaha's salon and ours, fill me with fear. So, I avoid them.

When Aunt Tuffaha died, she left everything she owned to the religious endowment instead of the poor people in her family, because the sins she had committed in her past were many. She had taken off her clothes and let the jinn fall in love with her pale skin; she had played with herself; she had fallen in love with a Frenchman, and she had also fancied an Italian aboard the ship to Brazil. She would often dream, as she lay under the sun in a bathing suit, that the man with the dark hair and smoky eyes was drawing close to her, kissing her all the way from her head down to her feet. There was too much that she had done, too much that could not be forgiven.

* * *

'Without people, even Heaven would be insufferable.' Aunt Naziha repeated the saying, after she too returned to ask God's forgiveness for her sins. Her dim eyes would not light up except when her memory delved into her shameful past. When she spoke of her memories, she lifted her threadlike brows over her black eyes cushioned in plump eyelids. Only when she recalled the details of her life in the world of prostitutes did her body stir, her face stretch in a smile and her hair shine as she tossed it coquettishly over her shoulder.

*

I had thought that the whereabouts of Aunt Naziha were unknown but everybody knew where she was.

Grandmother Ghaliya's husband, Naziha's father, and her maternal stepbrother Daoud—all went to have a death certificate issued by the mayor after Naziha's disappearance in the 40s. Her name was crossed out in red ink in the records of the living in the Civil Records Department as well as from the family's civil record. A little note was scribbled at the end of the line to indicate she was dead.

Naziha, like her father, had striking, dark features. The dusky tint of her eyes deepened the shine of her coal-black hair and accented the contours of the full lips which resembled two bars of chocolatey flesh drawn neatly then coloured. Her breathy voice became throatier with years of smoking. Even when she spoke about the most mundane things, her sentences broke and the words stumbled as she panted breathlessly. Not for a second did she shed the role of the seductress.

When Naziha's femininity exploded at an early age, it was accompanied from the start by an innocent shyness. Her voice was barely heard, and the cat could steal her dinner from her.

I thought she was lying about this, as I did about everything else she said—'In those days, the biggest personalities in Iraq and Syria would have killed to get as much as a glance from me.' When she raised her arched eyebrows, puffed on her cigarette and spoke, I thought I saw the truths and lies leave her mouth mingled with the smoke. Sometimes, it seemed to me—in fact, I was almost sure—that the picture she drew of and for herself in the stories was the picture she wished was real. She would hide in some words, then emerge in others, like the storyteller who makes himself a hero this minute and a victim in the next.

Naziha only became the victim of her imagination after her sisters turned her into one; it was then that she made herself the heroine of her story. Naziha went with her two sisters, Runjus and Samiyya (Runjus, Naziha and Mother were sisters from the same father and mother, whereas Samiyya was an older sister from Grandfather's first marriage), to Beirut in the late 40s, two years before the rest of Mother's and Father's families moved there. They went to work as maids in the houses of Beiruti families, so hunger would not eat at their bellies, minds or bodies.

In Beirut, they stayed in one of the rooms in a big apartment in Zuqaq al-Blat, where many girls lived together and paid the landlady jointly. Each girl would leave for work in the morning and return in the evening to spend the night in her room. But not all were maids. The gold bracelets worn by some made the others wonder about the kind of work they did and how their salaries could pay the rent, fill their bellies, buy gold and send money to the village.

'How?' Samiyya asked one of them, and the woman explained how she and some other girls worked in the apartments of Beiruti prostitutes on al-Mutanabbi Street.

'My God, what a job! That's blasphemy.'

The girl laughed and said to my aunt that their work was clean. They only had to clean the prostitutes' houses with soap and their bodies with sugar dough in order to cover their own arms with gold. And so it was that my aunts joined the group that earned more than the girls who worked for families.

They joined the workforce on al-Mutanabbi Street and began receiving their pay from the 'patroness' whom the girls called 'mother'. Each six or seven prostitutes stayed in a room and the patroness would find work for them and get her commission.

Every day, my aunts would go to clean the rooms and boil the sugar for whoever needed it. Slow Aunt Runjus would start boiling with anger and Aunt Samiyya would burn with jealousy towards Naziha whose sexy fifteen-year-old walk caught the eye of each pimp standing on the pavements when the girls entered the district on their way to the prostitutes' rooms. Runjus and Samiyya feared for their sister's safety but they envied her at the same time.

Every night when they returned to their room, they would give her a lecture about honour and decency, and they threatened to tell their father and brother to kill her if she were to commit a sin. But they wouldn't just lecture. Every evening, they assaulted her with the help of two relatives from the village, who lived with them in the same apartment. They would throw Naziha on the bed, take off all her clothes and pin her down so Aunt Samiyya could inspect her virginity with her fingers. First, they scrutinized her neck, breasts and belly. Then they turned her over on her back to check for traces of kissing anywhere. After they confirmed that there were no traces of anything on her body, they would start beating her pre-emptively lest she consider sinning. They'd noticed that her walk suggested a 'frivolous and indecent' character, and that the demons were thriving in her glances. Naziha did not know which part of her possessed body to guard against the blows and pinches that marked her skin instead of the kisses. They mostly targeted her large breasts and groin. Aunt Samiyya would twist her labia between her fingers, pressing her lips together, clenching her teeth, and widening her eyes. 'You whore! Say, confess! Did anybody say anything to you today? Did anybody do anything to you? Did anybody put something there?'

Every day it was the same story. At the end, she would put her clothes on, crying bitterly and covering her aching body after they had violated it.

After that, it wasn't hard for her to expose what was covered to the pimp who promised her marriage. After she let him deflower her, she ran away with him for fear that her sisters would discover what had happened when they examined her that night. Of course, the promise of marriage was never fulfilled, and soon the body parts that Samiyya and Runjus used to pinch every night became a job for her and a source of income for him.

She had disappeared.

Mother told me that only Naziha's mother knew where she lived. She visited her daughter in Iraq and Syria, or wherever she happened to be, and indulged in the money, servants and the big house furnished in the style of the *One Thousand and One Nights*, with the silk curtains, its luxurious sitting cushions, and the glimmering chandeliers which lit the parties she threw until the early hours of the morning.

Naziha did not only help her mother. It turned out that she was sending money secretly to each member in her family. Each one of them took the money and still denied that she was alive, just as they would have denied her help and money. They all claimed that they despised her and wished for her death.

Naziha also spent her money on two men, over the long course of her life. One was a Damascan youth who was much younger than her; she paid for his studies in America and loved him to death. The other was older; he died after loving her to death; she supported him, his wife and children, out of love.

During the Lebanese war, Aunt Naziha returned to spend all the money she had on her sisters and their children. But when she became 'Penniless, Your Honour,' they disowned her all over again. In spite of the poverty in her old age, she would only speak of her good old days, about the people who gave her clothes and jewellery. She would always speak distractedly, with an uplifted nose, as if whomever she was addressing was lesser than her. She would speak with disgust about the present and the poverty of the people surrounding her, perhaps forgetting that she was now poorer than them. She spoke as if she were still the empress of red salons, turning a blind eye to the state of her body and pocket.

I remember the day I took her, out of pity, for a walk on the beach. She spotted an old shabby woman whose dirty, fuzzy hair had traces of old dye on the edges. Her hands and feet had not met the clippers in ages. She walked with a bent back, her head lowered over her breasts, but her eyes kept looking upwards with a searching glance, as if looking for someone who might recognize her. A glance that said, 'No, it's not true what I've come to. This is just a mistake. I must have taken the wrong turn on my path and I will find my way back.'

'Do you know who she is, ya Maryam?' she asked me.

'Do you?'

'Of course I do. Look at her. Look what she's come to. This one used to be beautiful like the moon. Money ran in a stream between her feet. By God, how the days change people. It's a pity what's become of her. We worked together in Iraq. I wonder what changed her this way.'

Aunt Naziha said this with wonder and confusion, as if she herself had not changed. As if she was still the lady of beauty and seduction at whose feet the most important of men were ready to fall. She must have been blind to the black skirt and flowery shirt that she hadn't changed in years.

'Money from sex goes as it comes,' Mother said on the day Aunt Naziha visited us so she could smoke a few cigarettes out of my pack. She smoked one cigarette after the other until she finished them all and I had to slip a few packs into her tattered bag before she left.

The scene lives on before my eyes. The way she clasped her birth certificate in her trembling hands a few months before she died. Her eyes filled with joy when she regained the certificate that testified that she was alive. But her happiness did not last very long before she died alone in Aunt Samiyya's house.

Naziha is the only character in the novel who hurries back to Lebanon at the beginning of the war when the dream of securing a foreign passport troubled the beds of thousands standing in line at the embassy gates, like I was.

*

Aunt Naziha had returned with the goal of becoming a good citizen, after she spent her life moving from brothel to brothel, with no documentation but a prostitution licence.

After many trips back and forth, I drove her south to the Civil Records Department to finalize the necessary paperwork to issue her the birth certificate. I took her in my Renault 12, a model from the 70s. I remember how she kept looking at the car seats with disgust. Apparently, they did not live up to the standards of Princess Naziha.

'Don't you want to change this beat-up car?' she said finally.

'God willing, Aunt.'

'When?'

'When God wants. He is generous.'

'Yes, I didn't say He wasn't. Of course God is generous, but when are *you* changing it?'

I listened to her, with an eye on the heat arrow, as we stood in traffic on Awzai highway. I exhaled when we finally turned into the Khalde highway and the car temperature started falling after it had reached the red mark. We passed the little hotel where Abbas and I would meet once a month. I felt a tickle in my soul, so I accelerated, letting the cool breeze enter from the window and revive me after the sweat had glued my hair to my face and neck, and my bottom to the leather seat.

Aunt Naziha sat next to me in her tight shirt, her cleavage exposed, and her skinny bowed legs spread under her skirt. Every few minutes, she would rearrange her messy, 70s hairdo under the scarf she had tied at her chin in order for the bow to cover her mostly bare chest.

The hot air suffocated her, so she lifted her skirt periodically, without hesitation, to air her legs and what was between them. 'Oof, it's so hot. It's unbearable,' she said, fluttering what was left of her long lashes. Her glances wandered coquettishly, as if all the passers-by recognized her and were madly infatuated with her.

She sighed and pulled out the dark red nail polish from her hand-bag, and would crane her neck out of the window whenever we passed a pastry or sandwich shop along the coastal road. I realized that she was hungry and stopped the car to buy two thyme pies.

'Do you think Israel's bombing today?' she asked, biting into her pie.

'I don't think so, not today.'

'Then God willing we'll find the head of the Civil Records Department and hopefully he would be able to pull out the old note-books from Bint Jubayl, for the births of '25.'

Our trip was a success.

Finally, Aunt Naziha secured the certificate that proved she was still alive. She was happy, and I was happy for her happiness. But I nearly died of shame when she spoke to the clerk as if she were still a teenager and the most beautiful of girls. She even hinted at her profession and winked at him the promise of fixing him up with a girl, momentarily forgetting that she had 'retired' and no longer owned a brothel or a home. As she talked to him, she regained that voice, of a woman pleasuring a man.

When I pulled her away by her arm, she complained about my nervous behaviour. As I drove impatiently towards Beirut, she said, 'It's amazing how nervous you get. And for no reason! You're just like your mother.'

I didn't say a word.

But her happiness did not last. A few months later, she went for lunch at Aunt Samiyya's house. She walked the whole distance, from Ain el-Mraisi to Khandaq al-Ghamiq, repeating her famous prayer in her heart, 'Oh God. A day in poverty, another in goodbyes, and the next on men's shoulders.' She never gave up that prayer, neither in her heart nor on her tongue, so she would not have to beg from anybody.

In her sister's house, she went to sleep, coughing, after lunch, and closed her eyes for ever. She did not respond when Samiyya tried to wake her.

'Get up from the couch, Sister. Go lie down on the bed. You'll break your neck like this.'

'May God forgive her sins,' everybody said.

'Sleep, dear sister. What a waste, this gazelle's body,' said Aunt Samiyya, stuffing her mouth with cotton after washing the corpse and dressing her with the shroud. She tied the loose ends in a knot over Naziha's head to conceal that same body for which she was the fiercest assailant.

*

With slow footsteps, Slow Aunt Runjus hurried up the metal staircase to the aeroplane door. She carried her cane and her tears with her to America when her son sent for her to get a green card, just as Um Talal's son did for her.

My aunt, the wailer, did not cry for her plates and glasses, her furniture, blankets or virginity cloths. The only thing that pained her to the point of weeping was losing her shroud. 'The only thing that got to me, out of all the things stolen from the house, was my shroud. Of what use is it to them? I'd been keeping it for over ten years in the closet alongside the cup, the water of Zamzam and the incense. And my will was there too—I'd tucked it into the folds of the shroud.'

Of all the things she left behind in Lebanon, Runjus did not grieve except for her life companion, Um Yusuf. With her, she had shared a full life, and a life's worth of secrets. When word reached Runjus in America that Um Yusuf had died, her homesickness dried up for good.

Her next-door neighbour from the village, Um Yusuf, had died. She had barely absorbed the news when she heard that her husband, Abu Yusuf, had followed her to the grave six months after her death, months during which his strength failed him and his back became bowed after he had kept his posture until the age of seventy. After her death, he suddenly grew desperate. In fact, he became afflicted with something like madness once her shadow left the house. 'Where are you, woman?' he cried out into the empty rooms, to be answered only by the echo of her absence. At the shop, he would lift the meat cleaver in the face of any customer who called him Abu Yusuf. 'No. Don't you call me Abu Yusuf. Abu Yusuf is gone—he left with Um Yusuf. He died with her. The man you see standing in front of you is another man, not Abu Yusuf!'

'He wants to make her miserable in death as he made her in life,' said Aunt Runjus. 'May God have mercy on him. He knows that he's worth nothing without her, that wretched man. God save his soul and forgive him in this and the next life.'

She said this but she did not shed a single tear for him when she heard of his death. Her tears would fall in streams only for Um Yusuf, even six months after her death.

My aunt the wailer cried for Um Yusuf as if she was crying for the first time. This time, a bitter taste collected in the wrinkles on her cheeks and around her eyes. The verses dedicated to Um Yusuf's soul floated from Aunt's stereo in her American home and did not stop for forty days. When the cassette would reach the end, she would turn it quickly to the other side or replace it with another tape of Koranic verses in the voice of Abdel Baset Abdel Samad. She had carried these cassettes with her to America because only Abdel Samad's voice lifted the sadness from her soul. His voice would soothe her soul for a little while, as she sat silently on her sofa, but when her sadness overwhelmed her again, she would slap her cheeks with her hands and ask for God's forgiveness for what she had just done. The village Sheikh had forbidden slapping one's face when mourning the dead, and had also forbidden the women of the family of the deceased from dancing with his photograph in a golden frame.

Um Yusuf's sister cried out the day her son was martyred in a suicide bombing against the Israeli army in the south. 'Oh wretched me! You want to punish me for slapping my face and dancing with my son's picture? What else would you have me do? You want me to give out Baklawa like some others have done? I will do it, no matter what you say. Yee . . . Yee . . . ' she screamed, motioning with her hands right and left, then grabbing her son's picture from his aunt's hands to dance with it, in spite of the women who gathered around her and implored her, 'Don't blaspheme, woman. It's not right. Dancing with the photograph is forbidden and so is slapping the face. Be patient. God is on the side of the patient.'

'*If* they're patient, *if* they're patient, *if* they're patient,' she repeated, motioning and dancing. 'Eat the sweets of my son's death, God forgive him. This is what he asked for, that we give away Baklawa and Halawa when he is martyred, because he knew he was going to Heaven. He didn't want life—he wanted the afterlife, my son. Now he is happy in his death and comfortable in his grave, but my heart is on fire, for my baby, my life, the darling of my heart. Why did you deprive me from looking at your beautiful eyes? And now, they also want to deprive me from dancing at your wedding.'

My aunt Runjus the wailer was among the women who reprimanded her, 'It's forbidden to dance, woman. Your tears will fall on his grave like fire,' just like her own tears fell on Um Yusuf's grave. In America, Runjus found herself standing on her own and dancing with her frail body, mourning her friend as she pleased, with no memory of what is sanctioned or forbidden. She found herself looking at the floor in front of the sofa and imagining her friend's eyes closing for good. 'You waited for me to get to America, you virtuous one, you friend of my life, and did it? You beat me to it, my friend, without letting me see you, bid you farewell, mourn you or read you poetry as I've done for so many others. Is this possible? That I would lead the mourners for the whole world, read them verses, make the stone cry, except for you, my darling? I wish my eyes were dimmed and eaten by worms before your eyes . . . '

My slow aunt cried for Um Yusuf and all the memories that had been buried with her. As she cried alone, she looked back to a lifetime of shared suffering.

Living next door to each other, one would not eat a piece of bread without the other, especially after Runjus' children emigrated to America and she was alone in the house. Um Yusuf would stand in the courtyard and call out to her, 'Ya Runjus, come, take your milk before the children drink it all and leave you nothing.'

Runjus would come in the same black dress that she rarely took off, to drink her share of the milk that Um Yusuf had herself milked from her blonde cow.

To begin with, Um Yusuf was her milk sister. Then, the years blended their milk further in the world's cup, running from one open heart to the other, and from the courtyard of one home to the other.

They shared their childhood in the meadows, shared the harvest and shared the work of a lifetime. The stone bench would testify to it. The stone bench on the pavement in front of their houses, where they sat together each night, had been a witness to their secrets, unknown—except to them—to the night and the moon, and the late silence of the village. Scattered about the space of their sorrows, their whispers travelled only to each other.

Runjus could still conjure up that stone bench, built against the neighbours' garden wall on which they leant their backs, facing Abu Yusuf's dim butcher shop in the night. They sat shoulder to shoulder, hands pressed to their cheeks, the weight of their bodies heaped restfully on the stone. They spoke and fell silent, their glances always fixed at the end of the alley that led to the orchards, the graveyard and the village well.

Um Yusuf broke the night's silence a few months before Runjus left for America. She said to Aunt Runjus, as they looked together down the alley, 'Ya Runjus, which one of us do you think will be carried first along this alley to the graveyard? Me or you?'

'May my bones rot before anything happens to you.'

'No, may my bones rot first.'

'No, mine.'

'No, mine.'

Um Yusuf fell silent for a moment, then said, 'Ya Runjus, I have a feeling that my work's almost done in this world and I'm about to go. I've reached the end of my service. I feel like this is it, and I'm about to go and rest.'

But Um Yusuf could no longer sit comfortably on the stone bench at night after Aunt Runjus emigrated from the village alley to take a new turn in her life path, leaving Um Yusuf to be carried on shoulders along the alley to the graveyard.

For Abu Yusuf, the woman who served gladly as a ring on his finger was no longer. She would no longer run anxiously, tripping on the way, to entwine herself around his finger and turn at his behest. She would no longer circle like a cat his feet so her owner may feed her. Um Yusuf's true hunger, like Mother's, was not for food. Hers was an insatiable longing to obey her husband unconditionally, to fulfil the kind of obedience that knew no limit. She never yearned to be one of those women who had the reputation of ruling their husbands.

'He goes by his wife's word, poor soul!' She would say.

In fact, she only became jealous when she heard of another woman who had proven more obedient than her. She would then multiply her efforts until she regained her supremacy in the domain of marital servitude.

She felt no jealousy, even when she heard the rumour that her husband Abu Yusuf had contracted her relative Nabiha in a temporary marriage. Her true fear was that Nabiha would obey him more than she. Nabiha, who had reached the age of fifty and was still unmarried, may well have possessed a hunger strong enough to outdo Um Yusuf's obedience. Only then would Um Yusuf's life have been spoilt, only then would she have died out of despair, if Nabiha had showed perfect obedience towards their husband Abu Yusuf.

Nobody knew Um Yusuf's deepest thoughts except my Aunt Runjus. Nobody knew about her painful infatuation with Abu Yusuf except Runjus. Only she knew that despite their long years of marriage, Um Yusuf had never found a way to express her love for Abu Yusuf except by obeying him.

She would finish quickly with the cleaning, washing and cooking, in order to sit on the stone bench across from Abu Yusuf's butcher shop and contemplate him from afar as he trimmed the side of beef hanging in front of him from the ceiling. She could not get enough of his grave, virile posture—the slick waist that stood upright like an arrow.

His blue eyes would light a blue flame in her little brown eyes. She looked at him from behind her cataracts, as if looking through clouds at a sunny blue sky. She bathed in its warm glow and wished for many more years to better serve and obey him, much more than what she had done in her seventy years.

Abu Yusuf, the most handsome of village men, both in his youth and old age, flirted with the women who visited the butcher shop within earshot of Um Yusuf, and she did not say a word. He would work with the cleaver in his hand and recite poems to each one of them, diving with his eyes along their necks, breasts and the rest of their bodies. He explained why no other man understood a woman's beauty as he; that nobody worshipped or valued their beauty as he. As he sorted the meat, he composed verses on the beauty of the eyes, the splendours of the mouth, the perfect balance of the body's proportions, the magic of generous breasts, even on a delicate elbow or set of toes.

All women were beautiful in his eyes except Um Yusuf whom he rebuked in her final days as he watched the Mexican soap opera about the blonde Estrellita, 'That's what *real* women look like. Look at her beauty—how it opens your heart and goes straight to the soul. Not like you—neckless, shapeless, identical in width and height, lips three palms wide . . . '

She did not say a word in reply. She simply watched as he spat at his side and said, 'I spit on all ugly women. God shortens the life of a man whom he burdens with an ugly woman. God's wrath befalls such a man.'

In her eyes, the handsome Romeo had picked her out of all the women who dreamt of marrying him. In the end, she was the lucky one, as Aunt Runjus said to her, because he picked *her* out of the many. Even though she was not lucky in all things, and even though she never found the courage to express her love for him, she was the one who bore him twelve children.

When she looked at his arms as he stood in his singlet in the courtyard, she dreamt of touching the round muscles of that shoulder whose little curves she knew by heart. Even when she scrubbed his back in the bath, she was too shy or too scared to touch his ribs. She would take advantage of this opportunity to scrub his neck and arms, to pass her fingers slowly over them. At the touch of his skin, an electric current would run through her body and she would shudder. Whenever he asked her to dry him after the bath, she would pause at his ribs, pressing the towel on them slowly, until he yelled, 'Come on, woman, hurry up! Why are your hands paralysed all of a sudden? Come on. Finish up. Move.'

Embarrassed, she would speed up her work, lest he should get annoyed with her, 'No. It's just that there is some water left over here on your neck that I'm drying, so you don't get a cold.'

She dreamt of kissing his neck and felt a strange shiver in the dream. But in life, she never got to savour every inch of his body like she wanted or as she did in her dream. The urge became even stronger after she saw how foreign actresses expressed their love on television. Whenever there was a love scene, she would say 'Tfoo!' at the screen in front of her children, but inwardly she yearned for them. She wondered how other women could express themselves like that. Who taught them? How do these men let them behave in this way? And how do the women not become 'low' in their men's eyes?

'How clueless we've been,' she said to Aunt Runjus one day, 'how did we spend our lives like this, knowing nothing? Abu Yusuf would land on me like a hawk, peck me with his pecker, and end of story. I can't remember a single time when he said a nice word to me. Were we just stupid? I wish he'd just for once said, "You are the lady of all ladies," like he tells his clients every day at his shop, or smile to me the way he smiles at them. No, all he's said is, "Come, you donkey. Go, you ass. Thick-lips! No-neck!" All of that and I never said a word or even frowned. Instead, I just prayed to God to keep him for me. What could I do anyway? The man is the God of the house.'

Um Yusuf did not complain to Aunt Runjus except in her last days. She awakened to her body and other things only after her time had passed and she was preparing to leave this world. When she complained, Aunt Runjus would poke her in the thigh and say, 'What's wrong with you? You want to be young all over again? Be glad you got the best man in town.'

'I'm not saying anything but what can I do if I don't look like Estrellita? Can I say no to what God has given me? I don't argue with him when he says these things. I just smile and say, "Say whatever you want."'

At the age of seventy, she began imitating Estrellita, making childish faces as if she were the same age as the Mexican actress, or had the same eyes and mouth. Even Abu Yusuf noticed and started wondering. All her life, she had hidden her tears from him, because he didn't like a stony face. As soon as he would walk in through the door, she would relax her frown and put on an instant smile as if somebody was about to take a picture of her.

Sometimes, when she got up from her bed and found a tear at the corner of her eye, she would fear that Abu Yusuf might have awakened by mistake and caught a glimpse of it. She would look at him closely to make sure he was in deep sleep, then wipe it away and draw a fake smile on her lips. She would wake up more than once in the night for fear that the smile had been erased by sleep. She would stretch her long thick lips into a wide smile to make them thinner, and then close her eyes on the tears.

'What were you seeing in your dream?' He would ask her in the morning, 'What's with the smile, Thick-lips?'

'I wasn't seeing anything. It's just me—my face is like this, smiling and happy all the time, even when I'm asleep.'

'They say that "The odd smile is a sign of guile." Anyway, you're just stupid, like a madwoman, laughing in your sleep.'

'Whatever you wish. I won't smile again, day or night. Only when you want me to.'

The pleasure she took in obeying him was spoilt the day Nabiha walked into the butcher shop and Abu Yusuf sharpened his look by twisting the ends of his moustache, before lifting his knife to give her the meat she wanted.

'I'm at your service, you lady of ladies. You just give me an order and you won't have to make your request twice. Where do you want me to cut the meat?'

And Nabiha, whose famous pet expression was, 'No meaning,' would say to him: 'No meaning. Give me some of that, there at the bottom, or wherever you prefer. You know better where to find the tender meat—no meaning.'

Um Yusuf would start boiling as soon as he heard the words 'no meaning' come out of Nabiha's mouth. She would come and go, and call out to him from the shop door, 'Do you need anything? Do you want anything, ya Abu Yusuf?'

He would lift the cleaver angrily in her face and scream at her for cutting off the chain of repartee with Nabiha.

'By God you are annoying, woman! Did I call you? Get out of here this minute and leave me alone.'

Um Yusuf did not rest until Kameel, the idiot, exposed her relative Nabiha as well as four or five other women whose deviousness Um Yusuf had smelt around Abu Yusuf's shop. Only then did she relax and tell Abu Yusuf, 'My eyes could see clearly that Nabiha was not decent. Or did you think I was blind?'

But Abu Yusuf's eyes shone more brightly now, whenever he saw Nabiha or one of the other women who had been exposed by Kameel. Whenever Kameel would see one of the women in the village square, he would take off his trousers, hold his penis over his underpants, which was black with dirt, and stutter,

'H-h-hey you. Don't you wan-n-n-nt to come p-p-lay some m-more?'

'Go away, you dog,' she would answer.

'Go aw-aay!' He would repeat after her.

When Um Yusuf told her husband about Nabiha's scandal, to get the woman out of his mind, he said, 'Tfoo,' but his heart calmed once he discovered that Nabiha was not as hard as he had thought. If Kameel, who slept in the graveyard and whose clothes had not left his body in years, had tasted the folds of her flesh, how could he not? As he often said to his customers at the shop, he—Abu Yusuf—could pay the expenses of a temporary marriage with the best widow in the village, with only five dollars of what his son sent him from Saudi.

Abu Yusuf would talk about it proudly, even in front of Um Yusuf who also boasted of it in front of all people, as she did of his youth and blue eyes. Inwardly, she told herself that Abu Yusuf's talk was mere talk, because his dignity kept women away just as it attracted them to him. She found comfort in this idea, with which she shut the door of her brain to any lingering doubt—that perhaps he meant what he said.

But Um Nabiha, who lay paralysed in the little den where she lived with her daughter Nabiha, knew that the talk about her daughter was not mere talk but the truth of what happened that night. When she realized what was happening between her daughter and Kameel the village idiot, 'Ya Nabi-haa . . . ' she had called out, trying to lift her head from her pillow, lift her hand from the sheet, as she listened to Nabiha's moans.

But Nabiha did not answer.

Nabiha lay on her back on the tile of the passageway outside her mother's window with Kameel. She held his hand and said, 'Play right there.' 'Yes,' she moaned, 'rub right there with your hand.'

Earlier that night, Nabiha had been sitting with her hand on her cheek, all alone on the stone bench in front of the den. She was listening to the frogs and her mother's moans in the quiet night when Kameel was passing by her, scratching his lice-infested groin.

The devil scratched her head at that moment. The idea flashed in her mind as soon as he stood before her, a dirty rag in front of an infested soul. 'Is that you, ya Kameel? Damn you, you scared me.'

'You s-s-ca-a-red me,' said Kameel who was coming from the graveyard.

He smiled as he scratched his head violently, tilting it from side to side, and let his saliva dribble from the corner of his mouth.

'Come, follow me,' she said before she could think, and took him away by the hand.

'Fol-low yo-ou.'

'Yes, follow me, and don't say a word. Shhh.'

She dragged him behind her into the den where her mother was snoring loudly. She took Kameel into the small bathroom and closed the squeaking door behind them. She washed his body thoroughly, filling the little room with her panting. She could not bear to have sex with him covered in all the dirt.

She took his clothes off and threw them outside the bathroom.

'May God take you and this foul smell of yours. Do you ever take a bath?' She said as she scrubbed him.

'God ta-a-ke you!' He repeated.

'Shut up! Not a word. Keep quiet or Mother will hear us.'

'Mo-other will h-h-ear us!'

'I said shut up!' She pinched him, 'Talk in a lower voice.'

'Low!'

'Yes, you low man. Shut up. Whisper from the tip of your lips, just like you came in on the tip of your toes.'

'On the t-tip of your to-o-oes.'

'I said from the tip of your lips.'

She pricked him on his lips and wiped the spit on her dress, then put her finger on his mouth to silence him while she scrubbed his penis with her other hand. She stared at it, panting, while Kameel stood in front of her and she knelt before him on her knees, scrubbing the dirt away.

'Hee . . . hee . . . hee . . . That's what Kawakib and Diba did to me. Only Najiba the dog did not wash me—God take her—when she called me to play,' he laughed.

'Don't you dare telling anybody that I bathed you naked and played with you. You're a good boy. Or I'll bury you alive, you hear me?'

'Bury you!'

'Yes, I'll bury you, and I'll dig you a grave for real and bury you in it, not like the ones you sleep in.'

'I sleep in!'

'Yes, the graves where you sleep. But now we want to sleep and play in another way.'

'Play like I did with Diba, Kawakib, Najiba, and . . . and . . . and . . .'

He forgot all the other names as she poured the cold water out of the red plastic jug on his head to wash the soap away, his body shuddering from the cold.

'It's all right, I will warm you soon.'

'I will warm you, ya Kameel,' she said as she towelled him, then she wrapped his torso with the wet towel and held his hand as they walked together out of the bathroom.

The cool September breeze tickled her legs and belly when she lifted her dress above her breasts and lay on the stone bench in the open courtyard, after she had closed the gate. She pulled Kameel with one hand and undid the towel with the other. It fell and exposed his torso.

As Kameel lay on top of her, laughing, she lifted her head a little and said, 'Put this in your mouth and suckle at my breast, ya Kameel. Suck as hard as you can. You hear? Take it.'

She held her nipple between her fingers, pushed her breast into his mouth, and closed his lips on it. 'Suck as hard as you can, ya Kameel,' she said.

'Hard!'

'Yes, yes. Keep your voice down or Mother will wake up. Hard.'

Kameel started sucking slowly.

She hit him on the head and said, 'Damn you, I said hard. And press with your teeth on the flesh as much as you can. Put all of my breast in your mouth and suck as much as you can. Please Kameel, I'm begging you to suck. I can't take it any more. Come on now.'

'Yes, harder. Yes, good. Good, as hard as you can.'

Then she held his hand and said, 'Put your hand in there and play with it—play as much as you can.'

'Play . . . '

'Yes, play, you don't know how to play? Rub your hand there, up and down,' she said, and showed him with her hand what he must do.

'Oh! Yes! Harder!'

Then she held his penis in her hand and started playing with it with her fingers, and her eyes widened when she saw his erection. 'I underestimated you, ya Kameel. All this time your were this big, and I thought you were not a man.'

She held his penis and stuffed it inside herself, 'Do you know how to go inside, ya Kameel?'

'Go inside . . . '

'Yes, come on, come inside, ya Kameel. I can't take it any more. May God be good to you, ya Kameel. Go all the way in.'

'All . . . '

'Yes, all of it.'

'Like I did with Najiba the dog who didn't bathe me.'

'Deeper, please.'

Her moaning and talking woke her mother up, who started calling out to her, but she did not answer until she was done having sex with Kameel. After she put his clothes back on, she opened the gate and pushed him outside, 'Get out of here, and if you say a word, I'll bury you alive.'

Kameel did not tell anybody but every time he saw her, Najiba or Kawakib, he would start taking off his trousers and then say, 'Let's play like we did the other day.'

Once he stood in the middle of the square in front of the mosque and started moving his hands as if he were flying a plane. A man asked him, 'What are you doing, ya Kameel?'

'I am flying the plane.'

'Oh! And where do you plan to land this plane?'

'I want to land on the bums of Kawakib and Diba and Najiba and Nabiha,' Kameel stuttered, 'each of them has a bum this big,' he signalled with his hand and laughed.

During the war, Kameel's tongue loosened up quite a bit and the stuttering diminished. The improvement came about when many families fled the death and destruction of Beirut and moved to the village. After spending his life in the orchards and grapevines, the war turned him into the master of all ceremonies. His natural gift of entertainment became so high in demand that people started bidding for his presence at their parties. Urged to entertain night after night, his tongue became accustomed to the flow of words.

Once, Nabiha attacked him and started beating him when he started talking about how he had played with her. She cried to Abu Yusuf and said, 'No meaning—Kameel, all of him, wouldn't make me commit such a sin. If I watch my every word by saying "no meaning," don't you think I would watch my step too before doing something like that? And, of all people—with the filthy Kameel? God help me.'

*

When Abu Yusuf took her in a temporary marriage, she shed more tears than when she beat her mother that night as the old woman lay motionless in her bed.

She had knelt down and started beating her Mother unconsciously, on her face, breast, belly, lifting her head and hitting it on the ground, crying and screaming.

'You are the one who drove me crazy. You're the one who got me to the point where I'm sinning with a crazy, stinking man. You destroyed me and drove me to madness. When are you going to die and rid me of you? Talk to me, answer—when?'

Then she realized what she was doing. 'T-t, T-t, T-t,' stuttered her mother, tears flowing in rivers down her cheeks. Exhausted, Nabiha sat next to her mother and begged her for forgiveness.

But her mother could not answer. She looked blankly at her daughter, eyes clouded with fear. Nabiha asked her why she did not let her marry her cousin whom she loved in her youth and who, for years, had waited and asked patiently for her hand, to be refused again and again.

'It's out of the question,' Um Nabiha had said. 'No man deserves my daughter. There'll be no marriage.'

That was her mother's response to all suitors. Nabiha did not say a word. She bit her tongue and hid her wound for fear of her mother while her mother ignored her conscience for fear of loneliness and old age. She did not want a man to deprive her of her daughter, even if he was her sister's son, for Nabiha was more than a daughter to her; she had been her companion since her husband died. Um Nabiha had raised her in tears, believing that she would be the one to fill up the loneliness of her old age, and 'to turn her on her side' when she was on her sickbed.

When her mother became paralysed, Nabiha transformed from a dutiful daughter to a ruthless woman. When changing her diaper, she would pinch her mother in her thigh and say, 'When's God going to rid me of you? He is Great and He threw you in your bed, like you threw me to face the world by myself.' Then, each time, she would regret what she had said and done, and would ask for her forgiveness. She would kiss the hands of the speechless old woman who could only stare back at her with dry tears and utter, 'T-t, T-t, T-t, . . . '

*

Um Yusuf hid her tears from Abu Yusuf when she learnt that he had contracted a temporary marriage with Nabiha. She was afraid that he might say to her, 'What's with the pressed mouth, Thick-lips?'

Aunt Runjus told me that Um Yusuf's secret wish was that Abu Yusuf would not only obey her unquestioningly but also believe that she was the most beautiful woman in the world, that he would flirt only with her out of all women. She would have liked him to be blind to anyone other than her, deaf to all but her voice. In her dreams, she wore him like Solomon's ring on her finger, and it would take but a scratch for him to cry out, 'I am at your service, ya Um Yusuf.'

To realize her dream, she did what many women in the village did to bind their husbands to their will, and Aunt Runjus encouraged her. Secretly, she put a few drops of her urine in his tea and watched him with satisfaction from the corner of her eye as he drank it. The women were convinced that when a man drank his wife's urine, he became bewitched. After that, he would only walk obediently behind her, like the prey behind the beast after he urinates on him. According to Aunt Runjus, Um Yusuf went even further and gave him her monthly blood in the days when she still had her period.

*

It may be unlikely that Um Yusuf would do such a thing but why would Aunt Runjus lie? When I told her my aunt's story, Alawiyya had asked: Why would the slave give up the safe haven of loyalty to their master, especially Um Yusuf whose dream it was to serve her master?

But why would Aunt Runjus lie?

Even though I didn't feel certain about what Um Yusuf did, and of what the likes of her resorted to for revenge, I could imagine her reading about herself in the novel and flashing a smile that said, 'You don't know anything, Miss . . . '

And I don't know.

I no longer know anything.

As far as I know, my slow aunt was not lying. Um Yusuf gave Abu Yusuf her urine and her blood in his drink, and Abu Yusuf did not fall in love with her until she died. When he went mad after her death, he would lift his cleaver in the face of whoever called him by his name.

'You are a liar and the son of a liar! The man standing in front of you is not Abu Yusuf. Abu Yusuf died and left when the Lady of Beauty, Um Yusuf, died. The Lady of Beauty, my wife Um Yusuf. Look how beautiful she is. She is a fourteen-year-old moon, and glowing.' He asked the city photographer to enlarge her little ID picture and frame it in an expensive golden frame, no matter the cost.

'Look at my wife,' he said to the photographer, 'more beautiful than all the women in the world. By God, if you don't make her prettier than Estrellita who acts on television, I will bring your end.'

'But how, ya Hajj, am I to change her?'

'Change whatever you can. Make her pudgy cheeks thinner, enlarge her eyes, make them blue and bright instead of tiny like a scorpion's privates. I want to hang her picture on the wall during the funeral, for all to see how my wife was the most beautiful in the world.'

On her seventh day memorial service, he would point to the wall and say, 'Look how beautiful my wife is. Look how similar to the doe—her mouth, eyes and neck. Praise be to God for her beauty.'

But in spite of all the retouching, the picture of her on the wall retained the sadness of her eyes and the silence of her features.

Abu Yusuf waned like the light of a lantern when the oil is about to run out. He spoke to her picture and she didn't answer. 'You wretched man, how're you going to live your life without me? Remember how you tortured me during my life? God will punish you in what's left of yours. My heart aches for you, you wretched man, watching your youth dwindle this way. Who is there for you now, to make you feel your own strength? Who will say to you "At your service, my man," now that I'm gone?'

'Completely useless,' he said, 'I'm not worth anything without her. She was the lady of all ladies. But I was no good to her, no good at all. I was unfair, very unfair.'

*

In America, Aunt Runjus would also talk to herself. Even she, who knew all of Um Yusuf's secrets, could not understand the reason for Abu Yusuf's madness and death. 'There's no will or strength except from God,' she would say.

Sometimes Aunt Runjus wondered whether his devotion and death might have come as a delayed effect of the magic Um Yusuf had given him in his drink. And when the thought crossed her mind, she slapped one hand on the other and said, 'How wretched you are, ya Um Yusuf. What you worked for in life bore results only after your death. You did not live to enjoy it, to calm the fires of your anger. You never could reign and let him worship.'

But at other times, she said, 'No, that's not the story. He withered and waned when he found nobody to boss about. That's when he fell from his mother's lap, dropping like a cluster of ripe berries from the grapevine.'

Runjus kept coming out and going into her room, rubbing her hands together as she walked and stared at the floor.

'The wretched man made her miserable in life and now he has followed her to her death. Even there he needs her, to make him feel strong. He knows that without her he's nothing, nothing at all!'

Runjus cried and wailed for her friend whose body the men carried on their shoulders along the length of the alley to the graveyard, through the stage of their secrets, stories and memories from the nights on that old stone bench.

* * *

I told Alawiyya the whole story . . . I wish I could find her now to recover all the stories and anecdotes, which she surely has forgotten— the stories of my mother, of Aunt Runjus, of Yasmine, of Ibtisam . . . I must find them before I fly over the clouds, before the clouds of my memories turn to rain.

8

When I told Alawiyya about Ibtisam's story, she studied me carefully, then decided to go to her directly and hear for herself. She did not want to pay, she said, for fish that was still in the sea. So, after gathering all the words, still warm and stirring, she picked up the basket and left.

Now, how am I to find Ibtisam's story any more?

*

A couple of months after her marriage, Ibtisam's mother looked gravely at her daughter's body, shrivelled and wan, and said to me, 'The poor girl. That's her luck. She got a husband with a salty thigh.'

Ibtisam gave her mother a dirty look for calling her husband's thigh 'salty'. So, in order not to hurt her daughter's feelings more, she lowered her head and whispered to me, 'By God, look how salty it turned out to be. Remember her full, round breasts? Remember the hips that curved beneath the small of her back? Look how her belly almost presses now against her spine. Those bright black eyes, wide and dark like the night . . . Look how they've become two cold marbles made of glass.'

I did not understand her mother's theory about the salty thigh, so I asked her, 'What do you mean by his salty thigh?'

'A man with a salty thigh makes the woman rot from the inside until she becomes skin and bone, like my daughter Ibtisam.'

'But I thought that the man with a salty thigh drove his wife to an early death.'

'No. The difference is that she dies every day. Salt, you see, eats away slowly at the flesh.'

I tried many times to get in touch with Ibtisam in her new house but either I would get no answer or Jalal would tell me, as if trying not to taste the words, that she was out or in the bath or asleep. Then, when I finally reached her, what happened between us left me confused.

Until then, I had not considered, even for a moment, that she could be the one avoiding me. I, who had offered myself as a shade when life scorched her and she needed refuge, might have become a shadow that weighed on her.

I spent the evening pacing between my bed and the living room, trying to understand this change between us. I lay down on the living room sofa and, shutting out the sound of the generators, listened only to the silent passage inside me. From my parents' bedroom rose the rumbling of Father's snores, which for a time infected me with a childish laughter that alleviated my loneliness.

I gazed at the candle standing on the little coffee plate atop the side table, the flame shaking with each shy summer breeze that wandered through the window and through my white nightgown to my warm skin. I lifted my hair so the breeze would cool the wet skin on the back of my neck and play affectionately with my damp hair.

But my heart could not be cooled. Everything in the world faded and I thought only of Ibtisam.

*

Never had so long a silence passed between us.

Was she the one avoiding me? The one who didn't want me to talk to her or see her? Or did Jalal never tell her that I'd called?

I told myself that perhaps she was busy with her new life and imagined that her new happiness had taken her and flown her away, abandoning me and those who were still on the ground. If that was the case, fine. Her happiness was what I always wished for.

But if she was happy, why didn't she just answer me and say, 'I am happy, ya Maryam, very happy. And I am so happy that I have no time to talk to anyone, not even you.'

The fire burnt again in my veins. I stood beside the phone talking to myself, then looked at the time; it was ten thirty exactly. A feeling inside me told me she was at home, and that she would be the one to answer this time. I would check in on her briefly just to reassure myself that she was well.

I lifted the phone receiver and dialled her number. 'Alo,' answered her childish, bird-like voice. She said it and fell silent without hanging up the phone but the voice disappeared. I called out 'Alo' into the phone several times but she didn't answer. After a few moments, a man's voice—Jalal's—said, 'Alo,' so I hung up the receiver and sat at the edge of the sofa, astounded by what had just happened.

Sleep fluttered away from my eyes. The anxiety kept me awake till morning.

Why wouldn't she answer me?

How could I know if she was happy when I hadn't seen her since her wedding, since I bid her farewell in front of the main entrance of the hotel on Hamra Street, down the avenue near the Military Bath, where Jalal had rented a room for a few honey days.

We accompanied her all the way to the hotel lobby, the tail of the wedding dress dragging behind her. After the wedding procession had paraded down the Manara Avenue on the seafront, with all the decorated cars and horns, she and her groom retired to their room.

In front of the hotel entrance, I kissed her twice on each cheek and said to her, 'Mabrouk,' and pressed her hand.

She smiled and said to me, 'May you be wed soon. When we leave the hotel, you'll be the first person I call.'

Then she laughed and said, 'I might also call before then.'

Jalal also laughed as he stood next to her. Then they entered the hotel lobby, and he put his hand around her shoulder. I stood watching them until they disappeared behind the elevator doors. I was overcome by a strange feeling at that moment, the feeling of a mother parting with her daughter.

That day I returned home and felt the urge to call Alawiyya and talk to her. I wanted to ask her why she hadn't attended the wedding, and repeat the reprimands of Ibtisam who asked me more than once during the wedding, 'Where's Alawiyya? Why didn't she come? I gave her the invitation personally.'

Alawiyya said she was busy with family matters but she was lying for sure; for, such things had never preoccupied or even interested her.

We agreed on a day to visit Ibtisam and congratulate her.

The next day, Alawiyya disappeared as usual.

So, I decided to go by myself and called Abbas—asking him to arrange for me to be excused from office that day.

I washed my face, quickly threw on my clothes, then left for Ibtisam's new house near the airport. The whole area had grown and developed, reborn after the war.

Since the massacre of Sabra and Shatila during the Israeli invasion of '82, every time I passed through near there, the smells of death came back to me. For days, Ibtisam talked only about the stench that enveloped the area for quite some time afterwards. She would take a bath several times a day to get the smell of death off her body, and every time she washed her body with soap and her skin was clean, the pores reopened and the smell broke out again from within and became even stronger. And when the smell returned to her nose, the cloud of death covered the glimmer of light in her eyes.

*

On my way to see her, I imagined the smell of sex in her house, that odour I notice in every room when I enter the homes of newlyweds. I had not anticipated the scents of sadness, loneliness or fear.

I drove through the intricate web of streets that led to her house near the military headquarters of Fakhr al-Din and parked the car in a sandy corner. I knew her house room by room, for it was I who moved in her wedding gifts. I had hung her clothes and arranged her underwear in the drawers and the perfume bottles and make-up on the dressing table after I took them out of their boxes, so everything was ready for use.

I rang the bell more than once and knocked sharply on the wooden door of the flat; nobody answered. Impossible, I said to myself. She must be at home; the superintendent had just told me so. Besides, her gray car was parked outside. Why wouldn't she open the door?

I stood there for more than half an hour in front of the mute door; I was determined to see her.

At each moment, I felt that the door would open, and I fixed my eyes on the little circular light coming out of the peephole.

Then, at one point, I was almost convinced that nobody was there, and since I was beginning to feel tired and heavy on my skinny legs, I decided to leave. Carrying my disappointment home with me, I turned to head down the stairs to my car, but, for a second, I saw a shadow move across the peephole.

I could tell that it was she who had looked through, and I also heard soft steps behind the door. I froze in place; then, like a mad-woman, began banging on her door with both hands. I started talking to her and calling out to her, sometimes in a low voice and sometimes loudly as if I were talking to myself, 'Open the door, ya Ibtisam, it's Maryam. I want to see you. Tell me why you won't open the door. Open the door and talk to me, or talk to me from behind the door. I will listen. Tell me "Go away, ya Maryam, I don't want to see you," and I'll leave. Say "Come in and congratulate me," and I'll come in. Just say something. Just let me know that you're all right, just one word, and I'll leave.'

The door remained closed between us; she behind it from the inside and I on the outside, my face stuck to the door, as if I was trying to rest my head on a vacuum. The blood froze in my legs and ankles while cold sweat dripped from my temples. I spoke to her in one long confused sentence that broke down into shorter ones, until my words became a series of letters, then sighs, until my throat dried.

I gathered myself—my voice, body, words and despair—and returned home, asking myself all the way, silent with fear of the answer, 'Why did she not open the door?'

*

Two months had passed since I had seen her.

Waves of questions, longing and fear broke within me when I finally laid eyes on her. No, that face was not the bright face of Ibtisam that I knew. It now resembled a point of stillness, a face overwhelmed, without words, calm or anger, ebbing and flowing with the silence following profound sorrow.

I looked at her and saw a person in a stupor, present and absent at once. Her eyes were tepid, her glances vague. I could have never imagined how much a salty thigh could do to the flesh until now when she stood before me—it was as if she were a ghost speaking with failing words. She seemed to look without seeing, listen without hearing. Her breasts had melted, those round balls of flesh that stood firmly beneath her blouse had loosened in their journey, to become 'a cat's boobs' as her mother said.

The curtains were drawn in the living room where she received us, the room lit only by a single lamplight at the corner that allowed dim yellow beams that barely enabled me to see her face or Alawiyya's.

I felt like I was gradually suffocating in a tunnel. She spoke in measured tones, chewing on her inner lip on the left side as if she were eating herself.

That day I heard from her what I'd never heard before. She said she didn't want to see anybody or hear anything, not even the music she once loved.

She said she only wanted to sleep.

Her voice was barely able to leave the well of her chest, the words wet with muddied water. She dragged forth her sentences like someone lifting a heavy rock from the bottom of her chest. The words came up on a fine rope, and when she felt that it was going to break, she would slow down and pull it out of her mouth with difficulty.

She spoke a lot about sleeping as she chewed on her inner cheek.

She was not the bride to whom I had bid farewell and in whose eyes, despite her ambivalent feelings, I had seen hope on her wedding night.

I asked her, 'Are you sick, ya Ibtisam?'

'No.'

'Happy?'

'Fine.'

'What's wrong?'

'Nothing.'

I don't remember exactly what other questions I asked her and what answers she gave me while Alawiyya looked at her incredulously and looked at me beseechingly, to explain to herself what I needed explained to me. She looked around the dark living room, at the two windows and at the curtains drawn on Ibtisam's dark face.

I don't know if Alawiyya ever learnt that later Jalal's salty thigh became a sweet one for Ibtisam and that she grew back the flesh that had melted during the first years of her marriage, after having learnt to remedy her despair with food. Her belly became round and the flesh puffed around her bones. Her features transformed, gaining a harshness through days that I never imagined she could endure. Everything about her changed. Even her taste in clothes changed, so that she could better fit the role of the wife of Jalal Yunis.

*

And her past?

No, she came to reject it. She probably came to hate it too, like she began hating me, in order to reconcile with her present and become happy with her three sons. She learnt to find pleasure in food and complaining about maids. Who is better—the Ethiopian, the Sri Lankan, the Indian, the Bengali or the African?

She stared distractedly, spraying her asthma medication into her mouth, like our neighbour Um Talal. Ibtisam had not felt any symptom before marriage and did not cough before in her life. The doctor told her that it was an emotional condition resulting either from the pressure of maintaining a household or from the shock of the delivery of her oldest son Alloushi. She could have been afflicted with bronchitis that turned into an allergy and asthma.

Alloushi was also born with asthma, and his little chest knew suffering from the very first cry of his life.

I didn't see her during her first two pregnancies. She kept avoiding me, until the pain of contractions woke her in the middle of that night when she was with her third son, and she asked Jalal to get me.

'Sorry, Maryam, I know I woke you,' he said, begrudgingly. 'But Ibtisam wants you to come to the hospital. She's going into labour.'

I felt tears of true happiness roll down my cheeks for the first time in my life when she made it through the birth. But also for the first time I was invaded by feelings of jealousy, when I witnessed Ibtisam's birth pains, for I remembered the pains of my abortion and that distant day that she had shared with me.

*

I didn't know until the symptoms began that I was pregnant. It was the beginning of my relationship with Abbas and my period dates had passed without me noticing. I called Ibtisam, because for the first time in my life I hated the smell of the morning coffee. All I could think of at the time was my life and happiness with Abbas and his with me. But I knew he wouldn't consent to marrying me, so the decision was made. But how would I have an abortion? This is what I asked Ibtisam because I knew nothing about such matters.

In those months when I was pregnant, I became cognizant of those feelings that my mother surely had when she was pregnant, the feeling of thin transparency that turns the body into a non-body, to light, to air. During those two months that I was pregnant, not only was my body feeling changed but also my sense of the world around me. It seemed that I was standing on an elevated plane, with the whole world far below. All I could register was the feeling of a rose closed around its centre, sensing nothing except what's inside. At the doctor's office, I was surrounded by women of different ages, with bellies rounded to different sizes. Each one was stealing glances at the rest when she thought she wasn't being watched. I felt like they, sitting there with their happily married bellies, could tell just by looking at me that I was the one pregnant out of wedlock.

The doctor didn't say much. His mood had been marked by all the abortions he had to perform during the war. He was brief and direct with his summary questions and his methodical, detached manner was a relief to me. He didn't want to know any of his patients and I didn't want to be known. He asked me my name, date of birth and marital status while Ibtisam watched. When I left the examination room, he told me from behind his desk that I was two months pregnant. Blood rose to my head and boiled in my veins. I was in an alternate universe, swimming in my cold sweat. I'd been near certain of the pregnancy before the exam but the doctor's words made it final.

I asked him how fast I could have the abortion, but instead of answering the question he held the pen in his hands and looked at me as if apologizing for the impertinence of interfering in a personal matter.

He said, 'It would be a shame. You are already two months along.'

'I don't want a scandal, doctor.'

'I will call up the young man myself and convince him to marry you.'

'I don't want to, and I can't.'

'But it would be a shame.'

'It's okay, doctor, if you will. I would rather kill myself than ask him to marry me because I'm pregnant.'

'As you wish.'

And that was his last response.

The procedure took less than fifteen minutes, followed by sadness and tears. Only the doctor's tender hands—one holding mine, and the other brushing my hair away from my forehead—brought me back to the world. After that, I avoided Abbas. For the abortion had flushed out every dream connected to Abbas, and for a long time I roamed the streets, feeling pain and loss, looking at faces to find them empty and at buildings to find them dilapidated. The whole city, with its buildings and people, had aborted its dreams. I was merely like the city itself.

I told Alawiyya and Zuhair about the abortion. I sat in a cafe with them and said, while Ibtisam was watching, that the abortion did not break my relationship with Abbas. On the contrary, our relationship had become a lifeline for me which I couldn't cut; a lifeline for me alone.

Alawiyya looked at me with fear, soothing herself by caressing the skin of her hands, as if wondering silently to herself, 'What has she aborted?' As for Zuhair, he didn't care about my confession. I thought he'd wanted to hear the truth and only the truth but his indifference caused me regret and shame. My story scared him; and his reaction was simply to gather his papers and leave. 'What business of mine are these women's stories?' he muttered under his breath as he walked away.

*

My relationship with Abbas had not ended, and my friendship with Ibtisam only deepened, especially at that moment when her birth pains became mine, just as she had made my abortion pain hers.

I entered her room at the hospital and felt happiness upon seeing the boy. I kissed her and my eyes watered, like Jalal's. When I asked him, 'What will you call him?' he answered,

'Of course, Ali. Even if it had been a girl, I would've called her Ali.'

I laughed, and Ibtisam laughed, and so did he, as I caressed the sweaty hairs away from her face. Jalal ran his hand over his belly and said, 'My father, from the first day Ibtisam got pregnant, told me, "Your wife is going to have a boy, because our family has only sons."'

And so, she came to think of nothing but her sons. I would sit with her for hours and she would talk of her children without pause. Only when talking about them was she truly herself.

I don't know if, when I see her and embrace her tightly and say 'I am leaving', she will bite down some more on the inside of her cheek, or flee again from her thoughts by disappearing into her life with her children, her quarrels with the Sri Lankan maid and the gossip about her friends and family, like she did when I saw her the last time, when I had taken advantage of Jalal's absence during a trip he took to his village.

*

I went to see her that day, to have coffee, to see how she was and to listen to her news. That morning, she made me wait for more than an hour while she spoke on the phone.

I don't know why she showed me into the living room instead of the family room, like other friends and relatives. When I went into the room, I inspected the few books displayed on the shelves next to the antiques and silverware. I leant closer to make out the titles. Books about herbal and natural remedies, some about the interpretation of the Koran and others about home decoration. I also noticed *Path of Eloquence* by Imam Ali, and books about religion and tradition—in thick covers with titles inscribed with gold.

'Has Jalal read all these books?' I asked her.

'I'm not sure. I haven't seen him reading them recently. He's very busy.'

'So they are for decoration?'

'How should I know?'

She said it without looking at me, pulling her hair away from her face with both hands. Then she held it with one hand and tied it with the other using a black velvet hairband as I sounded out the titles.

I did not ask her about *her* books, the books of literature, philosophy, politics and feminism.

I remembered that her mother had burnt all her books in the bathroom as the Israeli tanks started moving into the streets and alleys of Beirut in the summer of '82, and the books transformed into a low mountain range of cinders while Ibtisam just looked on without saying a word.

'I can't *not* burn them,' her mother had said. 'Do you want them to burn down our house with all these Palestinian and Communist books?'

Ibtisam's heart smouldered with her books, and burnt even brighter with the crackle of Kalashnikovs in the night and the lonely clatter of guns and rifles being thrown out of windows onto the street in front of their building. The amplifiers on the tanks called out without emotion for surrender and non-resistance.

But Ibtisam never threw away her gun. She hid it in the little storage room next to the kitchen. The soldiers entered the apartment and searched the house room by room. They sliced open the mattresses, turned the closets inside out and did not leave a single spot unchecked. One of the soldiers prodded the sack of bulgur with the butt of his rifle, then, leaning his weapon against the wall, he opened the bag with his hands and asked Ibtisam's mother with an accent that betrayed years lived in Lebanon.

'What is this?'

'This is bulgur.'

'You store this?'

'Of course! Every year I store lentils and wheat and everything else.'

'You don't buy from the market, little by little?'

'We only buy what we need. What business is it of yours, what I buy and what I don't?'

'Where are you folk from, ya Hajji?'

'From the south.'

'So you are Shi'a?'

'If we are Shi'a, or Sunni, or Christian—what's it to you? Whatever we are, why these questions?'

'If you're Shi'a, it would mean that we are first cousins.'

Suddenly, her mother's tone changed. 'Why, why my darling would we be cousins? Did you think your father married my mother, or your mother married my uncle, or is it that my father and your father are brothers? What on earth would make us cousins, you unfortunate one? Or was the Imam Ali your first cousin? Listen to this talk!'

The soldier gave her a stern look; she, who always kept her calm, did not return his stare. He picked up his rifle again and jabbed at the sacks of sugar and bulgur with the muzzle of his gun and tore them open, making their contents spill onto the floor. Then he left with his friend who hadn't said a word.

*

I hate waiting. Ibtisam made me wait and wait, she who once told me that women's bodies move according to a clock whose time is 'waiting': waiting for her menstruation to begin, then waiting every month for the menstrual cycle to start, waiting for ovulation, waiting nine months to deliver, waiting for menopause. And every act of waiting, even the wait for death, is laden with pain, for pain is the tax of femininity.

But what are we, women, really waiting for?

Half an hour later, I was still waiting for Ibtisam to finish her phone call, and I was now becoming restless. I grew breathless in the chill of the living room. I decided to get up and leave, leaving behind my shadow to block the light that the sun cast on the floor. I sneaked out carefully, like one leaving her skin. Perhaps she would have expressed happiness for me, even if she said it with tearful eyes. She might have said, 'You're better off this way. Go away—at least you will feel safe. The government will protect you when you get the nationality. Here who protects a woman? A woman . . . her parents take care a little, her husband a little, and her children a little, and the law grabs what's left. Not one of us has a guarantee.'

Would she have said that, then fallen silent and wistful?

*

I woke up terrified from a dream in which I saw her sitting in a rectangular room with wooden walls. The room was the size of her body, no bigger. It was a box, like a coffin. She was screaming and knocking on the wooden door with both of her hands until they bled. When nobody heard her, she tried to open it from the inside, to free the birds in her eyes. But she could not. Iron nails had been driven into the edges, and they were much stronger than her soft fingers. Nobody answered.

When her voice reached me in the night, in my room in my bed, I went straight to the wooden room. I ran towards the coffin and broke it open with my hands. But when I pushed the cover aside, she was not inside. I couldn't find a single part of her. She had eaten herself up to the last morsel. The cheeks, the bones, the eyeballs, the hands, the fingers, and the voice.

I woke and started crying.

I too will soon eat my shadow as I leave, when I put my clothes and other belongings in the suitcase and say goodbye to Ibtisam, Alawiyya, Yasmine and the rest of the characters in the novel.

10

I know Alawiyya Subuh. I know her at least as much as Maryam does. In spite of her mysterious disappearance, I am certain that she is alive and writing. Without writing the word 'air', Alawiyya could not breathe. And if she did not write the word 'flowers', she would forget that the world has roses. She writes to remember the rose's smell, to feel the softness of its petals and to discover what it is that makes it perish—whether it is the hand that plucks it from the rose bush, the nose that sucks its smell greedily or the seclusion that it feels in the distant mountains.

I fear that she may have only smelt something of my story, without understanding. The day she came to observe my life with Jalal, I sensed that she had come in search of a glimpse of happiness, if only in the fate of one of her characters.

I told her everything so my story would take on a life separate from me, after my life and I had become separated. I wanted to draw Alawiyya as close to me as my secrets, as close as I am to my own story. But I must have been talking to myself.

I must have scared her away. I kept talking until she became lost in the details and the point of it all became incomprehensible.

Or maybe what scared her was that she heard and understood every word. She may have written my story and relegated it to one of the paper stacks near her desk. When she collected the papers to write the novel, she must have found my name mixed with other strange voices. And so I took on several names.

As she read the drafts aloud, it would pain me to hear my story wander and become lost among a host of names. I would stick my finger between the sheets of her manuscript, insisting, 'It is I, Ibtisam, ya Alawiyya. It is my story. It's the story I told you. Why do you evade my name and replace it with others?'

And she would say, 'But your story is not yours alone. I heard the same story from Huda, Jumana, Suaad, Samiha and many others whose names and faces I no longer remember.'

*

No, one can't be certain that she understood.

How is she to understand what I told her about Jalal when she has never been married? Just like I would not be able to understand the pain of loneliness, the price one pays for a life without marriage. She couldn't understand how I sometimes wake in a panic, sit up on my bed and look at Jalal as he sleeps undisturbed beside me, his snores reaching the other rooms. I ask myself after a marriage of fifteen years, 'Who is this man beside me? I don't know him and he doesn't know me. Who is this man who slept with me at the beginning of the night, wringing my body underneath him as our sweat and breath mixed? Who is this man to whom I gave my life, my body and everything I had?' Many times I fear the answer, and flee from him in order not to go crazy. I am afraid that after fifty years of marriage, I will still ask myself the same questions and still find no answers, like all the other women who told Alawiyya their stories. I never wanted this to happen. How did it?

*

'I like a girl like you, who is honest and has a personality and knows what she wants. I chose you because I want us to share one life in all its details. I want us to think together, take our decisions jointly and to stay close in everything we do.'

The day he said those things to me, I was elated. When he asked me about my past and I began telling him everything, he ended the conversation simply, saying, 'I don't care even if you're not a virgin.

You and I will start together from scratch.' But my honesty and Jalal's fear of it would later haunt this life he wanted for us.

Like the day we moved into our home and I rented the Egyptian film, *The Wife of an Important Man*. We lay together on the bed, his head resting on my shoulder. 'You know,' I said as I played with his blonde curls, 'I really like the acting of Ahmad Zaki. He has this authentic Egyptian look and his acting is amazing. He is so charismatic and so convincing.'

Jalal did not respond. The muscles of his face contracted as he kept his eyes fixed on the screen. Then he turned away from me and fell asleep.

He punished me for two days by avoiding my eyes and letting the words laze in his mouth whenever he spoke to me, until finally he could no longer control himself. 'Listen to me,' he said, shaking me by the shoulders, 'I don't need a dirty woman like you.'

'What do you mean by dirty? Dirty how?'

'Have you already forgotten what you said about Ahmad Zaki two days ago?'

'What do you mean? What about Ahmad Zaki?'

'Oh, poor you! You've already forgotten who Ahmad Zaki is. You've forgotten? You kept staring and gushing, looking at the television screen as if I were not even there. You didn't even respect my feelings while you played with my hair as if you were playing with his hair.'

'Me?'

'Look, your past is none of my business. But now you are my wife, my property, my responsibility. And I won't let you put horns on me, going on as you please about Ahmad Zaki or anybody else.'

He shook me so hard that for a second I thought that he had really *caught* Ahmad Zaki and me together in the house.

And so I learnt that I should never again talk to him or in front of him about Ahmad Zaki or any other man; but I hadn't realized exactly how extreme Jalal's thinking was until after a series of shocks that left me stunned and shaken by what I discovered in him and about him.

My body would shake like a prisoner being tortured in an electric chair. My desire for all things waned and dissolved so that even the light that I loved my whole life meant nothing to me except that it illuminated my pain. It was useless to fight when I was up against virtually a whole tribe embodied in one man. Like the day when his mother told me, on one of our weekend visits to the country, 'When a woman is not good to her husband, he should take her off like a shoe and throw her away.' And his father would say in front of me and all the other daughters-in-law, 'A woman is like a Persian rug—the more you step on it the better it becomes.'

I would stay quiet and watch Jalal turn into a different, more aggressive, man in front of his parents. Like a rooster, he would spread out his feathers and become compelled to convince his brothers and parents that their son was a 'man' who could put the fear of God in his wife. His tone would switch to the imperative so that even the word 'please' would disappear from his speech. He would sit cross-legged in his parents' country house—like an emperor—with his brothers while their wives and I spent the day in the kitchen. The men on the balcony or in the garden, the women in the kitchen, the food spread out all day, empty plates coming and full plates going out.

And when I would fall silent, he would also be silent with me. Dialogue was non-existent. The solution, in his mind, was to initiate sex. In bed, he was always silent, busy with his own pleasure while I drowned in the silent conversation with myself. I had no idea whether and in what he drowned when he was silent. While the sweat of my body spoke of the pain of my silence, his sweat spoke of the excitement of taking me like prey.

*

Something has broken in me. I don't know if it is Jalal or my dreams or my pregnancy or my children or the days and age, or every defeat—one after the other. I don't think I can start all over again. And when Yasmine said to me, 'Don't say anything in front of him. You can't tell a man everything,' I looked at her as she wiped the sweat from her forehead, to pin the grey veil with a safety pin to the side of her right temple. Before I could think, I answered, 'You're right. We live in a land of lies and more lies. For how long can one possibly fight?'

*

And my memories?

He tore all the pictures.

I was home, sitting on the bed with my albums, looking at old photos of Maryam, Alawiyya and me on a trip that we took during college. Jalal entered the room, looked at the photos scattered on the bed, and sat next to me, examining them one at a time.

Then suddenly, his silence turned into rage. He stood up and began tearing the pictures hysterically. 'I've told you a million times,' he shouted, 'that your old life is behind you. Now, you're my wife and my responsibility. If I see you even talking to Maryam or Alawiyya, I'll teach you a lesson!'

'Why? What did Maryam and Alawiyya do to you?'

'If Alawiyya were a clean woman, she would not sit in coffee houses with men, drinking coffee and reading newspapers. Alawiyya writes in magazines about love and men and couldn't care less about the rest of the world. And can you tell me what Maryam's life is about? How does she live? Who does she love? How is it possible that she doesn't have a man in her life?'

I didn't know what to say or do, whether to laugh or cry. I just kept quiet.

'Why are you quiet? Say something!'

'Nothing.'

'No, talk! You scare me more when you're quiet. Only God knows what you're thinking.'

*

More than once I tried to ask for a divorce but he threatened to deprive me of my children.

Who is this man? I would wonder.

I never understood how, in the evenings, when I dressed up as another woman to accompany him to his parties, he would suddenly transform into the model of geniality. I would look at him and see a man assembled of organs, limbs, a member, a brain, a voice and an imagination from eras and worlds apart. I told Alawiyya everything about that world of nightclubs and about the Jalal of the nightlife. How, in the night, I did not laugh. I just dispensed smiles all around, like Santa distributing gifts. Smiles that decorated my mouth like lipstick. Jalal would tell me a hundred times at home not to look stern at parties. He would say, as he bent forward a little in front of the mirror to comb his hair, 'Don't laugh too much tonight but don't frown a lot either. By now, you know my mind—what I like and what pleases me.'

He would turn back to me and say, moving his hand left and right, 'In other words, neither like this nor like that.'

Sometimes, at dinner, he would signal to me with raised eyebrows to lift the front of my dress if it had fallen when I leant across the table. At other times, he would nudge me to get up and transform myself into a private dancer for him near the table, like the wife of one of his friends. He would take away the shawl from my shoulders, tie it around my waist and say, 'Get up and dance like her. Now *those* are women.'

We would return at dawn and, after finally removing his mouth from my breast, Jalal would throw his heavy body on the bed and fall asleep. I would lie there and remember how all night he had devoured with his eyes the breasts of other women. I would get up and go to the bathroom, stand before the mirror and touch my face with my hand. For the first time, I noticed how pale I had become, how I was finally starting to look like my mother.

I pored over all the details of my face, scrutinized each detail. I contemplated my body. From the beginning, I had evaded my body. In college, I hid it under my jeans and threw over it a striped shirt, leaving the top buttons open to give a glimpse of my chest. I had glimpsed the tight skin through the shirt of Jalal's young friend and looked away in order not to compare it with Jalal's loose skin.

In the mirror, I noticed little wrinkles appearing at the edges of my face, as if waiting underneath the surface for my skin to weaken before attacking with their claws. A certain kind of bitterness overwhelmed me. I knew that when the body loosens with age, so do one's dreams. Time will not move backwards, nor will dreams look back. Desire starts dragging its feet sluggishly and cannot be fired except with a load of coal.

I pulled the skin back against my face, whispering to myself over Jalal's snoring. But my sentences made a rope that curled around my neck, an echo enveloping the voice and suffocating it, until a point is reached where the voice can no longer be told apart from the echo. 'Am I the voice or the echo?' I whispered to myself in the mirror.

After asking myself, I asked Alawiyya. But she did not answer. Her eyelids fluttered nervously; then, she fell into silence.

11

I don't know how Yasmine came to fear life altogether, as if crossing over to the other side—where there was only fear.

Yasmine wanted to be the one who would better the lives of those around her. It was neither pride nor shame that kept her from simply wanting to live among them. She would watch the children playing on the dirty streets and wish they had lush gardens with fountains, slides and games. It was never her wish to marry a man who would rescue her from poverty, the way it happened in the Egyptian films. She planned to walk along the path of women she had read about in books—fighters and revolutionaries.

But Yasmine's ideas always followed her feelings; and although she feared nothing, she worried about the judgement of her beloved. So it was that when she fell in love with Dr Kamel who had just returned from Paris at the beginning of the war, she quickly acquired his impatience for rebels. And it was for the same reason that she graduated from college with two honours: a degree in chemistry and a certificate in virginity. As a fighter, she willingly put her body at risk but she never endangered the delicate membrane between her legs.

'Even if I were stark naked with a man and we were deep in the ocean of desire, I still would not let him do anything below the surface. One must take risks only when it's safe. There's no reason a revolutionary should have to give up her virginity. Not at all.'

But when, on their wedding night, Yasmine boasted of this little victory over her will, Dr Kamel spoke to her soberly. 'All of that is meaningless,' he said, 'a woman is a human being with feelings like any man. This is rubbish.'

*

When I saw her in her grey robe and veil towards the end of the war, I did not recognize her. The new Yasmine smelt of ashes instead of jasmines and spoke to me about the comfort of death.

'It's so scary, ya Maryam, to live among people who are nothing like you, and to feel that you have no power to reach them. Do you know how it feels to be completely rejected?'

'But, all your life, you've never feared being rejected.'

'There was no longer a place for somebody like me. I had become irrelevant. Even my husband became frightening to me after he changed. And the people on the streets. How they stared at my body. Even my footsteps stuck out among theirs.'

'I don't understand . . . '

'You can't understand how hard it is to feel like a stranger within one's family and environment, to be rejected by your own people who live around you, to not understand them or be understood by them, to be different in one's language, dressing and thinking. The fear was eating me up because, in the end, I didn't have anyone else except them. It was easier to hide myself like the women around me, and when I took the veil and my body became hidden like theirs, I felt safe and at peace.'

'That's all? That's your reason to hide?'

'The world is full of monsters, the big eating the small, all preying on someone else. Why not hide to find peace? It's bad enough that the world consumes us. Do we need men's stares too, devouring our bodies? I'm tired, ya Maryam. All of my rights have been taken away from me. This way I kept at least one right, to be the only one to see my body, to keep it to myself. If they did not respect me before, now they have to show respect at least for my clothes.'

'And this is the right you've claimed for yourself? To be the only one who can see your body? Does that even count as a right?'

*

After that, Yasmine dressed up only on special occasions such as the parties given by her friends in commemoration of the Prophet's birthday. She would put her make-up kit, short dress and blow-dryer in a plastic bag and meet the other women at the reception hall in Burj al-Barajneh which specialized in weddings and commemoration parties. There, the corridors quickly transformed into a space like the catwalk of a fashion show: thick gaudy make-up, low-cut dresses, bare legs and shoulders. In turn, each woman turned her back to the others, took off her robe, slipped on her dress, and did not turn around until she was virtually unrecognizable.

'Who is it? Is that really you?' Someone would giggle.

'I did not recognize you either!'

'My God, you look so cute. This dress suits you so much.'

'You too, you look great!'

After the initial hunt for familiar faces under masquerades, they began the dancing contest where each flaunted her personal choreography to the rhythms of Prophetic songs. Bellies wiggled, hands flailed and feet stamped the floors until the chandeliers trembled. Yasmine climbed on top of the plastic table to attract some additional attention but she fell to the floor and sprained her shoulder.

'Who cares,' she cried, and got up gleefully.

'This way, you're not deprived of anything,' she said to me later. 'We do as we please, and since nobody sees us, we have not committed any sin.'

*

When Dr Kamel returned to Lebanon from France, he brought back with him the bright, cheerful face of his student years. In Paris, he had shed his timid glances, and anxiety had become defiance. His eyelids no longer fluttered with panic as they used to whenever the letters got tangled around his tongue. Now, his eyebrows arched confidently when he spoke or listened. His laugh quivered gently like a tickle in his throat, even at a time when solemnity was a laudable feature in the revolutionary's face. In those days, political speech was accompanied by a deliberate grammar of facial expressions in which the cynical, sideward smile was deployed only when necessary.

Kamel's dark skin was the first feature to draw Yasmine's attention. She liked the thick, black beard with the musky scent, and she loved tucking her face below it at the top of his neck.

The day she met him, she said to me, 'Ya Maryam, you should have seen those solemn eyes, the thick hair and that free mind. His thinking is so different from all the other men I've known. He is open-minded for real, not when it's convenient. He's not double-faced. He doesn't have a million faces! This is the *type* I would die for, this is the man I've always dreamt of—fighting by his side. That beard of his, my God is it sexy!'

After they got married, Yasmine asked him to spend more time in his private practice and less at the free clinics. She pleaded with him to raise his fees a little in order to cover their expenses.

'I became a doctor to treat the poor. Don't worry, no doctor ever starved to death. How can I charge a patient who swears he doesn't have any money in his pocket?'

'But we have to live too. How much longer can we run after every pound and let it run in front of us?'

'Ya Yasmine, we will manage between the two of us. Their suffering is not a product we can price according to our convenience.'

Dr Kamel was an idealist at the beginning. He came back from Paris with dreams of treating his poor patients, feeling a deep sense of belonging to them, at the same time a feeling of superiority that gave him the power and insistence to help them 'improve' their lot. But the war broke him. He could never accept how random death was and how cheap life was during war. He would go crazy whenever he heard the leftist leader boast about the number of martyrs that his party had sacrificed during the war. But he didn't truly go crazy until Israel, after invading Beirut, asked the Lebanese government for the remains of an Israeli soldier who had died in Tripoli many years earlier. He was ashamed of himself, as if Israel had made the request to him personally. He saw himself in the mirror like a cockroach, as the lowest of the world's vermin. He said to Yasmine, 'No, we are not cockroaches. The problem is that for us the more a leader kills people the greater he becomes in his people's eyes.'

And so, it took a couple of years after Paris to drive Dr Kamel to despair. He, who had gently led his patients out the door, began yelling at them, 'Now get the hell out of my office!' Above his greying beard, his sideward smile gained a new bitterness. The man of shy patience became an enraged cynic who unleashed a war on his patients, the embodiment of his defeat.

He began spending his nights playing poker after hospital shifts. When he drank enough, he told his friends about the microbes and bacteria of ignorance thriving in the minds of his patients, those resilient germs that defeated him before he could hope to find a cure.

Before long, Dr Kamel did not hesitate to throw his patients out. He no longer found tolerance for their stories, problems and mistakes.

'What can I do for you?'

'Before I tell you what hurts me . . . '

'I don't want to know what comes before. Tell me only about what hurts. Does each one of you have to tell me the story of your life?'

'No, I just want to say that I may have diabetes or a heart condition or something in the kidneys.'

'Since you know what's wrong with you, why the hell do you come to me? Should I lie down and let you examine me?'

'No, Doctor, with all due respect, my married daughter . . . she is very educated . . . and has a lot of degrees . . . I asked her what to take . . . then I asked my husband . . . and he said we had a lot of different medicines in the drawer . . . but I thought I would ask you first.'

'You beast! I asked you what hurt. I did not ask you about your daughter or your husband. Either say what hurts or get the hell out of here so I can deal with the next problem.'

'Wait, I am getting there. Why do you get upset so easily? Last week, when this happened, I boiled some camomile and after I went to the bathroom, I felt much better.'

'Get out of here! Out!'

'Wait, just a second, I'm finishing.'

'May Satan himself finish you! Get out of my face!'

He chased her out of the clinic and she cried out as she ran through the waiting room, 'This doctor is crazy. You can't have a normal conversation with him.'

'They've driven him to madness,' Yasmine told me. 'Even at home, he calls me a donkey like he calls his patients. And what am I supposed to say?'

*

The first time I took Alawiyya to see him, he and Yasmine had just been married. She told him about that chronic swelling in her intestines, and he looked at her and said, 'What is it with you, ya Alawiyya? You're always sick?'

'What can I do, Doctor,' she said, 'if the whole country is sick, how can one be expected to stay healthy?'

He pulled out his prescription pad and wrote, 'Don't see anyone who tires you. Don't listen to the news. No television. No newspapers.'

Alawiyya laughed and said, 'Is that possible? This is for the swelling?'

When we went knocking on his door a second time, many years later, Dr Kamel opened the door himself after looking through the peephole. 'Oh, it's you,' he whispered. 'Come in please.'

He listened to Alawiyya describe her intestinal condition again. This time, he listened to her silently, picked up his pen, scribbled on his prescription pad and handed her a slip. 'This is the only medicine for you,' he said. 'Pray five times a day.'

Alawiyya left the sheet of paper on his desk. Getting up, she said, 'Thank you, I've learnt it by heart. There's no need to take the slip with me.'

Towards the end of the war, this had become Dr Kamel's standard prescription. After a period of silence, during which he loathed the people he had sought to help, he returned to the clinics and never swore at them again.

After that, he could repeat the prescription calmly to his patients, explaining when to take the medicines, how to take it and when to come back. And when a patient would misuse a medicine, he would lift his eyes to the sky. In order not to say, 'You animal,' he would say, 'There is neither will nor strength without God. He is on the side of the patient if they are patient.'

His dream, that the earth could be Heaven, had been shattered. Now, his dream was in Heaven.

12

I have the ticket in my hand and Father's new wife is impatient to see me off to Canada.

She looked in my direction from the corner of her eye and pursed her lips as she explained to her sister what she had planned do to with my room after I left the house.

'I don't want it cluttered with anything. I'm going to send the bed and the closet to the village and turn it into an Arabic room. The Hajj likes to sit on the floor. You know how old age makes the bottom heavy.'

I kept quiet when she said that Father's bottom had become heavy, and so did he. But as soon as she said the words, she glanced at me fearfully, and Father's fingers stretched towards her from his place on the sofa, asking her to help him rise. This was his way of telling me that there was no need to reprimand her with a strong word or even a glare. I looked at Father. His fingers were no longer straight. They were bent awkwardly at the knuckles, like his back. His gaze was lifeless, and each time he tried to stand up, he struggled to raise his body from his seat.

After their pilgrimage to Mecca, he returned even more hunchbacked than before while she sat up proudly like a bride in the car that had been decorated by the family to carry them from the airport to the house.

His illness made him fear her and fear losing her care. After that trip, he said to me with tears in his eyes, 'Listen ya Maryam, my daughter, I made you a little hill of sand, for you, in your name, with my own hands, so it may be written in the heavens that you'll visit Mecca one day. I prayed for you and I cried as I asked God to make you happy with Amin and your future in Canada.'

My stepmother took this as an opportunity to join in enthusiastically, 'God willing. And just as his Canadian wife—God bless her soul—went to Heaven with her clothes on, God willing, your husband will veil you, ya Maryam, and you too will become one of the faithfuls. Or do you think one can enter Heaven with her hair, hands and neck uncovered?'

'You keep Heaven for yourself. When I get there, Amin and I will sort things out among ourselves,' I said.

Father interrupted, 'Did you get everything yet? What else do you need? Is everything packed?'

I had packed all my things in two blue suitcases, bought to match the blue suit I would be travelling in. I wanted to look elegant for Amin who would pick me up at the airport and smile at me shyly, just as he had done twenty-five years earlier. His smile used to tremble nervously in those days when I would not even look at his face, so he would understand clearly that I would never marry him or anybody else in the family. In those days, I dreamt of stretching my wings, flying as far away as I could from the family.

Amin, calm and rational as always, respected my decision. When I made my feelings clear, he did not even express his intentions formally to the family. Before leaving for Canada, he said to me, 'As you wish. If you change your mind, write to me.'

When he asked me to marry him the second time, I was stunned with happiness. This time, I was the one who said to him, 'As you wish. And if you change your mind after you leave, call me.'

*

The second time he asked, we were sitting together on the patio at their village house on a rather cool summer night. It was the same old fresh air and the same view of the vineyards except for the number of houses and villas that had multiplied in recent years. The seats had changed from chairs made of wood and straw to ones made of white plastic. I looked at his face which had grown tired and old in the four years since his Canadian wife had died, leaving him with two teenage boys and a ten-year-old girl.

This time, I consented without a moment's thought, and he put his hand over mine and gave me a smile that sat lightly on my heart. 'I miss you,' he said, and I looked at the lines the years had carved around his warm eyes, and anxious to hide inside them, I said, 'I miss you too.'

Father, his new wife, and my brother and sisters were all delighted that I was no longer a mysterious woman existing outside the authority of a man. In their minds, there was now a chance that I would take the veil like Amin's first wife. They forgot that Amin had never demanded it of her. In fact, his heart danced with joy to her brown locks and the little blonde eyelashes that she thickened with brown mascara. It was she who insisted on the veil after one of Amin's relatives had led her along that path during a summer visit to Lebanon.

At her funeral service, the village women remembered her fondly. 'By God, either be a Muslim like her or don't be one at all. She was a queen who outdid the king.' They all agreed.

Amin's wife would never skip a prayer. She fixed the veil into place with a pin just as the women advised her, and asked, to their delight, 'Which is more correct, to wear the pin on the right or the left?' They told her to wear the pin clipped under her chin, so the veil would not slip back from her head. Because if a strange man saw as much as a single hair, they warned, she would hang by it on doomsday, and each uncovered hair would burn in the grave.

When Amin's wife began to get sick with cancer, she asked to be buried in her husband's southern Lebanese village, even though there were many Muslim graveyards in Canada. As they walked in her funeral procession, the women imagined her lifting her arms upwards in order not to be dirtied by the wood. In their minds, she was lifting her body from the bottom of the coffin so she could meet her God clean.

*

Um Talal, too, eventually made her way to North America, long after she had told her story to Alawiyya.

For her, there was no difference between strangers, friends or distant acquaintances. She would tell and repeat her life story like a record, for anyone who would listen. She would roll the stories in her mouth and arrange them the way she might arrange stuffed grape leaves between her fingers. The women in the building would gather in her house in the morning to exchange stories of their problems, each carrying the ingredients of the big meal of the day on a tray to work as she talked. And Abu Talal, in his little room next to the kitchen, would hear everything she said about him, describing his penis, and would imagine her hands dangling from the wrists and swaying right and left to demonstrate how soft it had become, 'like a rag.'

After the women left, he would say, 'You are a woman who loves nothing in the world except money and telling tales. If you could count how many hairs you have on your bottom, you would have counted them and told the world how many.'

'I will tell the world about your testicles too that have become rotten.'

'And what about this woman Alawiyya? Haven't you told her enough already? I know that you love telling stories and she seems to love listening to them. Let's hope she doesn't print our stories in her book, or that would be the end of our reputation. You put Scheherazade and Reuters to shame!'

'If you hadn't started going around, telling people that I wouldn't let you near me, I wouldn't have had to tell any story.'

From his bed, Abu Talal would cry when he heard Um Talal beating their young son Hammoudi whenever she caught him with drugs. Or when she would invite the neighbours to help her with her daughter Zeina whose wails—according to the healer—were the work of spirits that would not leave her body until they were beaten and burnt out of it. The neighbours would descend upon Zeina with their shoes and cigarettes, and when she screamed, Um Talal was convinced that she had heard the voices of her mother, her sister, Zahra, and her grandmother. 'When they would ask me to drive Zeina to the hospital, I would go home with a stomachache that wouldn't leave me for days. Every time I thought of her little body, beaten.'

*

Abu Talal lost his authority with the coming of the war to his house and his street, where he was master. He retired after a militiaman slapped him in the face when he didn't stop at a checkpoint.

'I am a man of government, boy.'

'So what? You have to stop like anybody else. Show me your identification card.'

And when Abu Talal refused and said, 'I am Abu Talal and everybody knows me. You have the audacity to cross men of government? One day we will show you;' that's when the militiaman gave him a swift slap on the cheek. From that day, he did not leave the house except to go to the hospital. He never wanted to see the street again, where the government held no sway. And when occasionally he would put on his policeman's uniform and gallivant around the house, Um Talal would mock him to no end. With his pride gone, he lived and waited for the end, killing himself slowly—with sweets and scotch.

Gone was the Abu Talal of the old, who had one day married Hélène, an Armenian woman, and when she dared to complain he hit her on the head with his gun and made her bleed.

'If I agreed to divorce her, I would have to pay her 3,000 dollars alimony,' he would say. But when he did decide to divorce Hélène, he sent Um Talal to make her life miserable. Every day, Um Talal would go to Hélène's house and curse her at the top of her lungs, until *she* asked for the divorce and voluntarily gave up the alimony.

Abu Talal had been cruel to Um Talal from the beginning, but with time she had started seeing him as her man and feel inside his pockets for whatever his street rounds yielded that day. One day, he almost got her a precious little alarm clock which he tried to steal but failed.

'What did you bring home today, ya Abu Talal?'

'You won't believe what happened. I almost brought you a clock but it didn't work out.'

'Why not?'

'I was doing my round in the Mutanabbi market downtown, when the devil told me: "Ya Abu Talal, there is a new one in the district, beautiful like the moon." So I went down there as I felt a hankering for her.'

'You wretched man! And you tell me this to my face? Did you pay her too?'

'No, no. I'm getting there. I told her we could exchange services. Anyway, afterwards, she went into the bathroom to wash up, and as I was putting my clothes on, I saw the dainty alarm clock which I quickly hid under my hat. But as she was coming out of the bathroom and I was turning to leave, the alarm went off. Turns out, the bitch had set the alarm to go off at the end of our time together. So I ran out and she chased after me, screaming, "Thief! Thief!" I couldn't get away fast enough.'

'And you didn't think to turn it off before leaving?'

'I didn't get the chance.'

She taunted him about the clock, and forgot the part about his betrayal with the prostitute. But when he became impotent and started lying in bed all day, she would taunt him about the smallest thing, even a drink of water.

The day he drank a whole bottle of whisky, straight, and wet his bed, she lost it. When she approached him to move him off the bed to change the sheets and his clothes, the smell of whisky and urine in her nose, he reached out with his hand to grope her between her legs. 'Please, oh, please. Let me just touch it with my fingers.'

'I will show you what fingers can do!'

She left the room and came back with the rattan cane she used to hit her son with.

'Take this! And that! Begin counting the whippings you gave me when you were strong. Do you remember how you raped me? Do you remember how many times you made my head bleed? Do you remember when you made me sick in my youth? Tell me, who ever mistreated you and hurt you that way? Do you remember how many other women there were?'

Abu Talal's eyes swung with his head from side to side, and as soon as she walked out of the room, leaving him in pain, he crawled to the closet and reached for the small gun that his son Talal had found in an abandoned flat and left with him for safekeeping before going to America. Abu Talal shot himself in the head.

She mourned him, wailed and recited poems at his funeral. She asked for his forgiveness as he lay in his shroud. 'It's the children who drove me crazy, ya Abu Talal, and you drove me crazy. Forgive me; God forgive you. I still have to look after this addict of a son and a deranged daughter. But you and I are better off this way.'

Um Talal loved her son Hammoudi though, and boasted of his resourcefulness when he learnt to trade in the war. He would smuggle gas from the East to the West side and sell it at a high price, or roam the city in search of electric cables and cut them down to sell by the kilogram. When his pockets were full, his mother forgave him for the expensive treatment she had to pay for his addiction in Nabatiye. When he came back, healthy as an athlete, she said, 'Now you're well. Just don't go back to drugs. This is the last time I will pay for your recovery. I'm not worried about you. You will find a way to make money.'

'He's blessed, this child of mine,' she would tell the neighbours when they visited. Every day she would knock on my door, and update me on her news over a cup of coffee.

One night, Hammoudi was lying on a cardboard box, contemplating the city, and imagining his mother's breasts. His body felt numb, his eyes glassy, seeing nothing but her breasts in the dark sky. He could smell his mother's cooking that lingered on her clothes when in the night, afraid of the dark, he would go to her bed. There, in the folds of her full breasts hanging low on her belly, he would feel safe and fall asleep.

He would imagine himself returning to her belly.

He would imagine himself becoming a child again the next morning, to knock on the door and be welcomed by his mother like back in his childhood days. 'Hammoudi, you balm of my heart, how could you go wandering like this without giving me a clue to where you're going?' He would imagine her touching his chest back when he could stand in front of her mirror with his shoulders broad like a bridge. 'Are you a man or a bridge? May your height and breadth bury me first. There's no one like you,' his mother would say proudly.

That's when he felt that the whole world was his possession. Now, he was shunned by the world, by her, and by his body that had betrayed him. He put down his face on the filthy cardboard and fell asleep. The destruction of the city became the destruction of his soul, and the destruction of his body was but an extension of its rubble. And the punctures left by the morphine syringes could have been the holes made by bullets, explosions and shrapnel in the building walls.

But Hammoudi did not die of beatings, nor of an overdose of cocaine which almost stopped his heart several times. He was to die alone in the Monastery of the Cross, and it was a nun who covered his face with a white sheet and cried for him, for his lonely death without his mother at his side. She held him as he cried until the moment of his death. He said to her, 'I beg you, I want to see my mother before I die.' But the nun didn't have a phone number to call her or drive him home when the roads between the two sides of the city had been closed. She held his cold hands and didn't let go until she felt them turn into blocks of ice in her palms, and saw his eyes turn into clouds of death. She shut his eyes with her fingers, crossed herself, and mourned the boy who had said to her, 'Forgive me, Mother, why didn't you come and see me? Didn't you know that I was dying?'

*

Um Talal would travel to America to live with her son Talal. And Alawiyya? Did she flee after hearing the story of Um Talal? Or was she left with just another story to burden her—another story, with uncertain truths and motives, to find a place in her novel?

13

I don't know them.

Who are these people who can so easily get lost in the labyrinth of my fate? Why do they keep looking for me in mortuaries, asylums and women's jails? Do they fear that my disappearance would mean the murder of the characters in the novel, a final erasure of their names, faces and homes? They almost had me convinced that I had killed them all. For years, I would search my hands for the blood-stains and try to remember my victims. But it was pointless.

Who are these people who chase after me, demanding that I tell them their stories, when in the end they will only believe the tales they have told themselves? Frankly, I would love to convene a meeting with all of them and murder them all, one after the other, the way an author kills off his characters mercilessly to bring the action to an end.

Could I have already killed them by committing them to a distant memory? It's possible. And it's possible too that I may have followed them myself to their deaths when I buried their memories.

I do not know them, and I'm sticking to my story. Otherwise, I'd have to bear their long stares which confront me not only with dis-appointment but also pity—for her who has long lost her memory.

I admit that I fled from them.

I fled only because otherwise I would have had to devise a plan to corner each character and kill them separately. Dr Kamel, like me, considered writing a prescription for poison and dispensing it to the patients whom he had loved and who had failed him.

They will not be convinced that I don't know them. Like liars, they cling on and persist, denying that they were the ones who started it by muddling the peace of my seclusion and crowding my mind for years with their demands for stories with clear beginnings and endings. They will never admit that they asked too much of me. Who am I but a person who can hardly remember her own beginnings? Look at me. How I went missing. How I became a fugitive from my fate.

They only follow me because they think I can make heroes out of them. I am tired of running into them on the streets.

'Aren't you Alawiyya Subuh?'

'Yes. What do you want? Do you know me?'

'Of course I know you. I told you my story a long time ago, and I have yet to read it. Why did you lie to us, and burden us with the labour of telling and remembering? Where did you disappear?'

'God is on the side of the patient,' I say, turning away, in annoyance, from the question and the person asking it.

After scrutinizing the face, voice and features, I would start suspecting that I had once known that person. Or I may have known a similar name and face. For, aren't all women pregnant with the same story? The story of the foetus in one belly is the same one inside all women's bellies.

They follow me. Even when I stand in front of the mirror to look at myself, they crowd the view so that I cannot see my face. Sometimes I see the face of Ibtisam, and sometimes the expressions of Maryam, and at other times I make out her mother, or perhaps Um Talal. I put on my clothes and leave the house, and must look down at my feet as I walk, to check whether the legs carrying me are the skinny legs of Maryam or mine. At times, I get home and expect my mother's empty bed, empty as my heart after her death, is the bed of Maryam's mother, and I ask myself, 'Is the emptiness of this bed my mother's or Maryam's mother's?' Even when walking down the street, I look at the faces, get lost and wonder, 'Which one is Maryam? Who is Ibtisam? Which one is Um Talal? Who are they, all of them? How would I recognize them in the mysterious faces before me?'

One day, after a long search for her, I found Maryam on the street, and as soon as I started telling her story back to her, she ran from me, looking behind her with fear. I lost her again in the human profiles, some bent or slanted, others twisted or broken, until I could no longer tell her face apart from the other faces, or her story from the other stories. Then I saw a woman who looked like Ibtisam. Once I made sure of her features and she too smiled at me from afar; I asked her, 'Are you Ibtisam?'

'How did you know my name?'

'You're the one who told me your name and your story.' She looked at me, stunned, nibbling her lower lip.

'I'm sorry but I don't remember. Perhaps it's another Ibtisam who spoke to you?'

'No, it was you.'

'If you want to look for the other Ibtisam, I'm free today. I can use an escape from my housework and my husband Jalal who is at home today like a weight on the heart. I could use some down time if you need a partner for your search for Ibtisam.'

I could have been mistaken but it could certainly have been Ibtisam, for she was the one who was surprised when I referred to the day Jalal had beaten her when there wasn't enough meat in the bean stew. She looked at me with confusion, 'Jalal did that? By God, I had forgotten . . . ' Then she nibbled on the inside of her cheek and said, 'How can one be told their own story and listen as if they've never heard it before? Maybe it's thick skin that one grows but I don't remember growing any thick skin. On the contrary, when I touch it, I find it still smooth.'

My God, they're driving me crazy. They all laughed or smiled or grew sad when I asked them about their names. They were all scared of me, looked at me suspiciously, then hurried away from me and all my questions.

I went back to my old papers to make sure that the handwriting was mine.

I found neither beginnings nor endings, only a silence resembling that of Ibtisam, and an American passport with Um Talal's name and picture on it. I wondered, 'Who brought it to my drawer and slipped it between my papers? Did Um Talal go to America or did she give me her passport so I would keep it safe for her? How did she leave without it?'

Their words came back to me, this time with their voices, and I heard them much more clearly than I had read them on the yellowed pages. The scribbled letters looked like the new, unfamiliar signposts I now see on the streets.

I could hear Maryam and Ibtisam talking from inside my papers. I stopped and peeped in on their conversation. Maryam was saying, 'What's new about that playwright Alawiyya introduced us to?'

'I think he's gone mad. He's been writing the same play since the beginning of the war—about the war, but he hasn't actually written anything or managed to understand anything.'

'Do you know if his characters are the same ones as those in the novel of Alawiyya Subuh?'

'That's what they told people at the beginning. Nobody knows. Yes, that sounds right. Alawiyya Subuh. I've heard her name before.'

Maryam fell silent for a few moments, then she added, 'Maybe it's true. Who knows if I'll emigrate too? Thousands of people are leaving. But who is Abbas? Oh . . . Abbas. He's the one I loved for over ten years and met once a month at the hotel—in the novel.'

'What do you mean "in the novel"? You were just with him yesterday in the hotel, and you took sandwiches with you, and you slept together there.'

'Maybe in the novel.'

'Are you mad, ya Maryam? You've started forgetting even before you've left for Canada?'

'No, I'm not mad. Alawiyya is mad.'

'And Zuhair?'

'Zuhair has probably gone mad as well—nobody knows anything about him. I don't know if it was Alawiyya or his characters that drove him to madness. Zuhair's hero would go to sleep a communist, but when Zuhair would visit him the next day he would find that he'd become a banker, or a shoe merchant. Then Zuhair would start writing the story of the communist who became a merchant. But when he would go back to check on the fellow the next day, he would find him praying all day, that he'd become a fundamentalist. Then the next day, he would become something else, and so forth. How could he not go mad? How was he ever supposed to finish writing?'

'Do you think that is what really happened?' Maryam asked, 'Where is Alawiyya now, and where is Zuhair? What could have happened to them?'

I hear them arguing inside my papers and do not recognize the person they are discussing. Who is this Zuhair? His name sounds familiar. I seem to recall falling in love, a long time ago, with a man by that name. His anecdotes used to make me laugh, until he started making jokes about the comrades at the party newspaper. I did not find it funny when he said they made the office stink with their cheap Kufta sandwiches.

I think we left each other, in the end, because he made fun of the smell of poverty that reeked from my friends' mouths with the exact same laugh that Kareem gave when he discovered, on the first night they had sex, that Ibtisam was a virgin.

I left Zuhair for another man who smelt of Kufta when he laughed but I never noticed. I later left this man as well, after watching the vein thicken in his neck before my eyes. In the last days of the war, I was in the lift with this man, and I asked him as he was fixing his hair in the mirror, 'What's the first thing you will do, darling, when the war ends?' 'The first thing I'll do is leave you,' he said, without a moment's hesitation; then he turned and kissed me, as if he were joking. I did not laugh or return his smile, nor did I understand at the time what he had just said to me.

Whenever I think of those years, I remember his words, 'I love you, I love you, I love you. But I can't marry a woman from another sect. Love is one thing, marriage is another.'

'But I don't want to get married.'

'But I do. I want to get married and have children too.'

He cried as he spoke but I didn't join him. I laughed and lamented the years lost. And since that day, this man's memory brings back that stench of stale Kufta, which Zuhair hated, to my nose.

*

Too many faces, names, voices . . . I'm no longer sure whether Maryam is not the same person as Yasmine, whether Abu Yusuf died, or the playwright went crazy or simply disappeared. I'm no longer sure why I called him Zuhair in the first place, when that wasn't his name, and nobody ever confirmed his real name. I'm not certain whether the abortion was Maryam's or Ibtisam's, Yasmine's or mine, or of other women and men in the war whom I've never known. All of us aborted foetuses and dreams and memories. The city aborted the city, the street aborted the street and the buildings aborted their walls. The villages aborted the villages, and humans aborted their lives. I aborted my hand, so I wouldn't have to write.

I try to sleep to clear my head but, after a momentary reprieve from them and their questions, I feel Maryam poking me in the depths of my sleep to turn on the lights and listen to her talking. I go to my desk carrying her voice in my ears, suspended between drowsiness and sleep, pouring onto the page whatever the ink can remember, emptying it from her voice which has made it impossible for me to sleep. I go to bed relieved but Maryam again draws me out of my sleep. She asks if she can borrow my bed, if I can leave my house for some time and go to the street or a cafe or any other place, so she and Abbas can make love one last time before she leaves the country for ever. Then comes the memory of Jalal and Ibtisam on their wedding night when he discovered that she wasn't a virgin. How he lied to himself when he said that he did not care about her past, yet how for years thereafter he would enter her as if into a crevice teeming with demons.

And just when I think Maryam is gone, she returns to ask me, 'Should I tell Abbas that I'm leaving, or should I save him the sight of my tears? Will he find another Maryam to cut the nails on his feet, toe by toe? Will he find a Maryam who can make him a hero and a king in her bed when he meets her once a month? Or will he just go to his wife and make out of her the heroine of the forbidden, a mother-wife of no sexual urge, who can please him with her modesty as she curses at the television during the "shameless" advertisements about sanitary pads?'

No wonder I cannot sleep when they crowd my head so. What business is it of mine to keep track of who lived, who changed, who went crazy and who died? What I want is to watch the trees and the colour of the sea. I want to listen to the quiet I dream of and care for nothing but the trees growing on my new street, in a city without trees. The trees are still very small; they need a long time to grow and cast a shadow over me while I walk, a long time until I delight in the leaves being played with by the breeze. I want to follow the growth of the tiny trees that the city has planted. Will they grow fast enough so I can enjoy them before I die?

14

Was Alawiyya erased in the water and mud? I know that if I should find her, I would say to her, 'Underline what you have erased, ya Alawiyya.'

No, it is not I who says this but Zuhair who said and wrote.

His neighbours gathered the papers of his play spread all over his house, floating on water and mud, the colour of his blood. After his disappearance, they found a single sentence repeated, its letters sitting over the erased words, 'Underline what has been erased, ya Alawiyya.'

And so, the neighbours began asking one another with curiosity, 'Who is this Alawiyya? Is she the one who made him disappear, or the one who killed him? Is she the one who erased his play? Why else would he ask her to confess to the secrets and underline what has been erased?'

When I find her, I will ask Alawiyya, 'Are you scared of underlining what has been erased, or are you scared of divulging all those secrets?'

*

Zuhair too disappeared. He exited the novel after telling Alawiyya that her imagination was weak, that the play he wanted to write must follow the imagination of the war and absorb it as a whole. As he took out the papers of the novel, he reprimanded her, 'Believe me, even if I wanted to write about the same characters, I would never write about them in this way! Not only are you conspiring against me, to make me hear only what you hear, and see only what you see, the target of your scheme is also the common people. Maybe Interpol has sent you to drive me crazy and make me write what they want me to write!'

At first Alawiyya thought he was joking. Clearly, he was mixing up theatre and life, just as she sometimes could not keep apart the lives lived from the stories written. I too thought Zuhair was joking when he said, 'Don't tell Alawiyya anything any more. Don't even greet her. She wants to drive me crazy with that novel. God knows what she has in mind for you. Everything about our old agreement turned out to be lies.'

'All right then, you can keep the characters including me. But choose other ways of telling their stories.'

'No, none of these stories interest me. They have no value or consequence.'

In Dr Zuhair's (he had finished medical school after all) search for the theatre of war, he became scared of Alawiyya and me, so much so that if he saw us on the street he would cross to the pavement on the other side. He wrote as a way of understanding the war; but when we spoke to him, the words would hit against his ears and fall to the ground. And so, he stopped talking to everyone, and would only talk to himself, alone at home. Clearly he had gone mad, though I'm not sure why. Even his patients, when they began telling him about their troubles, became suspicious of him, and he of them. So he stopped practising, just in case they too were spies.

But he saw Alawiyya as the primary threat. So, one day, he invited her to dinner at his house, and after they peeled the garlic together and put the stew on the stove to simmer, he handed her a glass of beer with a small plate of peanuts. And just when she relaxed, he confronted her with questions about whom she was working for and what scheming he was the target of. She couldn't run out the door fast enough when she realized that he was serious and he, who was already terrified of her, felt the same.

After that, Zuhair would sit in his house alone, reading and rereading the newspapers he had kept since the beginning of the war.

He would cut out reports of politicians' press conferences and news of massacres, as if to understand them. He would cut dates in red and black, stack the snippets on his desk and read them again before writing through the night. Occasionally, he would go to the door and look at the people on the street, and hide the sentences with his hands from spying eyes, like a little boy hiding the answers during an exam. He would fall asleep at dawn and wake up in the afternoon to write again. No one expected to find him at his clinic any longer. Every time he checked the writing of the night before, he would find that the number of casualties had changed. It seemed futile to write down an account that would soon erase itself. He would turn left and right and pretend to fall asleep in his bed, to see who would try to enter his house in secret to make changes on his papers. Who changed the leftist protagonist into a fundamentalist? Who changed the patriot into a traitor? Who changed any sense of standard he could hope to find in his papers?

'It must have been Alawiyya,' he would say to himself. 'I wish I knew how she entered my house and played with my writing. Tell her, I never knew her nor do I want to know her. Nor do I need her characters, for I will find my own. She must leave me alone. Every time I look in my papers, I find that she has put in there what she wants. She changes everything or erases the words with water and mud.'

*

'Poor Zuhair,' Alawiyya said to me, 'but why did he fixate on me in particular? All I ever wanted was for us to work together. I never doubted his gift or sincerity. If he hadn't insisted on confronting the war, he could have written something beautiful. I wish he had stuck to medicine and left the business of writing alone . . . '

It was true. If I ever loved Zuhair, it was because of how much Alawiyya adored him. For a while they were like twins. Each would run to the other the moment they heard something worth telling.

I saw him standing next to Saint Rita Church near his house in Ras Beirut, carrying a stack of pamphlets in his arms, which he was handing out to passing cars. I drove up to him and rolled down my window. It was raining hard but he didn't care that his head and clothes were wet. His face had grown sad and pale, his body emaciated. He handed me a pamphlet without recognizing me. I took it from him without trying to start a conversation or look him straight in the eyes. 'There you are, madam. Here's a letter for you madam. See to it that you read it,' he said and turned to the car behind me. I saw him banging with his fist on the next car's closed window when the driver refused to open it. I parked my car by the side of the road and began reading his letter dated 19 March 1990.

*

This letter is the summary of the facts surrounding the problem of the exploitation of some of the unnatural circumstances in this country, and the immersion of citizens in the concerns of daily survival, and the dangers confronting the nation. Its purpose is to illuminate the various contexts of recent events.

*

I have already clarified the problem in a letter dated 20 November 1988 and in another dated 28 October 1989, both of which I delivered to authorities on all levels, and to officials charged with matters of security, spirituality and unionization, including unions (of journalists, doctors, lawyers, writers, intellectuals, educators), student associations and committees of higher education as well as foreign embassies that have expressed interest in restoring the local situation to normalcy, and to the board of trustees of the Arab University, which has always called for conferences in matters of communications and education in the intellectual resistance to Zionist propaganda. The report goes as follows:

I was working in the field of medicine and had intended to transition into dramaturgy with humanistic motives that aspired to a total view of the human condition. From my experiences, reflections and first-hand exploration of the lines of conspiracy facing the country, I had ideas for a play that might serve man in the values of justice and all that is good, and of peace everywhere. I began recording my impressions, memories and ideas in addition to clippings from newspapers in a log that would form the basis for my writings. But in April 1987, certain individuals began entering into my flat in secret, where I lived by myself, during the day when I was away or at night while I slept. They began leaving signs and symbols until I realized that all I had written had been stolen and replaced by fraudulent documents. Since then, various international agencies began contacting me, indirectly, through the media—TV and the newspapers—using coded speeches and messages whose veiled meaning would escape the normal reader or listener. But they had intended for these messages to catch my attention as they meant for me to notice when they added dots on words, or complete sentences. They wanted me to collaborate with them intellectually and literarily in the service of Zionism, convincing me either by promises or status or threats of death. They pointed out to me that I was like an island surrounded by sea, with no hope of escape, to which I responded with several points, including the following:

That work in the field of theatre and literature is a noble aspiration motivated by a feeling of internal well-being of the kind that a writer feels in the search for truth and the contribution of good to the people, and which he would inevitably lose should he diverge from the path or be tempted by profit.

You have the power to obliterate my body but I refuse to give up my freedom.

For five months, their dispatches continued to arrive until they realized that they wouldn't be able to realize their goal or impose their views. And so, since September 1987, they have resorted to a new method, which is invisible harassment and physical harm. They have used modern and advanced devices to send radio waves that press on the skull, the bones and sometimes around the heart or the eye or the area around the gut. Intensifying this activity during the night has been their way to inflict sleep deprivation on me.

*

Many times, I ran away from them in Beirut, and escaped to other countries, thinking that I could be far away from their invisible reach. But, their practices followed me on my journey on the plane and abroad. It became clear to me that Interpol was following me, so I sent letters to the American Congress and the United Nations, and the permanent members of its Security Council by way of foreign consulates, explaining the problem to security agencies in possession of modern equipment, satellites, the goal of which is the maintenance of security but which some big countries abuse in contradiction with their official stance on global terror and what they profess on the subject of human rights and the freedom of thought and conscience. In view of their continual harassment despite my clear response that I refused to surrender to become anyone's puppet or parrot or spy, I am threatening to perform a hunger strike to the death if the agencies in question do not stop targeting me and meddling with my papers.

*

I will stop eating completely in twelve days, drinking only small amounts of water during this period. I put these facts before all. And I am ready to present documentary evidence to any formal investigative committee that would look into the signals that have been sent through various media to effect the terrorization of the mind and the piracy of the brain in order to generalize the law of the jungle and transform the world into a theatre of the absurd.

*

Finally, I say to those who are behind all that is happening: you have
fallen prisoner to your lesser nature, crossing the line from agents of
the dark to authors of the absurd, which no theatre in the world has
depicted. Beware of reducing the mind to the justification of all,
because when justification becomes the absolute horizon for action,
from this only absolute evil can follow.

*

I read the letter underneath his pale stare. There goes the fate of
another one of Alawiyya's protagonists, with a sad beginning and
end. Either she told me about his ending or I told her after she had
forgotten all about me.

I must bid him farewell. Something inside me tells me that I must.
I went to the street and entered the building, knocked on the door of
his flat on the main floor, and imagined that he would open the door
and not recognize me. Or that he wouldn't open the door after seeing
me through the peephole and assuming that Alawiyya had sent me.
His white door was covered with dust and a big lock hung from the
gate. The doorman, the neighbours—all had a different version of
what had happened to him, who he was and what his name was.
Some said he had fasted until he died, and that when the smell of his
corpse left the flat, they entered to find him lying on the floor with
his burnt papers all around him. Dates, defeats, massacres, names,
addresses were scattered about in black and red and grey.

'But when did he commit suicide?' I asked the neighbour who
described how he was found.

'I'm not sure. Early 90s, or perhaps the late 90s—I no longer
remember.'

Then another neighbour volunteered that the reason someone
had entered his flat was not the smell but a flood in his bathroom
which spilt into the hallway—a mixture of water and blood. But a
third neighbour said, 'Lies!'

They all disagreed and each had their own version to tell. According to one story, he never died but left for Saudi Arabia to practise medicine. And according to another, he walked to his village in Mount Lebanon during the 1983 war, where he was found murdered. And according to yet another story, that flat never belonged to a doctor by that name but was left empty at the beginning of the war by a man who went abroad and left the place in the care of a woman who would clean it once a month. In all these stories, I got lost. Whether he walked South or North, eastward or up to the mountains, he had gone in search of the country that was his dream to write about in a play. Could it be that he was the victim of nothing more than his delusion that a play could bring back to a citizen his youth or sanity, or restore his sense of right and wrong? Who was Zuhair after all—a man who was a doctor or a playwright or a standard citizen or Alawiyya or me? We may never know, for no story is more plausible than any other. Even if he is not one of the thousands swallowed by mass graves, wells and valleys full of skulls, and if his body were to be found, according to General Abu Suleiman in a report I read recently: 'It is impossible to identify the bodies. And he who has not appeared by now is considered legally dead;' and so, it would be impossible to verify that he ever existed. The man could have existed to whom I told these stories, or he could be a figment of my imagination. More reason to find Alawiyya. For when I told her everything, she made me a promise I believed—that she would be the keeper of our stories.

15

That night, I couldn't believe my eyes.

I could not believe I was watching Alawiyya talking on the television screen. She was wearing make-up, something that I'd thought was alien to her. There was a thick line of kohl on her eyes and a coat of mascara weighing heavily on her eyelids, so much that it seemed to slow down her eyes' movements and threaten to make them fall any minute to the ground. Her hair was not scruffy and wild as usual. It was coiffed and fixed with hair spray. Her long tight dress had nothing to do with her. The only thing in that frame reminding one of Alawiyya was her voice and the motion of her eyes.

She was promoting a magazine she had started editing and the show's hostess was asking her about her opinion of newly famous singers, other women's magazines and several topics which I no longer remember.

I couldn't believe my eyes and ears. Was it really Alawiyya speaking, or another woman carrying the same name and voice? Had she fled into a safe world where she could write forgetfully?

I don't know.

It's hard to tell.

The last thing she had said before disappearing into her bottle was, 'Ya Maryam, the large voids have filled up my chest and I'm suffocating. I can't fill up a single sheet of paper, even if it's a matter of finding out whether I am dead or alive. First, I have to empty all the voids from my chest. But how can they leave me, ya Maryam, if I haven't even understood what they are about? I am terrified to think that it may take as many years to get rid of them as I have carried them inside me.'

She stood up, looked around and found nothing but voids. Each of us had dug a well inside her body with our own hands, then dived into it, closing the lid behind us until the city became an upturned one and the facades of the tall buildings began to look like the walls of wells. We could see our faces and bodies on the city walls like we saw in the wells' waters.

Just like us, Alawiyya had dug a well for herself with her own hands, and when her hands and feet grew tired, she leant on her eyelashes, her mouth, her tongue, her ears. Every now and then, she would lift her face over the threshold to check if we had climbed out of our wells. When she did not find anybody standing, she lowered her face to our wells' mouths and shouted our names, one by one, and waited. But all she ever heard was the echo of her voice; and in our wells, we heard our voices in it.

*

Before she left, I would sometimes run into her on Hamra Street and we would greet each other like formal acquaintances.

'How are you?'

'Fine. I'm all right. And you?'

'Fine, I'm right where I was the last time you saw me. And you?'

'All right. What's new?'

'What can I tell you? I'm just like myself, and I'm doing as well as this country. I teeter this way and that,' she would laugh, 'but I'm managing.'

'It's fine. We're all in the same boat.'

'Let's keep in touch.'

'We'll see, God willing. Call me.'

'Definitely.'

She would then go on her way and I'd go on mine, and looking back for a moment at her broad shoulders walking away from me towards an unknown, I would feel a certain chagrin. I would wonder, like Ibtisam, 'Is it the war or the years? Is it defeat or just life?'

I did not know.

I don't know.

*

When I decided to leave the country and went looking for Alawiyya in her house where she lived with her mother, I found myself invading the privacy of their kingdom. But I needed to tell somebody, and who else was there to talk to?

Ibtisam no longer listened and even if she heard, she would choose not to understand; and Yasmine could not care less about the outcome of my worldly journey, for she only cared about my ending in the heavens.

Abbas maybe? Should I bother telling him that I'm leaving him to emigrate and marry another man? Should I tell him that if I hadn't had him in my life all those years, my soul would have been torn away from my body and my shadow away from any light? But what could he say in reply? Who could I talk to among my relatives and friends? None of them was interested in leaving the bottle in which they hid, in smelling an odour other than that of their limbs, in touching a space beyond their body's surface, or feeling anything with the tip of their fingers other than tired folds of their own flesh.

As she listened, Alawiyya at least seemed to care about the fate of her friend. She kept asking me the same question, 'Even you are leaving? Can that be possible?'

I can't remember whether she tried to dissuade me once she realized that the decision was final. Instead, she began lecturing me about life. Imagine! She, Alawiyya, who had spent the last few years hiding in her flat! I listened to her and did not raise questions, either about her wisdom or her writing. I felt certain that she would not be able to handle it. During the war, when she saw the posters of martyrs covering the walls of the city, she would look the other way and cross quickly to the other side of the road. Their stares demanded of her that she ask them to descend from the walls.

* * *

Who was the one writing then, she or Zuhair? The handwriting on the pages in front of her was illegible. She began reading the story from the beginning but the tales overlapped, and the names of Ibtisam, Maryam, Yasmine, Zuhair, Kareem, Mustafa, Abu Yusuf, my mother and her mother and the others did not behave like a list of names entering the story in a sequence. At times, we all became Maryams, Alawiyyas, Yasmines, Fatimas, Samiyyas; and Zuhair, Kareem, Abu Yusuf, Abu Talal, Dr Kamel would become different names for the same protagonist. She pored over her papers in search of clues. Her fingers felt sore and her hand feverish. But she could not be certain of anything.

Nothing was certain.

GLOSSARY

Abu. Father of. For example, Abu Ali, or Father of Ali, is used to refer to the father by his relation to his oldest son, his anticipated son, or his daughter if he has only daughters.

Bayk/Bey. Title for the governor of a district or province in the Ottoman Empire.

Dabka. A folk dance performed by men and women in much of the Arab Middle East.

Durzi. A member of a political and religious sect of Islamic origin, living chiefly in Lebanon and Syria. The Druze broke away from the Ismaili Muslims in the eleventh century; they are regarded as heretical by the Muslim community at large.

Fatiha. The opening chapter, or sura, of the Holy Koran.

Habibi. My dear.

Hajj. The Muslim pilgrimage to Mecca that takes place in the last month of Islamic calendar, and that all Muslims are expected to make at least once during their lifetime.

Hajji. An honorific given to an elderly person or a person who has performed the pilgrimage to Mecca.

Hula Massacre. The Hula Massacre took place between 31 October and 1 November 1948. Hula, a village in Lebanon, 3 km west of River Litani, was captured on 24 October by the Carmeli Brigade of the Israel Defence Forces without any resistance. Women and children were expelled and most of the males, aged between 15 and 60, were shot. Between 35 and 58 men were shot in one house, which was later blown up along with their bodies.

Ibtisam. Smiling.

Kamel Bey (and his father **Ahmad Bey**). Ahmad al-Asaad was speaker of the Lebanese parliament from 5 June 1951 to 30 May 1953. His son, Kamel al-Asaad, was speaker for three terms between 1964 and 1984.

Lebanon War. A multifaceted civil war in Lebanon, lasting from 1975 to 1990, in which local, regional and international interests competed for power.

Nakba. Nakba Day, meaning 'Day of the Catastrophe', is generally observed on 15 May by Palestinians as an annual day of commemoration of the displacement that preceded and followed the Israeli Declaration of Independence in 1948.

Najaf Pilgrimage. Najaf is a city in Iraq about 160 km south of Baghdad and the capital of Najaf Governorate. It is widely considered one of the three holiest cities of Shia Islam and the centre of Shia political power in Iraq.

Qana Massacre. The massacre took place on 18 April 1996 near Qana, a village in Southern Lebanon, when the Israeli Defence Forces fired artillery shells at a United Nations compound. Of the 800 Lebanese civilians who had taken refuge in the compound, 106 were killed and around 116 injured. Four soldiers of the Fijian United Nations Interim Force in Lebanon were also seriously injured.

Sabra and Shatila Massacre. The Sabra and Shatila Massacre was the killing of between 762 and 3,500 civilians, mostly Palestinians and Lebanese Shiites, by a militia close to the Kataeb Party, also called Phalange, a Christian Lebanese right-wing party in the Sabra neighbourhood and the adjacent Shatila refugee camp in Beirut, Lebanon. From approximately 6 p.m. on 16 September to 8 a.m. on 18 September 1982, a widespread massacre was carried out by the militia virtually under the eyes of their Israeli allies. The Israeli Defence Forces (IDF) ordered their allies the Phalanges to clear out Sabra and Shatila from PLO fighters as part of the Israeli manoeuvring into West Beirut. The IDF received reports of some of the Phalange atrocities in Sabra and Shatila but failed to stop them.

Seven Villages. The villages invaded by Israel in 1948.

Sharaa. Female name for one who is prone to argue.

Temporary marriage. *Nikah mut'ah*, or a type of marriage, permitted in Twelver Shia Islam, in which the duration of the marriage and the dowry must be specified and agreed upon in advance. It is a private contract, verbal or written. A declaration of the intent to marry and an acceptance of the terms are required (just as they are in permanent marriage). *Nikah mut'ah* was also practised by the pre-Islamic Arabs.

Tuffaha. Apple.

Um. Mother of. For example, Um Ali, or Mother of Ali, is used to refer to the mother by her relation to her oldest son, her anticipated son, or her daughter if she has only daughters.

Ya. Exclamation used to draw a person's attention to the speaker, as in 'Hey, Peter!' or 'Oh, Katherine!'

Zamzam water. Water from the Well of Zamzam, located within the Masjid al-Haram in Mecca, Saudi Arabia, 20 m east of the Kaaba, the holiest site in Islam. It is the well of Ishmael the son of Abraham, from which God quenched the thirst of Ishmael when he was an infant. According to Islamic belief, it is a source of miraculously generated water from God. Millions of pilgrims visit the well each year while performing the Hajj or Umrah pilgrimages in order to drink its water.

TRANSLATOR'S NOTE

There are some deliberate inconsistencies in the plot to make the stories seem jumbled, as if confused in many memories, as if they are not necessarily one person's story. The author has done this in the original Arabic text to stress the individual memory/collective memories as part of the complexity of the narrative.